The Shie

By: Will

Visit the author's website **htt**

William Kelso is ...**or of:**
The Shield of Rome
The Fortune of Carthage
Devotio: The House of Mus
Caledonia – Book One of the Veteran of Rome series
Hibernia – Book Two of the Veteran of Rome series
Britannia – Book Three of the Veteran of Rome series
Hyperborea – Book Four of the Veteran of Rome series
Germania – Book Five of the Veteran of Rome series
The Dacian War – Book Six of the Veteran of Rome series
Armenia Capta – Book Seven of the Veteran of Rome series

Published in 2011 by FeedARead Publishing – 2nd Edition
Copyright © William Kelso

British Library C.I.P.
A CIP catalogue record for this title is available from the British Library.

To: Barbara Johnson and John Kelso

Chapter One – Young Titus

(Early on the 2nd August 216 BC)

The massed ranks of heavily armoured Roman infantry stood densely packed together in neat, straight lines, as if the whole vast multitude of men resembled a single impregnable metal beast. It had taken the Tribunes nearly three hours to get the huge army into position, but now all was ready. Across the plain, separated by half a mile, through the swirling clouds of dust, Titus could make out the enemy. The sight of the Carthaginians seemed to have a sobering effect on the Roman soldiers. Titus licked his lips nervously. Fear and tension had tightened every muscle in his body. There was no escape now from the approaching battle. No way out. It was going to happen. His heart was thumping wildly. He licked his lips again and thought of his family back in Rome. As long as he was thinking about them and could picture them in his mind he knew that he would not panic.

He was tall for a seventeen-year-old, powerfully built and his skin tanned by much hard outdoors work. His short hair was black and his eyes even darker. In his hand, he gripped his long throwing spear and his large oval shield, with two lightning bolts emblazoned on it, rested against his legs. Around his neck, his Focale, the soldiers scarf, protected his skin from chafing on his body armour. It would not be long now before the Centurion signalled the order to advance. Ahead of him were seven lines of Legionaries, proper Roman citizens unlike himself and the second Cohort of Samnite allied infantry whose equipment betrayed their provincial origins.

3

"For Samnium, for our gods," the soldier to his right cried. The man caught Titus' eye and winked encouragingly.

"Boy, don't fear them, honour your ancestors." another man behind him said reaching out to lay a sweaty hand on Titus' shoulder and gripping him tightly.

"Silence," the Centurion bellowed in Titus' native Oscan language. Titus said nothing. His dark eyes watched the enemy line. The sun beat down on his head and he felt the sweat on his neck and back where the close-fitting armour gave him no respite from the searing heat. Whatever happened today he thought, he had to stay alive. His mother and sister were relying on him to come home. They had no one else to support them. He had to stay alive for them.

The Romans had begun to chant their battle cries and rhythmically crash their weapons into their shields and from the Carthaginian ranks a similar roar rose until the 135,000 men packed into the tight space between the hills and the river were all shouting. It was a tremendous noise and Titus was only aware that the forward ranks of Legionaries had started to move when his own companions lifted their shields from the ground and began to advance.

"Carthage must die! Carthage must die!" the Legionaries began to chant. Titus did not join in. The skirmishers, lightly clad, agile men, armed with all types of missiles were filtering back through the solid ranks of the Roman infantry. Their job had been done but it was impossible to see what they had achieved.

"Carthage must die!"

Titus glanced to the right and left but clouds of dust, kicked up by thousands of hooves obscured what was happening to the cavalry on the flanks. He was swept along in the remorseless Roman advance that was taking him straight into the centre of the Carthaginian line. He kept his eyes on the enemy ranks until he could begin to pick out individuals. The men facing him were Celts, wild looking men, some naked from the waist up, other's at least a head taller than the Legionaries. No easy looking opponents. They may be bigger than us but always remember, his instructors had told him, in skill and bravery they do not compare to the Roman soldier.

The front ranks of the two armies closed to within ten paces of each other and then halted. For an instant, all was silent and in that moment, just before the first clash of arms, an unknown Roman raised his voice, cursing the enemy. Then the air was filled with spears and with a loud cry the front ranks charged at each other. Titus watched mesmerized, too far back to take part in the initial contact.

"Ready your spears!" the Centurion bellowed.

Titus raised his spear above his shoulder like he had been taught. In front of him the Roman Hastati, the youngest and fittest soldiers, who always formed the front line, were pushing and stabbing at the enemy with their shields and short swords. The fighting line rippled forwards and backwards like the tide on a beach. A man fell to the ground clutching his stomach and was swiftly lost and trampled to death under the feet of his comrades. The clash of metal on metal could hardly be heard over the din of thousands of voices. Titus edged forwards as the second and third Roman lines became caught up in the melee. The Romans pressed around him eager now to get on with the fighting.

Some of the men beside Titus glanced nervously towards the flanks where the distant noise of battle was obscured by the dust and the thousands of Roman infantrymen moving forwards. Then, just as Titus was expecting the order to throw his spear, the Celts in front of him began to give way. Around him Roman voices cried out in triumph. The enemy was beginning to crack under the weight of the Roman assault. Titus was ten paces from the fighting line and sure enough the Hastati were beginning to drive the Celts back, step by step. A soldier directly in front of him threw his spear into the enemy mass without having been ordered to but the Centurion was too busy to notice. Then the whole line was throwing their spears and Titus, with a savage, liberating cry, followed suit.

The Centurions and Tribunes, identifiable by their plumed helmets and splendid armour were urging their men onwards. Titus could see many of the officers already bore wounds. Their men edged forwards, thrusting and stabbing at the enemy with their short swords or smashing their shields into the faces of the Celts and slowly the enemy retreat began to gain momentum. Titus however never managed to reach the fighting. When his maniple was two lines away the cohesion of the Celts finally broke and they turned and ran, routed. It happened in an instant. One moment they were fighting. Then their line was crumbling and breaking up into individual groups.

With a triumphant roar the Romans set off in pursuit and suddenly Titus found himself running, carried along by the vast numbers pressing from behind. In an instant the neat maniple lines of soldiers dissolved and he lost sight of his Centurion. The only way he could go was forwards. He ran and nearly tripped over several bodies. The Romans were crying out to each other sensing victory. A wounded Celt tried to rise to his feet but a soldier at Titus' side ran him through with his spear. Up ahead the Celts were running for their lives now. This is the moment when the enemy is vulnerable. This is when they will die in huge numbers his instructors had told him. Titus charged deeper into the enemy centre.

But something was not right. Gasping for breath Titus suddenly halted and turned to look first to the left and then to the right. All around him the Romans were surging forwards in great disorganised masses. Then suddenly he gasped. A hundred paces away to his left a solid line of men, some dressed in Roman uniforms were advancing into the Roman flank. With a shock Titus suddenly realised they were Hannibal's men.

"Libyans." a soldier at his side hissed.

"To the right also," another man cried in alarm.

Titus stared with incredibility as the front line of the Libyans cut straight into the flank of the mass of disorganised Romans and kept on coming towards him. Up ahead the Roman pursuit seemed to have run out of steam and the Celts were reforming.

"Form a line. Form a line!" a Centurion shouted but no one was listening to him. The men around Titus were staring at the new threat that had appeared on their flank.

"This is no good," an old soldier muttered.

"Forwards, keep advancing men." a Tribune yelled urging the soldiers onwards with his sword. The next moment his voice ended in a rattle as he was hit in the throat by a spear.

"Run lad, get to the rear now!" the old soldier who had spoken earlier now raised his voice in alarm. "Nothing is going to stop those cursed Libyans. We have run into a trap!"

And with that he pushed Titus backwards.

The masses of Romans milled about in confusion. They were being attacked from three sides and the sudden reverse of fortunes was completely unexpected. Yet they did not give up, and here and there, individuals and small groups began to form up to try and stop the surprise attack on their flank. Titus did not know what to do. There were no officers to give commands. He had no idea where the men from his maniple were. Everything was a terrible mess. He felt panic starting to rise in his stomach.

A howling, shrieking melee broke out twenty paces away from him as a group of Libyans attempted to punch through the thin disorganised Roman line. Titus screamed as the adrenaline surged through his veins. Then he charged straight into the melee. It was as if he had hit a brick wall but he didn't feel any pain. Fear gave him a desperate strength. Wildly he thrust his sword into the struggling group of men, without thought or aim, and felt the blade strike someone's armour and slide away. He took a step back and rammed his shield into the nearest man but no one was taking notice of him. Then a Libyan was suddenly upon him and Titus, dropping his shield, grabbed the man by his hair and sank his teeth into the exposed neck. With a moan the Libyan fell to the ground. Titus stepped back his mouth and chin covered in blood.

A yard away from him on the ground, a young Roman equipped with very fine armour was wrestling with a Libyan. Both men had lost their weapons and were trying to throttle each other. Titus lunged with his right foot and caught the Libyan square in the head. Then he stabbed him in the neck. A fine spray of blood shot up into the air and the Libyan collapsed backwards without a word taking Titus's sword with him. The young Roman who had nearly been strangled was on his feet in instant, pale faced and panting for breath. It was only then that Titus saw that he was a Tribune, a senior officer of the Legions. The Tribune looked just as young as himself.

"Scipio of the Cornelii," the man gasped. Then before Titus could do anything else the Tribune had snatched up an abandoned sword and was struggling towards the rear calling for Titus to follow him. Whether it was the officer's natural authority or the deeply ingrained army drill, Titus obeyed, knowing somehow in that instance, that the battle was lost.

Chapter Two – Cannae

Late on the 2nd August 216BC

Hannibal leaned forwards on his horse and adjusted the eye patch that covered his blind eye. His breath came in short, sharp gasps as he studied the dusty plain below in utter disbelief. His earlier exhaustion was forgotten. He said nothing. His armour was covered in dust, and in places dented and damaged. Sweat streaked his face. A group of Numidian horsemen had gathered around him on the small hillock. No one spoke. All were staring at the incredible sight that stretched before them.

Across the plain to the north east, between the hill top town of Cannae and the Aufidius river, groups of Carthaginian soldiers had flung themselves onto the ground to rest. The great battle they had just fought had exhausted them. As Hannibal sat watching, a young Roman soldier with a focale tied around his neck, rose up from a pile of corpses, pointed his sword at Hannibal and tried to attack. The boy's face was smeared with blood and there was a crazed look in his eyes. He managed a few paces before he was set upon by a gang of Iberian swordsmen who cut him down. The soldier's body vanished under a flurry of blows.

Hannibal didn't seem to notice the soldier. Across the battlefield he could hear the cries of the wounded and the dying. But Hannibal was not interested in them either. His eye was fixed on the huge piles of dead Roman soldiers that covered the plain as far as he could see. The dead did not just lie side by side on the ground. They lay in great bloody heaps, in some places stacked as high as a man's head. Others he'd been told, in their desperation to end their suffering had dug holes in the ground and had suffocated themselves. And spread throughout this sea of lifeless bodies was the wreckage of a great army, heads without bodies, torsos without limbs, swords, cracked helmets, broken spears, mutilated horses, battered shields, proud unit standards and in the summer heat, the gathering, overpowering, stench of death. In the end, it had not been a battle. It had been a massacre on an unprecedented scale and now when it was finally over, fifty-six thousand corpses lay packed into a space no larger than a square mile.

"They are all dead Sir," a bodyguard muttered.

Hannibal leaned back in his saddle and slowly wiped the sweat from his brow.

One by one his generals gathered around him and Hannibal turned to look at each in turn. Hasdrubal, the aging cavalry commander, who had forced the crucial breakthrough on the flank, old enough to be his father, blushed in awe like a young maiden. Gisgo, the politician's son smiled slyly. Maharbal the African, whose Numidian cavalry had routed one of the consuls, came with wildness in his eyes as if he was suffering from fever, and Mago, the last to join them, young sensitive Mago, his younger brother, looked up at him in astonishment. Dust, sweat and blood covered their faces and Hannibal could see fatigue etched around their eyes but they didn't seem to know they were tired. No one wanted to be the first to speak.

Then as the silence lengthened Hannibal started to laugh. In that moment, those clustered around him knew that their leader, Hannibal had become a legend. And as his laughter grew they all joined in turning to look at each other, eyes flashing wildly, filling with relief, awe and the fierce elation of knowing that they had won. They had won! They had done what the politicians back home had said was impossible.

Across the battlefield soldiers paused to stare at the group of laughing generals.

"They have lost four consular armies in a single battle," Hasdrubal cried. He turned to Hannibal. "I was with your father in Sicily and again in Spain but I have never seen a victory like this. As Tanit is my witness, I swear that you Hannibal are the greatest general Carthage and the world has known."

"This is just the beginning," Gisgo smiled slyly.

Hannibal felt the fierce surge of euphoria slip away as fast as it had come. Suddenly he felt his aching and bruised muscles again, the dryness of his mouth, the sweat stinging in his eyes. Mago, noticing the change anxiously touched his shoulder.

"Are you wounded brother?"

"I need to rest," Hannibal sighed. "But it can wait."

He raised his spear above his head. He had worked for this moment ever since he'd been a boy.

"Tell your men this. Tell them that today, here in this field, we have avenged our father's defeat and humbled our enemy. Tell your men that all the good friends we've had to leave behind during these past two years have not fallen in vain. With this victory, I have given Carthage back her pride, her power and her dignity. The might of Rome is broken. She is finished."

Hannibal paused and then continued in a softer voice.

"My one regret is that my father is not here to see this day for this was his dream and my inheritance."

"He sees you now Hannibal," Mago said quietly.

"What shall we do with the prisoners?" Hasdrubal said, "We have taken fifteen thousand so far," and before anyone could reply he added his own suggestion. "Let's bury them alive so that we won't have to fight them again. I am sure I recognised a few who fought us at Trebia and Lake Trasimene."

They laughed at that, all except Hannibal.

"No," Hannibal shook his head, "we shall ransom all Roman citizens according to their wealth and class. The Italian allies shall be sent home unharmed bearing our usual message of good will to their community."

"Again?" Hasdrubal groaned.

"General," Gisgo interrupted smoothly, "Fostering a reputation for clemency will gain us more allies and cities than your blunt sword ever will."

"Ha!" Hasdrubal snorted and shot Gisgo a contemptuous look.

"You have said that before and how many came over to us after Trebia or Trasimene? None."

"It will be different now," Gisgo nodded confidently, "the Greek towns have had enough of Roman rule. Once they learn that the largest army the Romans have ever fielded has been totally wiped out they will desert the Republic in droves. Hannibal's war strategy will work."

Hannibal ignored Gisgo and his veteran general. Instead he turned to Mago and laid a hand on his brother's shoulder. With his index finger, he pointed at the battlefield.

"Go back to Carthage, brother, and tell them what you saw here today. Gather the gold rings of all the Roman senators and knights you can find. When you are amongst the council of 104, in the great hall, pour them onto the floor so that all will see what we have done to Rome. Urge them to send us reinforcements at once. Don't let them delay you with excuses."

"Reinforcements, what do we need those for?" Maharbal now spoke up for the first time and there was no mistaking the fiery passion in his voice and eyes. He rounded on Hannibal.

"Let me take my Numidians and ride on Rome tonight. In five days, Hannibal, we could be feasting in the forum. The city is defenceless." Eagerly Maharbal extended an arm towards the battlefield. "The flower of the Roman army lies dead in those fields. This war could be over in a matter of days. Let's end it now." His voice rose in excitement, "for how else will this war end if not with a victorious march on Rome?"

The others remained silent as Maharbal's plea trailed off.

Hannibal sighed wearily. "I hear you Maharbal and your part in this great battle will not be forgotten."

But his reply was not enough for Maharbal.

"The very sight of our army at her gates will crush any remaining Roman will to keep on fighting," he said fiercely. "They will capitulate. They are ready to run like never before, Hannibal."

Hannibal smiled gently at his general's enthusiasm.

"Don't you think, Maharbal," he said wearily, "that I too would like to ride on Rome and end this war? But it is not so simple. The road to Rome from here is a long one, her walls are still standing and our army is not in any fit state to move. We have many dead. We have even more wounded; many more than we had at Trebia and Trasimene and the men need to rest and recover their strength."

Hannibal paused to glance at the battlefield. "Besides maybe there is no need to march on Rome. The Romans know they are beaten and have lost the war."

"So what do we do?" Hasdrubal said gruffly.

Hannibal paused again and then seemed to make up his mind.

"Gisgo, select ten Roman nobles from the prisoners and send them to Rome with our terms for the ransom of the prisoners." Hannibal glanced carefully at Gisgo who nodded in agreement.

"We need the money," Hannibal said turning to Hasdrubal, "but with the Romans will go Carthalo. He will have the authority to present our conditions for peace to the Roman Senate."

Then Hannibal turned to Maharbal with a perplexed expression. "They are beaten, old friend. They will make peace. No city can keep on fighting after what we have done to them today. They have no choice. The Romans are a rational and practical people. They will recognise a hopeless situation when they see it. Then we shall take back all that is rightfully ours and the name of Rome will soon be forgotten by history."

The others nodded in agreement, all except Maharbal, who frowned in exasperation.

"Truly Hannibal," he cried, "you know how to win a great victory but you don't know how to use it."

Chapter Three – Hannibal's gamble

11th August 216BC, the battlefield at Cannae

The flames licked greedily at the body which was carefully wrapped in white linen cloth and placed on a large heap of dry wood. Blood seeped through the linen. Hannibal stood close by waiting for the priest to finish the sombre burial rites. In a mark of respect, he had removed his helmet and held it tucked under his arm.

On the funeral pyre lay the body of Lucius Aemilius Paullus, Consul of Rome. The Consul's body had been found by chance and some Roman prisoners had confirmed that it was indeed their former leader and general who had fallen in battle. It was right to honour such a man and send him on his way to his gods, Hannibal thought. He had no quarrel with brave men who fought for their country like he did. His quarrel was with Rome and what she had done to his native city, Carthage.

As the flames began to devour the body Hannibal turned away. His army had not moved since the battle and his men were scattered across the plain, looting and recovering from their ordeal as he himself was. The vast numbers of Roman dead still lay where they had fallen. He was not going to bury them. Let the dead be a warning and a reminder to the Romans of what he could do to them. But he would not be able to stay here forever. In the hot August weather, disease could strike at any moment and Hannibal feared disease. He had heard his father's tales of what disease had done to a Carthaginian army in Sicily some forty years before.

He caught sight of a group of horsemen threading their way from the river towards the Carthaginian camp. He frowned as he thought he recognised one of them. Then as the riders drew closer Hannibal stirred uneasily. Too soon he thought. They had returned too soon.

Seeing him the riders immediately changed direction and urged their horses up the hill towards him.

"Well?" Hannibal said with a growing sense of foreboding, eyeing the tall sweating officer who stood before him.

Carthalo looked uncomfortable and took a few moments to catch his breath. His clothes and face were caked with dust and his lips cracked by thirst, but he asked for no water.

"I took the road to Rome, with the prisoners, to give the Romans our peace terms and ratify the ransom, as you instructed," Carthalo said. "I reached the city gates but they would only allow the prisoners to enter. I gave them our peace terms and told them I would wait for an answer. Later that day a senator came to see me. He gave me a message which I am to repeat to you."

Carthalo licked his lips nervously.

"Well?" Hannibal demanded.

"To Hannibal from the Senate," Carthalo said reciting from memory. "The Senate and People of Rome refuse to discuss the possibility of peace as long as an enemy army remains on

Italian soil. Rome will negotiate with you, Hannibal, only when it has won the war. The ransom for the prisoners will not be paid, nor will any private Roman citizen be permitted to pay for the release of men who, like the consul Paullus, should have died nobly on the battlefield. All the prisoners who came to Rome will therefore be returned to you."

Carthalo cleared his throat. "That is all Hannibal. I was told to leave Roman land before nightfall if I valued my life."

Hannibal gaped at him in shock.

"They refuse to make peace?" he bellowed. "After we have just utterly destroyed the largest army they have ever fielded. What madness is this! They have lost the war. What more do I have to do to make them realise the truth?"

Carthalo bowed his head and remained silent.

Hannibal frowned unable to comprehend the message. In later years Carthalo would remember this moment as the only time he was ever to see the great Hannibal look shaken.

For a long moment, no one spoke. Then Hannibal's face darkened.

"Fabius", he hissed. "You are behind this foolishness!"

He spun on his heels and stormed towards his tent.

"Execute a hundred Roman prisoners," he shouted at Gisgo as he passed him. "Do it now. Fabius has condemned his own people to death. Sell the rest of them into slavery. By the great Baal, I shall teach these Roman jackals the meaning of fear!"

Hannibal's tent was furnished with looted Roman objects. In a corner was the camp bed taken from Consul Varro's tent. Beside the bed was a wooden table for writing dispatches, a chair, washing bowl and from a hook at the top of the leather canvas hung his armour and weapons. Alone Hannibal paced up and down his fist tightly clenched in anger. But mingling with anger was something else. He felt it in the pit of his stomach. The Roman refusal to make peace had not only shocked him, it had rattled him. The balls of it! No nation had ever continued fighting after suffering such a crushing defeat. Only one man had ever managed to rattle him like this before. His old enemy, the aging senator who three years earlier had come to Carthage with the temerity to ask for Hannibal's surrender in exchange for peace, after Hannibal's destruction of the Roman allied city of Sagunto that had started the war.

Quintus Fabius Maximus!

Hannibal's thoughts turned to the past two years. His army had been in a dreadful state when it had at last descended from the Alps. Winter was closing in. There was a shortage of food and he'd lost over half his men on his five month journey from New Carthage and only one elephant out of 37 was still alive. But the punishing journey had weeded out the weak and those mercenaries, Iberians from Spain, Carthaginian citizens from the heartland and Libyans and Numidians from North Africa who still remained with him were the best of the best. He could rely on their fighting skills and they in turn would follow him into the gates of hell.

The Celtic tribes, whose hatred and mistrust of the Romans was well known and who lived amongst the slopes of the Alps and in the Po valley flocked to his banner by the thousands. He had expected them to, it had been part of the invasion plan but it hadn't stopped him worrying about their fickle nature. Too often, when he was still in Spain, he had seen the local tribes switch sides for a handful of Gold. This too had been the time when Roman arrogance was at its highest pitch and he'd eagerly looked forward to the day when he would teach them a lesson about warfare.

That first sharp lesson had been taught to the Consul Sempronius Longus, an aggressive and impulsive man whom had rashly committed his army and had been soundly defeated at Trebia in the Po Valley. Afterwards Hannibal had moved south, carefully making sure that his new Celtic allies did not have the chance to desert or leave the army to go raiding the Roman towns and farms. Crossing the marshes in northern Etruria, Hannibal lost an eye to a painful infection. Then the following year he'd ambushed the Consul Flaminius and killed him and fifteen thousand of his men by driving them into the waters of Lake Trasimene. It had been another splendid victory but some of the more uncharitable Celtic chiefs had commented that Hannibal only knew how to win a battle by unfair tricks and ambushes.

And then a new Roman commander had been sent against him. This man, Quintus Fabius Maximus had been a dictator, combining the power of two consuls in one office and elected by the Senate for a term of six months only. On the dictator's approach, Hannibal had immediately drawn up his army and offered to fight a battle but the dictator's decision had surprised him. Fabius and his army had remained safely on the high ground and had refused to fight. The Romans had contented themselves by shadowing and watching the enemy from a safe distance. Surprise had turned to grudging admiration as Hannibal had begun to understand the dictator's strategy. Instead of risking a battle with his half trained troops Fabius planned to starve Hannibal into submission by denying him access to food. Without food to feed his thousands of men, Hannibal knew that his army would melt away like the spring snow.

On numerous occasion's he'd tried to lure Fabius into battle but the old man stubbornly refused to be baited and the Romans had given Fabius a nick name, the delayer. Hannibal had pillaged the Roman countryside far and wide hoping to provoke a reaction but there had been none and as the months had passed, without a decisive battle, his admiration had turned to anger, born from increasing desperation. It was a cowardly way in which to conduct a war Hannibal thought but an effective one. He'd known that he had to force a battle and destroy the Romans before they starved him into surrender for Fabius had abundant supplies and could afford to wait.

It had therefore been with considerable relief that he had learned that the dictator's six-month term had expired and that new more aggressive commanders were being sent to face him. Of those Consuls, two were now dead, one had retired and the other was severely discredited.

Hannibal stopped pacing and slowly unclenched his fist. Yes he knew why Fabius had got under his skin. The man knew how to defeat him.

Hannibal slowly became aware that a man was standing in the entrance to his tent waiting to be noticed. It was Gisgo. There was a cruel gleam in the Carthaginian politician's eyes.

"I have executed the prisoners," Gisgo reported, "the slave merchants are nervous though Hannibal. They say that taking so many Roman prisoners in the heart of Italy will not be good for the market. They are refusing to buy them all."

"Lower the price per man and if that doesn't work kill the ones that are not sold," Hannibal snapped.

Gisgo paused, seeing that his general had something weightier on his mind. "What's the matter Hannibal?"

Hannibal glanced at his subordinate and sighed.

"We have a problem," he replied.

***

Gisgo stayed silent as he waited for his commander to speak. Hannibal unrolled a scroll of parchment and spread it out on the table. It was a map of Italy. With his finger Hannibal jabbed at Neopolis on the west coast of Campania.

"I need to capture a port," he muttered. "Without a port Mago will never be able to land his reinforcements from Carthage."

Then his finger slid northwards and came to rest on Rome. He tapped the parchment. "Or, we can march on Rome like Maharbal suggests." He looked up and Gisgo could see the sudden indecision on Hannibal's face. "We may not be able to take the city by assault without suitable siege equipment but that's not the point. The objective would be to destroy Roman morale and their desire to keep on fighting. With our army at their gates so soon after they have suffered catastrophic defeat; it may be too much for them to bear and their morale will collapse. Then they will sue for peace like they should be doing now."

"It's a gamble Hannibal," Gisgo frowned. "If the Romans continue to refuse peace talks and move to defend Rome, we will only be able to remain outside their walls for a few days at the most before we start to run out of food."

"Yes," Hannibal sighed, "and if we had to retreat from Rome it would be a humiliating blow. It would look like we were not capable of taking the city. How many potential allies would we then lose by such an action."

The tent fell silent as both men studied the map. Hannibal was conscious of the great decision he had to make, a decision to which his fate and the outcome of the war now surely depended.

He turned to Gisgo with sudden ruthlessness.

"Find me a man who can do a job," Hannibal muttered.

Gisgo' face slowly broke into a smile as he understood.

"You mean an assassin?"

Hannibal nodded looking uncomfortable.

"I have been away from Carthage for a long time now," he muttered, "but I understand that the use of assassins is still a normal part of doing business in our city, is it not?"

Gisgo nodded looking pleased, "You hired me to advise you on political matters. There is no dishonour in using an assassin during peace or war. Every tool has a purpose and should be used when necessary. It's a splendid idea and will not stain your reputation. Our citizens will understand."

Hannibal grunted and for a moment he looked embarrassed.

"Roman morale may be close to collapse," he muttered to himself, "but as long as Fabius remains to rally the Senate, they will never surrender." He paused hunched over the map and his face darkened.

"He's back in charge, I can feel it. I cannot march on Rome whilst he still lives".

He glanced up at Gisgo. "Our prestige cannot be seen to suffer. If we, at any time, appear to be weak then our allies will desert us. This war Gisgo will no longer be settled by armies, it has become a contest of wills."

Gisgo dipped his head in salute. "Leave it to me," he replied, "I know just the man who can solve our problem."

Chapter Four – A good horseman

2nd August 216BC, the battle of Cannae...

It was getting harder to keep up with the Tribune. Titus struggled with increasing desperation through the great mass of Roman soldiers trying to keep the officers tall plumed helmet in sight. Everywhere there was chaos. Those men who could still fight did so bravely but increasingly a sense of terror and panic was spreading amongst the Roman troops. They were being attacked from three sides and slowly the great disorganised mass was being squeezed tighter and tighter until the centre of the shrieking mob was so tightly packed together that no one could use their weapons or defend themselves. Dust billowed into the air making it hard to see for more than twenty paces.

Titus fought to keep his balance using his elbows to hack his way through the ranks of desperate men. If he stumbled and fell now he would be trampled to death in an instant. Follow the officer he thought. The man seemed to be the only person who knew what he was doing.

On the edges of the Roman mass he caught a glimpse of the enemy. The Libyans were cutting the Romans to pieces. Hundreds had to be dying every single minute. Without space to move the Romans had become helpless targets, unable to fight or flee. Heaps of the dead were forming and in places the Carthagians were climbing over the bodies to get at the living. Titus felt another spark of panic and fought for control. The carnage was too awful to look upon. It was a scene that belonged in hell and not in the world of the living.

Suddenly he felt the press of bodies around him start to slacken. The Tribune had disappeared into a cloud of dust. Titus wrestled himself free, treading on a corpse. For a moment, he nearly lost his balance and wildly his fingers clawed at the heads of the men around him. Up ahead the crowds of men were starting to thin out. A group of Romans ran past with drawn swords. Titus plunged on and caught sight of Scipio, the Tribune. The officer was running flat out now. The thunder of hooves was coming from his right and a moment later a troop of riders, foreigners with dark beards and alien clothing flashed past cutting down everyone in their path before they vanished into another dust cloud. Titus ran on, grateful to find more and more open space ahead of him.

The Tribune was making for the river. Titus caught up with him and saw that he was bleeding from a wound to his head. Blood had soaked one half of Scipio's face but it hadn't slowed him down. The two of them dashed through groups of running Roman soldiers. It seemed that everyone had the same idea. They had to get to the river where the terrible Carthaginian cavalry would not be able to pursue them. It seemed that the enemy encirclement was not yet watertight for it was mainly cavalry who were trying to close the last Roman escape route and they couldn't stand still for very long without becoming vulnerable. Titus and the Tribune burst into a clearing littered with corpses. A hundred paces away was the river lined by green bushes and small trees that looked out of place in the parched countryside.

A Numidian was wheeling his horse around to make another charge. The beast was small and scrawny unlike the big Italian animals Titus had helped rear at home. Unable to change direction, Titus bowled straight into the rider catching him in the flank. The collision sent both of them crashing to the ground. The Numidian cried out and tried to rise to his feet. He was armed with a spear but Titus was quicker. His hob nailed boot caught the man in his groin with such force that it knocked him senseless. Titus shrieked in pain at the contact and hopped on one leg, grasping his foot with both hands. It felt as if he had broken a bone. The Tribune had already swung himself into the saddle by the time Titus let go of his foot. Then the officer was galloping away. Titus's chest was heaving with exertion and he was nearly exhausted but the adrenaline was pumping and with a cry of pain and a grimace he forced himself onwards, half running, half limping towards the river.

Horsemen seemed to be all around them, charging down the fleeing Romans and the cries of desperate and terrified men could he heard everywhere. Yet somehow Titus managed to make it to the river. The water level was low for it was August and he plunged into the river using his hands to propel himself forwards. All along the bank other Romans were doing the same, splashing through the water, desperate to get to the other side. Titus began to feel the weight of his armour beginning to drag him down and desperately tore his helmet from his head and flung it away. Yet he could not undo his torso armour. His breath came in gasps and he spluttered as he gulped in a mouthful of water by mistake. His feet scrabbled wildly on the smooth pebbles of the river bed and he was sure now that he had broken a bone. The stabbing pain was shooting through his whole body. As he splashed, gasped and struggled in the water, Numidian riders appeared on the bank and some in pursuit, urged their horses into the water killing their desperate and helpless quarry with single thrusts of their spears.

Titus staggered onto the far bank. The Tribune had disappeared. Despite the dry hot weather Titus was shaking from the cold mountain water. He stumbled and whirled round at a sudden noise close behind him. A rider less horse came cantering past and without thinking Titus grabbed the reins and in one fluent and practised movement swung himself onto the beast. It was an Italian horse, larger than those ridden by the enemy. It was not a moment too soon. Titus groaned as he saw the three Numidian horsemen charging towards him. The Carthaginians had crossed the river. He dug his knees into the animal and felt the beast surge forwards. A spear flew past his head clattering harmlessly onto some rocks. Titus swerved and hugged the horse tightly as they began to pick up speed. He had been brought up with horses and had ridden them since the earliest possible age. He sensed the animals fear but the beast was an army horse and trained for war and it responded to his commands. They thundered on across the desolate, rocky plain. Titus did not have time to look behind him. All his concentration was needed to keep control of the horse and evade the many rocks and obstacles that littered the ground. Another spear slammed into the earth just behind him.

Fear gave him added strength and made everything seem very simple but he refused to panic. He clung to just one thought. He had to live. His family were relying on him to survive.

"Run, you lazy beast." he screamed at the horse.

Up ahead the ground was beginning to rise to a line of hills. A solitary red tiled farm stood some way off surrounded by neat rows of vineyards. Roman stragglers were everywhere. Some were running but others had given up and were sitting on the ground, too exhausted to continue. There was only so much a man could endure. It was a sorry end to what had once been the greatest army that Rome had ever fielded. Titus felt the horses pace start to slow as the ground began to rise. He risked a glance over his shoulder. His pursuers had given up and turned their attention to easier prey. He raised his arm in the air and screamed in triumph. He had gotten away. He had out ridden Hannibal's cavalry.

***

The Roman stragglers were still coming into the town as night fell. Canusium was crowded with thousands of shocked and exhausted survivors. They came in as individuals or small groups, many wounded and without weapons. Then when the night was well advanced the magistrates of the town ordered the gates to be closed and armed men to be posted to the walls. Hannibal's army was only a few miles away and there was a danger that the Carthaginian would be tempted to try and take the town by force.

Titus sat cross legged on the ground in the forum, the market square, and watched as the town folk lit torches along the walls of their small settlement. He'd said a prayer to Minerva for his safe deliverance, and if he'd had his baggage with him he would have offered her a coin too, but his baggage had been left behind in the army camp, which by now would have been looted by the Carthaginians. He had lost everything he'd possessed. But he was alive. That was more than he could say for his friends. They were all dead. He'd searched for the men in his unit amongst the survivors but he'd found no one. The second Cohort of Samnite heavy infantry had simply ceased to exist. He seemed to be the sole survivor.

The glow of the fires cast an eerie flickering light across the paved forum and the brick houses that surrounded it. A cool easterly breeze had brought some welcome relief from the heat of the day but the shutters on all the windows of the houses remained firmly shut.

An aristocratic woman, clad in a blood red toga and followed by her slaves was picking her way through the long lines of weary soldiers who were sitting in the forum. As she approached Titus saw that she was distributing food and wine to the men. There was a grace about her that seemed to calm the traumatised soldiers and Titus found himself thinking about his women back in Rome and their home, a crumbling, unhealthy and dangerous one room apartment, on the fourth floor of a block in the Subura neighbourhood. The new Insulae, apartment blocks that had started to spring up all over Rome had been sold to the rural community as a dream home in the city. A dream home my fat arse he thought. Yet the rent was all he could afford on his wages as an apprentice blacksmith. His mother had made a little extra repairing clothes but it was a pittance, barely enough for a loaf of bread a day. He wondered if they would think that he had been killed.

The pain in his foot was a dull ache now. The town's only doctor had been far too busy looking after the more seriously wounded and Titus had not thought about bothering him. Maybe the bone was not broken after all he thought hopefully.

His attention was suddenly drawn to a small group of officers who had emerged from one of the houses. They spoke in urgent, hushed voices as they made their way through the lines of soldiers. As they passed close to Titus one of the officers stopped. It was Scipio, the Tribune whom he had saved on the battlefield. The man had a bandage around his head but the dried blood still caked his cheek. The officer had recognised Titus. He grinned conspiratorially.

"I am glad you made it," Scipio said and although he was practically the same age as Titus he sounded like a father speaking to a son.

"Sir," Titus replied bowing respectfully.

Scipio glanced over Titus' head in the direction of the battlefield.

"The battle was lost when they attacked our flanks," he declared, his face growing solemn. "That was our mistake. I won't allow that to happen when I am in command. You did well today soldier. It was important that I survived. Rome will need me more than ever now."

"Yes Sir."

"The boy came in on a horse, the beast was one of ours," one of the staff officers beside the Tribune interjected.

"Did he now," Scipio bent down to give Titus a closer examination. There was a sudden interest in the young Tribune's eyes.

"Horses are valuable military assets. I shall see that you are properly rewarded for your loyalty to me and your bravery. What is your name and unit soldier?"

Titus gave the Tribune his name and Scipio frowned as he realised Titus was not a citizen but belonged to the Italian auxiliaries.

"A Samnite boy from the mountains," he muttered. "Well it doesn't matter. Where is your father, Titus? I would like to meet the man who has raised such a fine and loyal warrior."

"He is dead Sir."

"A pity," Scipio straightened up with a disappointed look, "But he will be proud of what you did today", he continued. "War teaches a man more about himself than he could hope to learn in a hundred years of peace. That is why we, men, shall never grow bored of war. In war a man will learn whether he is brave and noble or a wimpering coward. Two years ago, I saved my father's life in battle, and since then I have not worried about my fate, for whatever happens to me, I shall be remembered as the son who risked his life in order to save his father."

"Sir," Titus said.

Scipio turned sharply to one of his officers. "Give the boy ten silver coins," he said.

"Please Sir. Teach me to write and read instead," Titus replied looking up boldly.

Surprised the officers and men around him fell silent. Scipio frowned again. "You refuse coins as a reward?" he muttered.

"I do Sir. I would do better if I knew how to read and write," Titus said feeling his cheeks beginning to blush furiously. It was a gamble to ask the officer for so much but he may never have a chance like this again.

There was a stir amongst the soldiers who could hear the conversation.

Scipio' face was disapproving. He glanced at the mass of soldiers sitting in the forum.

"No, you would have done better to have taken the money," he snapped. "It was offered fairly. The army has no time to be a school teacher." Scipio paused to study Titus and as he did so an amused look crept onto his face. He continued in a lighter voice. "Tell me Titus, do you like horses?"

Titus looked up at the young officer. He'd asked for too much and now he'd lost his chance. He'd blown it.

"I do Sir and I out rode the foreigners. I have heard that they pride themselves on their riding skills but today they could not catch me."

There was a sudden pride in Titus' voice as he spoke.

Scipio laughed and the sound was so alien amongst the wretched survivors that heads turned to look at them from all over the forum.

"Good," he said, "From now on you are to be a dispatch rider. I need a brave and competent man who knows how to handle a horse to ride to Venusia with a message for the Consul Varro. You will leave at first light."

"Sir," Titus nodded rising to his feet and rapping out a quick salute.

Scipio turned to leave but then hesitated.

"You are the head of your family," he said with his back turned, "and the father of a Roman household has duties. Above all things, boy, you must learn to lead. Do that and you will become a true Roman."

Titus watched Scipio walk away. Fool; silently he cursed himself. To be rewarded by an officer was a rare occurrence in the army. It was considered a once in a life time opportunity and now he had blown it. In his bungling haste he had thrown away the only chance he would probably get at advancement.

Annoyed he slapped the ground with his hand.

An arrogant ass his army friends would have called the officer. His fellow soldiers had always been moaning about their officers and the harshness of army discipline. Their desires overwhelmingly had been confined to wine, money and women. Titus had grown up around such men all his life. The boys from his village were for the most part destined to follow in their father's footsteps, dull, back breaking work for a local land owner who paid them a pittance and sent them to an early grave. Titus had no interest in that. From an early age he had known he wanted to be different.

He remembered the day when, aged nine, the road had come to his home in the mountains. His father had taken him down to see it. The road builders had been led by a solitary engineer, a young man in a red cloak. The town's folk had been hostile to the road builders, seeing its construction as a sign of foreign occupation but the cool, dogged professionalism of the young engineer had impressed Titus. He had refused to join in the taunting of the road builders. For him the real heroes had become the men who held civilisation together for civilisation gave a man a chance to better himself. Civilisation was worth fighting for.

Chapter Five - His name is Adonibaal

The Carthaginian mercenaries were in a boisterous mood. They sat around the crackling fire passing around flasks of captured Roman wine. Some had started singing songs from their distant homelands, ballads about lost love and triumphant hunts. Night had fallen and across the plain Adonibaal could see hundreds of Carthaginian camp fires. He sat a little way back from the fire so that his face was hidden in the shadows. He didn't like to attract attention. Adonibaal was a loner. Slowly he sharpened his sword on a stone. The metal scraped and grated on the rock. Now and then he paused to scratch the old white scars across his arm. The scars had been inflicted by a whip. There were more whip scars across his back but he did not care to show those to anyone. He was a big handsome man, deeply tanned and muscular like a bronze statue of Hercules; and for a fortyfour year old, he'd kept himself in excellent physical condition. His hair was tied back in a pony tail and fixed with a small string. The Iberians had worn it like this in order to keep their eyes and faces clear during battle. Sharp swords and good physical health mattered for that was how he made his living. Adonibaal was a professional swordsman, not a gladiator, but a mercenary, a knife for hire. It was a profitable business too and it had made him a wealthy man.

He lifted the sword and ran his finger down the edge, testing the sharpness.

He knew that he was good at his job. Amongst the Gallic mercenaries, whom he'd got to know, it was common to give ones weapon a name and Adonibaal had named his Centurion after the first Roman he had slain in battle. It had been a strange experience finding himself on the opposite side to his countrymen. From the start when he had signed up to Hannibal's army he'd known that if the Romans caught him he would be executed as a traitor. A man like him could never surrender. A man like him could only kill or be killed. That was the law by which he had to live. During the next eighteen months he had killed every Roman he'd come across. He'd shown no pity or mercy and had robbed the dead of everything they possessed. A hard and bitter man, the Gallic mercenaries had muttered behind his back, a man with a heart of iron, and they had learned to avoid him.

Around the camp fire the mercenaries had started to recount their exploits during the battle, each speaker trying to outdo the other but Adonibaal was not listening. Idly he grasped a handful of dirt and let the soil slip away through his fingers. It had been twenty-four years since he had been forced to flee Italy. The city of Carthage had granted him asylum and for that he was eternally grateful. In Carthage, he'd found a new home in a multicultural society. The Carthaginians had not judged him on his looks or background or asked awkward questions and he had been free to do what he pleased as long as he'd obeyed their laws and customs. Carthage had been a splendid place to make ones' fortune and that suited him just fine. Money, he had learned, was a fugitive's best friend. Money earned him respect, money never let him down. Money and Centurion were his only friends.

The first time he had seen the great city of Carthage he'd approached from the sea. He had been barely twenty. His galley had nosed its way into the grand circular harbour. Ships of all sizes and nations had filled the port and amongst the workers he'd heard a half a dozen foreign languages. The sea had been a brilliant, sparkling blue and the massive, solid walls of the city had towered over him, their strength a proud reminder to all visitors that this was a city which controlled its own destiny.

Carthage was one of the true great cities of the world. There was no doubt about that. He had taken the main street from the harbour that led up to the Byrsa, the ancient citadel, feeling a strange mixture of emotion. Had it really been just more than a year ago that he had been fighting these very same Carthaginians and preying for their ruin?

The first Carthaginian ruler and founder of the city, Queen Dido had established her home on the Byrsa some six hundred years earlier, when Rome was still a barren uninhabited hillside covered with sheep shit. Tall apartment buildings had kept the street in shade from the burning African sun and in the malls and markets there had been people and products from all over the world. It had been an exciting place. Traders had mingled with philosophers, soldiers, mercenaries, fortune tellers and prophets, all competing to take away a man's hard earned money. That was what Carthage was all about, her heart and soul, the pursuit of wealth and pleasure. People came to Carthage to make money. How unlike Rome he had thought, where people just wanted to rule the world.

It had been a turbulent time when he had first arrived. A widespread rebellion had been on going throughout the countryside and it had not been hard to find work as a bodyguard to a rich merchant who owned several country estates in the highly fertile valleys beyond the city walls. The work had been well paid but boring and soon he'd caught the eye of the merchant's young wife. The affair had been fierce and wild and he'd revelled in the secret knowledge that he was screwing his master's wife but there had never been any love, he'd done it for the power it gave him.

A few months after the affair had started she had demanded that he murder her husband. The wife had long had her eye on her husband's wealth and she had promised Adonibaal a share if he agreed to her plan. So he had entered his master's bedroom at night and strangled him and dumped the body in a well but he'd underestimated his lover's ambition for on the next day the wife had recovered the body and accused him of murder. She'd gotten everything she had wanted and Adonibaal had only narrowly managed to escape with just the shirt on his back and a price on his head. The experience had turned him into a loner and had fuelled his hatred of any type of authority. He fled to the Carthaginian town of Utica, just up the coast and found work as a thug for a business rival of his former master.

The years had passed and he'd become an expert at killing and catching wanted men for his employer but the price on his head had never been lifted and he'd continuously been forced to watch his back, in case some desperate character tried to cash in and bring him in. It had been a violent life. His victims had often pleaded for mercy, some had tried to bribe him with sex, slaves or whole estates if he would let them go but he never did. He was a professional. It was the one thing he was proud of.

Women had been attracted to his wolfish good looks but he'd had no desire to form any relationships and he had treated them as if they were a commodity until his reputation was such, that the only women who bothered to hang around him were the prostitutes in the alleys in which he worked. But occasionally, just sometimes, when he was alone at night, when his employer's house was fast asleep, he would lie awake and think in despair about the monster that he'd become. He had betrayed his country. He was a murderer and a fugitive. He had thrown away all the promise of his youth and alienated his family. His life hadn't needed to be like this but he couldn't go back and undo what had been done. When he died there would be no one to remember him and make sure that he was properly buried. That was the law by which he had to live. In those moments of dark despair there was only one source from which he drew the strength to keep going; the memory of a young woman from long ago.

Then the day had come, whilst hunting for a man through the narrow alleyways of Utica, when his past had finally caught up with him. Adonibaal had been surrounded by a gang of men led by a Carthaginian nobleman called Gisgo. He'd presumed they had come for the price on his head but after he'd been taken to the noble's house Gisgo had made him a surprise offer. The Carthaginian had described himself as a spy master and a politician. He'd long kept an eye on Adonibaal and had been impressed by Adonibaal's growing reputation as a killer but what had interested him more was that Adonibaal was Roman, spoke fluent Latin and knew the city of Rome inside out. The choice he'd offered Adonibaal was between, being handed over to the family of his former master which would mean death, or he could come with Gisgo and join Hannibal's army which was assembling in Spain. I can use a man like you Gisgo had told him, especially where we are going. It hadn't been a hard decision to take and Adonibaal had been impressed by Gisgo's influence with Hannibal but soon he'd understood the full personal price he'd had to pay for Gisgo's protection. On the first night after their arrival in the town of New Carthage, Gisgo's men had forced him into their master's room where Gisgo had raped him. It had been a devastating and humiliating experience made worse by the money he'd been given afterwards, as if he were a prostitute, and the warning that if he deserted the Spanish tribes, who lived in the mountains around the town, had orders to track down deserters and mutilate them. Not that he had considered deserting. He was tired of running and hiding. He had been running for twenty-four years. Instead he'd resolved to kill Gisgo but the nobleman had always taken great care to protect himself and no opportunity had come his way. He had realised bitterly that there had been nothing he could do but take the humiliation.

Gisgo' talent, he had observed, was to know who to support in the fractious, violent and forever changing world of Carthaginian politics. That's how he had gained his influence over Hannibal but the man had another talent too, one that Adonibaal had grudgingly come to admire. Gisgo knew how to spot weakness in other men and ruthlessly exploit it. It had turned the Carthaginian spy master into a feared man. A few weeks after the rape, the army had begun its epic march and Adonibaal had realised that he was finally going home.

***

Adonibaal was suddenly conscious that the mercenaries around the fire had stopped singing. He glanced in their direction and to his surprise saw that the men had vanished into the night. His shoulders sagged with a sudden sense of foreboding.

"There you are," a voice called out from the gloom. A figure appeared. He was dressed in a long cloak. The man crouched down on his hind legs and watched, from a safe distance, as Adonibaal sharpened his sword.

"Still not forgiven me have you," the stranger chuckled.

"Come a little closer Gisgo, and I shall," Adonibaal growled.

Two years had passed since the rape and the two men had grown familiar with the tense standoff which always developed whenever they met. Gisgo would come protected by his bodyguards to find Adonibaal and tell him what he wanted. For Gisgo it was a fairly safe way of doing business and he revelled in seeing Adonibaal's humiliation every time they met, but on each occasion there was just the off chance that Adonibaal would do something crazy and unexpected. Gisgo loved the danger and the excitement of getting close to someone who wanted to kill him.

For Adonibaal seeing Gisgo was a source of depression for he knew he would have no choice but to obey him or be put to death for disobedience. He had conceded long ago that the Carthaginian spymaster was an expert at torture for every time he saw the man it reminded him of his humiliation. And there was another reason why he hated seeing Gisgo. The Carthaginian was toying with him, enjoying his power, but at anytime he could grow bored of the game and have Adonibaal murdered.

"I am surprised that you haven't deserted and gone over to your countrymen," Gisgo chuckled.

Adonibaal didn't reply but went on sharpening his sword.

"Ah, of course, they would have you executed for being a deserter wouldn't they," Gisgo laughed, "Fine mess you have got yourself into isn't it?"

"What do you want?" Adonibaal looked up.

"I have work for you, Adonibaal. A job that will require all your qualities and genius," Gisgo replied smoothly. "I think you will like it."

"No," Adonibaal shook his head, "My mercenary contract expires next month. When it does I intend to take my money and leave."

"Really," Gisgo eyes widened in mock surprise, "And where will you go, back to Rome, to Utica, Carthage and retirement? You have enemies in all those places."

Adonibaal nodded solemnly, "I will go to the east and find work."

"Yes well," Gisgo smiled, "my orders come directly from Hannibal himself so I am afraid that I won't be letting you go next month. Hannibal himself wants you to do this job."

Angrily Adonibaal pointed a finger towards Gisgo. "What's this, would you cheat a man out of his rights?"

"You will obey," Gisgo raised his voice sharply.

For just a split second Adonibaal was tempted to go for it, to drive his sword into the Carthaginian's stomach and gut the bastard, but by a supreme effort he held back.

"Yes still want to kill me don't you," Gisgo sneered, "but that won't do you any good my friend for I know what a man like you needs." He laughed and the laughter was cruel and mocking. "After all this time you still think like a Roman, don't you? Contracts..." Gisgo spat the word out scornfully. "The only contract you will obey is the contract you have with me and that ends when I tell you that it ends."

"Go and find someone else," Adonibaal retorted bitterly knowing that he was losing the verbal exchange.

"I want you," Gisgo snapped, "You are the ideal man for the job." He paused. "This job, this is the reason why I rescued you from that shit hole where I found you. Now are you prepared to listen?"

Adonibaal remained silent knowing he had no choice.

"Good, that's better," Gisgo said. He paused. "I know what a man like you thinks of a man like me and to be honest I don't give a damn." Gisgo licked his lips. "All you Romans are as straight as your roads but I know something about you too Adonibaal, I know what a man like you needs."

Adonibaal spat onto the ground and finished sharpening Centurion. Around him he could sense Gisgo's bodyguards watching his every move.

"You lost everything when you fled from Rome didn't you? Oh I know your story and what you did Adonibaal," Gisgo grinned. "So what would you say if I gave you the chance to get it all back, to regain everything that you lost? Isn't that what you have always desired?"

Adonibaal laid down his sword and a single bead of sweat appeared on his forehead. He stared into the distance.

"Who is the target?" he said slowly.

"Good man, I knew you would accept," Gisgo clapped looking pleased with himself. "Come, you already know who he is, the man belongs to your clan, Adonibaal, or should we use your real name from now on Caeso Fabius Vibulani?"

Adonibaal sat very still and stared into the night. No one had called him by his real name in twenty-four years.

"You want me to kill Quintus Fabius Maximus, senator and ex consul of Rome," he said at last.

Gisgo's face lit up in delight. "Very good," he said clapping again. "Hannibal wants him dead within a month. If you manage it I shall see to it that in the new Roman administration, which Hannibal will set up, you are restored to your former position. You will once again be one of Rome's leading men. Your wealth, property and titles will be returned and you will finally be able to give up this awful life of yours and be the man whom you were always meant to be. Is that not what you have dreamed of for so long?"

Adonibaal swallowed and stared moodily into the camp fire.

"I will kill the bastard and you will keep your promise," he snarled.

Chapter Six –The story of Caeso and Numerius

Numerius lay on the couch in his house shaking and shivering with cold despite the hot clammy august weather outside. His head rested on a cushion and three woollen blankets had been draped over his body. His eyes were closed and beside him a bowl of porridge and a cup of wine stood untouched. The chattering of his teeth was audible to the young freedman, Publius who sat at his former master's feet bearing a worried look. The freedman had laid down the stylus and the parchment he had been writing on.

"Sir," Publius said laying his hand gently on the shivering figure, "the doctor is right. You sh…sh…should," he stuttered, "leave Rome for a healthier climate. At least until the heat of the summer is over."

Numerius' eyes remained closed and Publius knew the man was trying to hide the pain he was enduring.

"I will not go," the rasping words slipped out barely audible.

Publius sighed and bit his bottom lip. "The doctor s…s…says," he stuttered again," that you may die if you stay in Rome. He says you suffer from bad air, Sir. Please…"

There was a touching concern in the young freedman's voice and eyes but the stubborn old man beneath the blankets was unmoved.

"I was born here and I will die here," the voice whispered.

Publius hung his head in defeat. His patron was known to be a stoic and would not change his mind after he'd resolved on something, but Publius knew that he'd had to try. The shivering and shaking had started early that morning and had been followed by a fever, coughing and intense sweating. It had been necessary to have the gardener and the cook's assistance take turns fanning the master of the house.

Publius had called the doctor right away and the man, an old learned Greek had arrived and after a quick examination had pronounced Numerius was suffering from bad air, Malaria. It had been a completely unexpected and devastating announcement.

Later that morning the fever had faded until Numerius was feeling strong enough to rise to his feet and Publius had hoped that the worst was over but Numerius' face had looked grey, haggard and resigned.

"Fetch a stylus and some parchment," he had ordered, "I wish to record the events of my life before it is too late."

Publius had protested but Numerius had silenced him.

"There is no cure for malaria, Publius," he had said. "Fetch the parchment and send word to Pompeia, that she should come at once."

That had been in the morning. Now Numerius was asleep again snoring gently. Publius glanced down at the parchment which lay in his lap. He dared not leave his master's side in case

Numerius woke suddenly and needed him. After five years as a slave and ten as a freedman, Publius thought he'd known everything there was to know about the family he served. Numerius had been a good master, strict but fair. He'd given Publius his freedom on the day the boy had officially become a man and had paid to have Publius taught to read and write. In Rome such generosity was rare and Publius knew he was lucky to have a master like Numerius. As a free man Publius would have been able to go his own way but he had decided to stay and work for his former master. It had been a good decision.

Numerius was a lawyer who had made a reputation defending the poor in the city; giving a voice to those who could not afford it or did not dare to speak out. It had made him revered in some quarters and hated in others. But Publius was proud of Numerius and had resolved to follow in his former master's footsteps and so had trained to be a lawyer. Soon, he hoped, he would ask Numerius' permission to conduct his first trial but his patron's sudden illness had made everything uncertain.

Publius glanced at the manuscript again and touched it with his fingers tracing the lines of neat writing. The texts were disjointed, the memories and thoughts mixed randomly together, sometimes rambling, written down just as Numerius had spoken them. It was not the smooth story the playwrights in the theatre would create and yet there was something irresistibly fascinating about it. In the fifteen year's he'd been with Numerius, he'd never heard his patron speak about his family like he had today.

My name, reader, is Numerius Fabius Vibulani, younger son of Marcus. I was born into the clan of the Fabii, the noblest of the great families of Rome during the fifth year of war with Carthage. We are descendants of Hercules. My family are guardians of Rome and can trace our ancestry back to the founding of our blessed city. We have shed more blood for Rome than any other. Three of my forefathers held seven consecutive consulships, three hundred of my kinsmen died nobly at Cremera and a Fabius defended the Capitoline against Brennus in the terrible days when our beloved city was sacked by the Gauls. We, Fabii have a sacred duty to protect Rome and greatness is expected from us from an early age.

So, it has been for more than fifteen generations, thus it was until the day my brother and I were born. This is the story of the downfall of our house.

I shall remember the 10th March in the year of Atticus and Cerco with special care for it was the first time that I went into battle. The trumpets called us soldiers down to our ships and it was here that I embraced my older brother Caeso, possibly for the last time. We were going to war at last. He was a year older than I and held a more senior rank. He shook my shoulders and I remember the excitement in his eyes. He had trained all his life for this moment. He always did love the pursuit of glory. He told me that today we would learn of what iron we were made. Like Hercules.

I tried to remind him that there was no need for foolish heroics and that our father expected to see us again. To this Caeso answered and I remember his exact words. "Leave the old bastard out of this. He never cared for us." He was wrong about that but at the time he didn't know it.

My position was as a staff officer on the flag ship of the Praetor Quintus Valerius Falto but Caeso had been assigned the command of his own vessel, even though he was only nineteen and had never set foot on a ship until a few months ago. But such privileges are the natural right of a patrician family which has protected Rome for over three hundred years. Falto had been given command of the two hundred Roman ships that made up our fleet which had been besieging Lilybaeum since the previous year. It was an odd arrangement for his superior, the consul Catulus should have been in command but had been unable to do so because of wounds suffered in an earlier engagement. Nevertheless, Falto proved to be a competent leader.

I was eighteen years old. The first war with Carthage had been dragging on for twenty-four years. It was a miracle that we had a fleet at all as at that time our treasury was empty and the state as good as bankrupt. Our fleet existed because of the patriotic donations from its wealthier denizens.

The enemy had borne down on us, with the wind fair behind them, long vertical lines of sails, intent on running for the harbour of Carthaginian held Lilybaeum. As a staff officer, I was not expected to fight, but it still takes a strong nerve to stand and watch the enemy approach and not feel the fear in the pit of your stomach. It's a fear borne from not being in control and of not being able to do anything but wait. Caeso was right. We were going to know of what kind of iron we were made of.

I knew from the first day, as a boy, when my teachers first started to instruct me in the art and skill of fighting and war, that I was no warrior. I lacked the killer instinct that my brother had. I was not confident with the sword or the campaign map. How different I was to my brother Caeso who immediately excelled at everything to do with combat and physical exercise. Perhaps my teachers noticed but I never gave them cause for complaint or ridicule. I never asked to be excluded from the training. Life was easier when I did not complain even though I did not enjoy the labour.

Falto, our fleet commander, despite the unfavourable wind and being out numbered, attacked and in the battle that followed our ships and men proved their quality. There was little time to worry about Caeso. It was only when with the fading light and the remnants of the Carthaginian fleet fleeing westwards that I learned that he had won himself great fame by capturing three enemy ships. They told me that he had been the first man to board them. For this action, he was rewarded.

So, I suppose I can claim to have taken part in the final battle that decided that first war with Carthage. There are some, now that we are once again at war with our old enemy, who deplore the futility of war and point to the human cost. These voices do not consider that sometimes war is inevitable, sometimes war is foisted on a man against his will and once engaged, the only strategy that makes sense is to win. Soon afterwards, our year's service completed, Caeso and I were allowed to return to Rome. Little did we know it at the time but our troubles were just about to start.

After my father's death, I became a lawyer. Our family wealth meant that I was a rich man but I felt compelled to defend those who could not defend themselves, to do right like Ambustus did all those years ago, and in time I made a reputation for myself.

My father was a strict disciplinarian. He used to tell us that the first duty of a Roman was to obey. We were always being reminded of the Roman general who executed his own son for disobedience before a battle. My father's household was run like an army camp and as boys Caeso and I were beaten for the slightest offence. The man who carried out our punishment was called Janus. He was a slave, a dull stupid brute from the mountains of Liguria. When my father died, he was given his freedom.

The only fond memory that I have of my father is when at night he would come to our bedside, when we were still young, and tell us stories about our ancestors. Both I and Caeso loved those stories. They were full of heroics and great deeds of valour and nobility and we would spend all night talking about them. Our ancestors were our heroes and both of us wanted to be like them. In our house, we had a library and on one of the walls, hung up in a long line, were the death masks of our ancestors going back fifteen generations. We were not often allowed into that library but when we were, we entered as if in the presence of Jupiter himself. On feast day's my father would hire men to re-enact the deeds of our forefathers. The actors would wear the death masks and Caeso and I would sit and watch. We each had our own champion, Caeso chose Hercules, the founder of our family, a half man half god with strength beyond any mortal soul. I chose Marcus Fabius Ambustus, the man who helped reconcile Patrician and Plebeian interests and so allowed our city to avoid civil war.

It gives a boy courage and purpose to know that he lives amongst such illustrious company. Yet it places an expectation on him too and that is a heavy burden to bear. Caeso was forever deriding me for choosing Ambustus but it takes courage to go against your class and peers, risking your reputation, alone and abandoned by ones friends, for the sake of the common good. Caeso never did understand that kind of courage. For him courage could only be shown on the battlefield.

I never knew my mother. Her name was Lydia. Caeso claimed to remember her but I don't think he did. She died when we were both very young but it is from her that I inherited my love of words and our Latin language. Caeso grew up as a rebel. He was too proud and confident. Whenever he could he would argue and refuse to follow our father's orders. He was beaten a lot and there was always a bruise or a scar on him but the punishment didn't work. I don't think anything could stop him. He was headstrong and fearless. In many ways he was just like my father.

As a boy I did not have my brother's physical strength and self confidence. But my father's rules taught me the difference between right and wrong. I learned about what a man could and could not get away with. I became good at speaking. I learned to obey my father and I took my punishment in silence even when I knew that it was not justified and because I never challenged my father's authority, he began to treat me with less severity than he did Caeso. I think he found it hard to argue with me. So, I began to speak up in my brother's defence. I knew just the right tone to take and what words to use and by my action I saved my brother from many a beating but Caeso was never thankful and he made my task no easier with his behaviour.

Looking back now I know my father did love us. He was just no good at showing it and now I shall admit, that a day does not go by during which I hope to be reconciled with my brother again.

We returned from Sicily in high spirits. Caeso had been rewarded for his bravery in battle and news of his exploits had already travelled on ahead of us. We were expecting to enter the city in triumph. It is odd what things a man remembers. I was with Caeso on the Appian Way as we approached the Capena Gate. He was nineteen and he had just announced to me that he was going to marry his woman. Her name was Flavia. She was a cattle driver's daughter, a sweet girl with a beautiful smile and jet black hair that always smelled of roses. I had actually known her before Caeso had. In those days when we had reached maturity, my brother and I had started slipping away from the house at night and spending time in the taverns and bars of the Subura. I had a group of friends who did this regularly and she had been part of this group. It was on such a night when Caeso had joined me that he had met Flavia and he'd fallen for her right away.

I told him that our father would never allow him to marry Flavia. She was from a poor family, utterly unsuited to be a wife for a young nobleman. I told him that he could not marry without our father's consent. Such is the law. It would be impossible for me to speak up for him against my father on such terms. By tradition our father would choose our wives from our own class. I told him to forget about Flavia. Ofcourse he was not happy with me. He was stubborn, and like my father, he had to win at all costs, no matter what damage he did in the process. He said that he didn't care about our father's opinion. He said that he and Flavia had sworn an oath of loyalty to each other. He was not going to break that oath to spend the rest of his life married to a wife he didn't love because it suited his father's ambitions. If it came to it he was prepared to run away with Flavia and forsake his title and inheritance. He would go north taking Flavia with him and would find some land on the Gallic frontier that needed a brave enough man to farm it. It was after these comments that I started to worry.

I tried to reason with him. Flavia was going to bring him trouble. She was going to ruin his life. I knew he didn't stand a chance of winning the argument and that the law would decide against him. Caeso would have none of it. His mind was made up and we nearly came to blows there and then on the Appian Way. He accused me of taking my father's side which was unfair for I had always tried to speak up for him. For all his qualities, my brother was not a sensitive man. He never did care much, or bother, about how other people felt. That was his greatest weakness. It was after this conversation that I suggested he petition Quintus Fabius Maximus. My father was a supporter of Fabius and Fabius was a close family friend. My father would listen to Fabius and I thought it may work.

But Caeso disagreed. He said he didn't trust Fabius because he was too close to our father. He called Fabius a slow dim witted child stuck in a man's body. There was a section of the nobility at this time who agreed with this description. It was not an uncommon view. Eventually Caeso swore me to silence on the matter.

Throughout the weeks that followed our return to Rome, Caeso would not change his mind about marrying Flavia. The three of us would often go up into the hills above the city and wander around aimlessly amongst the forests and fields delighting in our freedom. But soon things became awkward and I stopped going. I knew by then that it was useless to try and change Caeso' mind and his decision hurt me deeply.

***

Publius looked up as Numerius stirred on the couch and muttered in his sleep. Anxiously the young man watched for signs that the malaria had returned but all seemed well for now.

***

On the ides of the March in the second year after our return from war, Caeso came to me and told me that he was marrying Flavia the next day. He wanted me to be his witness. I hadn't seen her for a while so I asked him why he was in such a rush. She was only fifteen after all and too young to marry in my opinion. I remember the look on his face. We were lying beside the pool, all alone. Our father and Janus had gone to Ostia on business and the slaves had been dismissed for the afternoon.

He told me that she was pregnant and would give birth within days. He did not want his son or daughter born as a bastard.

So I made my final appeal knowing it was pointless. I reminded him that our father had the right to put him to death for disobedience and that I thought he may do so when he found out. But this was Caeso I was talking to and he just laughed and said that he was not afraid. He had friends amongst the officers with whom he'd fought with in the war. They would protect him.

He asked me again to be his witness and eventually I agreed.

I heard him shouting that very same evening. It sounded like he was in a fight with someone. In the atrium of our house I came across Janus and my father. They had just locked Caeso into the room where my father kept our money. It's a strong room ringed by masonry two feet thick. I could hear him hammering on the door. He was shouting every obscenity he knew. My father glared at me without saying a word whilst Janus stood guard at the door. Janus had done well from my brother's downfall. I could see the delight in his eyes and it angered me. But there was nothing that I could do.

They kept my brother locked up for five days. He was guarded day and night. On the morning of the sixth day a distraught man presented himself at the entrance to our house. My father would not allow him in. But I knew who he was. He was Flavia's father. The news he brought gutted me. Flavia had given birth to a daughter, a healthy daughter, but she herself had died in childbirth. Her father had come to ask if Caeso would accept the child as his own. My father threatened to have the poor man flogged if he dared show his face here again. Flavia was a sweet girl and I mourned her loss greatly, but she had made a poor choice in Caeso. She deserved better than what fortune gave her.

It was Janus who told my brother the news. He did this from behind the locked door and the manner in which he spoke showed the evil that lurked in his soul. My father knew by now about my brothers plans and he was livid. He stalked the house breaking everything in his path but it was but a small rage compared to that of my brother. I suppose I should have realised what was coming. But none of us suspected at the time what he was capable of.

My father decided that Caeso would be punished. The next day my brother was taken from his prison and given twenty lashes. It was Janus who carried the whip and the punishment was carried out in the garden by the pool in front of all our slaves. It was humiliating to watch. Afterwards my father ordered that Caeso be stripped of all his honorary armour, weapons and awards and that from hence onwards he would serve as a common soldier in the Legions when we were required to go to war again. My brother would serve as a common soldier until he had learned to obey.

Caeso took his punishment like a man. He took it like I knew he would take it. He did not flinch or cry or beg for forgiveness. He was silent throughout the whole ordeal. But when he caught my eye I could only see hatred for me in that look. He hated me from that day onwards for I suppose he thinks that I betrayed him as I was the only one who knew what he was going to do. I do not blame him for it is the truth.

The next morning when I woke I found a bloody knife lying beside me on my bed. I knew immediately who had left it there. Why he did not kill me is something I still don't really understand. Maybe the madness that came over him had passed. Maybe deep down he did realise that I loved him, that is what I would like to believe, but I don't know and now I will never know. What however is irrefutable is that I have not seen my brother since that day, 24 years ago. He perished most probably a long time ago in some lonely forgotten corner of the world and maybe that was best for him. I shall meet him again in the afterlife where I shall explain myself to him.

We searched the whole house and then the city but we did not find him. He had vanished and so I went to the Senate and told them what had happened, for my father was a senator then, and they agreed to list Caeso as a fugitive, with a price on his head, for the murder of his father.

Chapter Seven – The gods have deserted us

Numerius stood waiting in the atrium, in the hall of his friend's house. The atrium was the central room and at his feet a rectangular basin filled with water had been sunk into the beautiful mosaic floor. Opposite him, in a niche in the wall, standing on a ledge, were the statuettes of the various household gods. Above him the atrium was partially open to the sky to allow for rain water to collect in the basin. Surrounding him on all sides were the doorways to different rooms, an office, the kitchen, bedrooms and the dining room and towards the back of the house he knew there was a colonnaded garden, although he had never been invited into that part. The slaves were all busy in the kitchen preparing breakfast and for a moment they were alone.

It was early morning but he could sense it was going to be a hot day. His face looked pale and weary, yet there was alertness in his eyes. At fourty three he was considered an old man in a city where the average life expectancy was thirty years and one in two babies died in infancy. He was slimly built with short greying hair and wore a simple white tunic with a belt from which hung an old army sword. On his feet, he was wearing a pair of army sandals that had seen better days.

"Not a word about my condition," he glanced at Publius who stood waiting beside him carrying a stout stick and a leather satchel.

The young freedman nodded and kept his eyes lowered. It was strange, Publius thought, that he still thought like a slave even though he was a free man. Old routines were hard to break. Should he swagger around like a wealthy patrician or like the rough soldiers he saw in the street? All Publius knew was that he liked to serve his patron. If there ever was a man who combined decency and compassion with the ways and haughteur of an old fashioned aristocrat, then it was his patron. Publius had long ago started to copy Numerius, using the same phrases and even the same poses. It was his way of showing his devotion to the man to whom he owed everything, but it had not stopped his friends in the city from mocking him. His city friends were always urging him to broaden his ideas, telling him that there was more out there than just service. Publius understood them but he didn't care, he knew his own mind and he was happy. Why should he change when he was happy with the life he had chosen to lead?

But now he worried about Numerius. His patrons fever had faded just as the doctor had said it would but the physician had also told him that it would return and keep returning. Publius kept his eyes on the floor, tracing the fine patterns in the mosaic. That was the nature of the disease the doctor had said. It would return and go away and return again in a few days, like a cat playing with a mouse, before eventually it would cause a major organ to fail and death would follow. There was no cure and it would be a painful death. He'd asked the doctor how much time his patron had left but the physician had shrugged and told him it depended on how strong the patient was but that death would be certain within a few months. Until then his patron would experience periods where he felt much better.

Publius worried what would happen after Numerius died. What would he do without his patron's guidance and support? His life was about to change and the change had come much faster than he had expected. His friends had urged him to try and get himself written into Numerius will. It was possible he would be left something. The man had no sons and only a daughter and he was wealthy, maybe not as wealthy as the man in whose house he now stood, but still...wealthy. However the thought of asking to be included in Numerius' will left a bad taste in Publius' mouth. If it was meant to be the old man would make provisions.

Footsteps were coming down the corridor from the garden and a moment later the venerable white haired figure of Quintus Fabius Maximus appeared. He looked sombre and serious, dressed in his fine white toga. Numerius stepped forwards and embraced his kinsman.

"Good to see you Fabius," he said.

Fabius raised his eyebrows as they parted. "Gods, you look terrible," he murmured taking his time to examine his friend. "And why the sword," he added, "All we are doing is going for a walk to the forum."

Numerius shook his head, "I thought it best to come armed, what with the city in such uproar. You never know what the people may do."

Fabius grunted. "Yes I suppose you are right. Come, we should not be late, that would not do today."

He extended his hand to Publius and rested it on the man's shoulders. "I trust you know how to support an old man with a bad foot blister," he said to the freedman, without looking at him.

"Of course Sir," Publius replied and so the three of them stepped out into the street.

***

Rome was in the grip of panic. As the two old men and young Publius struggled down the Sacred Way towards the forum they could see and hear it everywhere. In the narrow twisting streets and alleys people thrust past, shouting and gesticulating that the enemy was approaching the city. Some were already pushing carts filled with personal belongings before them. In the houses and tall apartment blocks, the high pitched, dreadful wailing of women in mourning had begun as soon as the news of the terrible, unexplainable disaster of Cannae had reached Rome. The wailing had grown like an approaching thunderstorm until it seemed every household in Rome was caught up in it. Could it really be true, Numerius thought, that the greatest army Rome had ever fielded had been completely destroyed? He tried to ignore the wailing but it was difficult. He glanced at Fabius who was still leaning for support on Publius' shoulder. Fabius had thrust his jaw forwards and moved along at his usual slow but steady pace, his face unreadable but confident and Numerius was suddenly glad he was there.

"Yesterday," Fabius muttered, "I was an old man who many thought was politically finished, past his prime, but today," he grunted in a deep voice, "today these same critics come running back to me like children seeking comfort from the advancing night. Isn't it strange how a man's fortune can change so swiftly?"

"It is the same for nations," Numerius sighed. "They should have listened to you. Your strategy for dealing with Hannibal was sound. You should remind them of that today."

"I think they already know," Fabius muttered casting around him. "Today, Numerius," he added, "we shall find out the true nature of what it is to be a Roman."

Numerius nodded. "Has there been any news at all from the Consuls?"

"None," the old man shook his head, "We must assume that they have perished along with every able bodied soldier that we had."

"Varro was a fool then," Numerius exclaimed, "You warned him not to risk battle with half trained men and now we must pay the price for his rashness."

"No, this is not the time for recriminations," Fabius replied, "If anyone should be punished then let it be the enemy and not our common cause."

The forum was a scene of wild, nearly hysterical disorder. It was market day, the day upon which the farmers came into the city to sell their wares to the town dwellers, but today hardly any of them had bothered to show up. Instead it seemed as if every lawyer, financier and businessman who normally filled the forum was packing up his belongings and fleeing towards the nearest city gate. As the fine stone statues of past heroes and the deities of a hundred different professions looked on in silence, property, privileges and belongings were sold at huge discounted prices. Through the crowd a thin trickle of men clad in white togas struggled towards the Curia Hostilia, the Senate house and seat of government. Numerius glanced up at the temple of Jupiter on the Capitoline hill. The doors to the temple would be open and he wondered what the patron god of Rome would make of the scene. The doors to the great temple were only closed in times of peace. He shook his head in disbelief. It had taken nearly all of Fabius' authority to just get the senators to attend a meeting, such was the fear and panic that now gripped the city.

"I have never seen anything like it," a white-haired senator gasped as he ran into Fabius.

"The gods have deserted us!" another man called out hysterically as he too recognised Fabius.

The three of them entered the Comitium, the large open paved space with circular steps cutting down into its centre. It was here that the Roman people would gather to listen to their magistrates who would speak from an elevated platform, the Rostra. Using his stick, Publius tried to clear a path through the crowd. The Comitium was packed and it was only after some difficulty that they finally mounted the broad steps leading up to the Senate house which rose above the circular open space opposite the Rostra.

"Make way there!" Publius cried out as a woman tried to grab hold of Fabius' toga.

***

As Numerius was not a senator he was not allowed to have a seat on the benches or take part in the debate and instead he and Publius hung around the doorway into the building. They were joined by the sons of various senators out to see how the Senate worked. When the Senate was finally gathered together the scale of the disaster had become unmistakeable, one that every man in the house could not ignore. Out of the 300 members who would normally have been present barely two hundred senators had taken their seats. The gaps between the rows on both sides of the great rectangular building testified to the terrible slaughter that had occurred. On the benches the senators glanced uneasily around them and gasps of dismay could be heard as the truth sank in. The speaker, an old stooping, grizzled man opened the session and in a voice whose tone rose and dropped he asked if anyone had something to say. The two Praetors, the most senior magistrates left in the city and who had called the meeting on Fabius' urging, looked utterly bewildered. No one replied, for no one seemed to know what to do about a disaster on this scale, and the great hall remained silent but for a few stray pigeons who fluttered high up amongst the ceiling and the wailing of women in the streets outside.

Then Fabius rose, nodded to the speaker, and taking his time made his way to the speaker's platform at the far end of the hall. There was no procedure or agenda. Fabius would speak because he was one of the oldest members of the Senate and because he alone had managed to face Hannibal and not be utterly ruined.

"It seems," he said with a mild voice, "that we have suffered a great defeat. Possibly the greatest defeat and slaughter in our history."

A murmur rose from the gathered senators but no one spoke out.

"I can't say with certainty what has happened to the Consuls but we must assume that they are dead and that it is up to us to decide the next move, and we must decide today." Fabius paused watching his audience. "Time presses us and we must act with vigour and courage, nothing less will do. So I propose that the following measures be immediately taken. Firstly that soldier's be placed on all city gates to prevent the people from fleeing the city. Secondly that the period of mourning be restricted to a maximum of thirty days and that all women be banned from leaving their homes. Their wailing does no one any good. Thirdly, that we immediately send scouts down the Appian Way to find out where Hannibal is and whether he intends to march on Rome or is already doing so."

Fabius stopped as a senator rose from his seat. "You propose to continue the war?" the man exclaimed.

Silence fell in the great hall. Fabius leaned forwards to peer at the senator who had stood up.

"Of course," he replied in his mild-mannered voice, "We are going to win this war if it takes us a hundred years. What other outcome would you desire?"

Not a man made a sound. Then slowly and with as much dignity as the man could muster, the senator sat down.

"Fourthly," Fabius continued, "the severity of this crisis demands that all able-bodied male citizens of the city be at once conscripted into a new army. In addition, I propose that those slaves and debtors who are willing to fight, and take an oath to this effect be granted their freedom and enrolled in the army. Finally, that Marcus Junius Pera should be elected dictator at once with Tiberius Sempronius Gracchus as his Master of horse."

Fabius paused as a hush suddenly broke out in the house. Another senator had stood up. It was Quintus Caecilius Metellus, secretary to the Pontifex Maximus, the high priest. A man seated beside him tried to pull him back into his seat but Metellus, a man in his late thirties with black curly hair and small pig like eyes shrugged off the restraining hand.

"The Pontiff, our father," he declared in a confident voice, "wishes to complain about the inauspicious date of this meeting. As you all know, it is market day today and the law clearly states that it is forbidden to conduct a public meeting of the Senate on market day."

Several senators jumped to their feet to protest but Metellus ignored them and addressing the speaker continued, raising his voice boldly so that he could be heard, "It is the opinion of the college of Pontiffs and our father that the ill fortune that has befallen our city is due to the lax and careless way in which our magistrates have gone about honouring the gods. Many are the ill omens which have recently been observed in the city. I shall not burden you with examples but nevertheless their meaning is clear to our father. The gods are angry with us," he bellowed suddenly, "for the disrespect that we have shown them."

He managed to compose himself quickly, so smoothly that Numerius who was watching knew then that he was feigning his anger. Metellus was a well known figure in Rome. He was hated for his arrogance and alleged cruelty but mainly he was feared for he was the second most powerful man in the college of Pontiffs, after the high priest himself. The college of Pontiffs, the priests who regulated and carried out all the higher religious rituals were in turn the most important and powerful group of the four colleges into which Roman priesthood were divided.

"Watch him," Numerius whispered to Publius, "and you will see how an expensive oratory school teaches its students."

Metellus' pig eyes turned to old Fabius. "Fabius here," he pointed, "is a practical man and has proposed certain measures which he wants us to pass. Let us pass them I say. However know this, know that the high priest has decided to send an ambassador to the shrine at Delphi in order to consult the oracle on what we should do. Until our ambassador has heard the Oracle's words there can be no ratification of any proposals in this house. To do so will inflame the anger of the gods even further."

"We can't wait until he returns!" several voices cried out in protest.

Metellus turned aggressively towards the house ignoring the protests that seemed to grow around him like a storm. "However," he whined, "in the meantime we can consider the disrespect that has been shown to the gods. Someone," he thundered waving a finger in the air; "is responsible and must be punished for this disrespect. For if we do not placate the gods with a suitable sacrifice, a sacrifice so great and potent, that they will not be able to refuse it, then gentlemen, our current misfortune can only grow worse. Someone is responsible for the neglect of the sacred duties. I do not know who, but I know that we cannot tolerate it any longer."

Metellus shook his head as his voice grew in passion and volume and again he waved his index finger in the air in warning.

"I, like you all, do not wish to see a Carthaginian enter this city but without a suitable sacrifice Rome will be doomed. I demand punishment, the college of Pontiffs demands it, the high priest demands it and the gods demand it."

Then abruptly Metellus sat down.

"Bravo," Numerius muttered sarcastically under his breath.

As Metellus sat down another senator rose to his feet. "What hope do we have," the man cried, "Thrice now Hannibal has defeated us in the very heart of Italy. Our best men are dead, our city is defenceless; we have no armies left, our leaders have proved incompetent. I say that it is time to make peace before all is lost."

A few voices joined him calling out the names of their sons who had been lost and their estates which had now passed into enemy hands but most of the senators, stunned and sullen, remained in their seats.

Fabius remained silent until the tumult died down. Then he looked at Metellus taking his time to size him up.

"Yes it is market day," he said slowly, "And yet even you have shown up to this meeting."

There was a smattering of laughter amongst the benches and Metellus shifted uncomfortably in his seat.

"Presumably you have the names of those you accuse of dereliction of their religious duties?" Fabius asked him.

Metellus managed a smile and nodded.

"The high priest will declare them in due course," he replied.

There was an angry stir amongst a section of senators and some shouted obscenities in Metellus' direction.

Fabius raised his hand for silence and as he did so his eyes seemed to pick out Numerius from the crowd.

"Go on," Numerius muttered with a sudden up swell of emotion, "give it to them."

"You speak with authority Metellus," Fabius said with a dignified voice, "but you are wrong. This is no time for punishment. This is the moment when only our unity and resolve will save the Republic. I will not support any witch hunt whilst we are in such mortal danger. Even if it angers the gods, we are men and we are all still the leaders of this great city for which our forefathers did so much to raise her from the ground. We must, all of us, now stand firm and if we can do this, then I am confident that we will survive and prosper."

Metellus' face darkened and he folded his arms across his chest as Fabius turned to address the house. And as he spoke it seemed to Numerius that the old man's words began to lift the mood of his fellow senators. It was true Fabius said that maybe one day they would have to seek terms from Hannibal but that day was not today. The Senate had to keep its nerve. He would ask for no peace as long as Rome and the Roman people still remained free and considerable strength remained within the city. It was time for Rome to show it was worthy of being a great people, worthy of its great destiny. The gods were indeed watching, waiting to see what we would do and they would reward those who were steadfast and faithful. Leadership would come from no other place but from us he warned; for the aristocracy of Rome owed its greatness, privilege and honour not to an accident of birth but to its willingness to lead the nation in battle. That willingness had already made casualties of a third of the Senate's members and if the Senate were not prepared to lead once again it would be the people who would throw us aside for what use to Rome would we be then. His speech had concluded with a call for a vote on the measures he had proposed. No one had opposed him, not even Metellus and so the poll had been duly and solemnly taken, but a murmur had risen when the motion had passed but with only a narrow margin.

***

Afterwards as the meeting broke up and most senators headed for the door a group of glum faced men gathered around the figure of Fabius.

"I have just heard that the town of Arpi has gone over to Hannibal," one of the senators said. "The traitorous son's of whores! They closed their gates on our envoys."

Fabius nodded solemnly. "I fear that much of the south will go with Hannibal now. All the Greek towns and maybe parts of Samnium too but Capua should remain loyal, they are in our debt more than most."

Numerius hung back. It would not be proper for him to act as an equal to a senator by voicing his opinion. Yet he was angry and saddened at the same time. The vote on Fabius' proposals had shown that many senators did not really believe that Rome could win the war. What signal would this send to the people if they ever heard how narrow the margin had been?

"Capua, you say," a new voice spoke. It was Metellus who now approached with a few of his supporters. The man's eyes glanced at everyone around Fabius as if he was making a mental note of their faces. "I would not be so sure that Capua will remain loyal, Fabius; these Campanians have Greek blood in them and as we all know the Greeks can never be trusted. They are like corn, blowing in one direction and then another when the wind changes."

Fabius looked at Metellus with an expression of sudden distaste. "It is a shame that you managed to split the vote Metellus," he said gruffly, "did I not say that we must remain a unified force. The survival of the Republic is at stake man!"

The sudden anger in Fabius' voice took everyone by surprise. Metellus raised his eyebrows but he didn't flinch where a lesser man may have blushed.

"Split the vote," he repeated, "I did no such thing. Did you not hear me say that I wished to have no Carthaginian enter this city?" Metellus face darkened. "As for your words about not being worried about angering the gods," he growled, "The high priest shall hear about them. I would watch yourself next time you speak such blasphemy."

And with that he and his supporters stomped off.

"Cock," one of the senators around Fabius grunted.

"I see what you mean now master," Publius whispered as he stood at Numerius side. "The man is an actor but why does he not realise that others can see it?"

"Maybe he doesn't care," Numerius shrugged.

Fabius, Numerius and Publius were the last to leave the Senate house. At the great double doors leading out onto the steps and the bright sunlight Fabius turned and gazed back into the house and the empty benches. "At least we have set something in motion," he sighed. "Maybe our activity will encourage us to continue the fight."

"Metellus was a disgrace," Numerius muttered, "but are you sure that it was he who split the vote. There were others who spoke against you."

Fabius seemed to consider the question.

"No it was him. He is a dangerous man," he said wearily. "His purpose today was selfish and partisan. He has already begun to bargain with us. The man cares only for his own and his master's interests. He split the vote alright. His support is stronger than I had expected and remember this," Fabius said laying a hand on Numerius' shoulder, "the Pontifex Maximus is an ambitious man. He is always looking for ways in which to grow his power and influence." Fabius raised his eyebrows. "Maybe the high priest even wishes to be crowned king, if Hannibal were to occupy the city such a thing would not be impossible."

"Crowned king of Rome," Numerius gasped. It had been nearly 300 years since the last king had ruled Rome. The idea of a return to a monarchy was such an abhorrent idea to any Roman that it had never crossed his mind.

"There are enemies in our midst," Fabius muttered darkly. "Some men have stopped believing that the Republic will survive. They are already actively working on what will come next. Be wary of them. What we saw today was an attempt to settle political and personal rivalries using our current ill fortune as an excuse." Fabius sighed. "What kind of man thinks about growing his power base when the city is in such mortal danger?"

Numerius glanced at Publius who nodded and patted the leather satchel he had been carrying.

"I have made a note of everything that was said during the debate," Numerius said to Fabius. "When the time is right you can present your case. The city should know how much regard their priests have for them."

"Good man," Fabius replied. Then he gave Numerius an inquisitive glance.

"Are you sure you are alright. You look dreadful."

Chapter Eight – Daughter of the state

The sacred fire of Vesta had nearly gone out and it was all the fault of Opimia and Floronia, Pompeia thought as she fed the dry sticks into the fire. Those two were useless. Always chatting away, gossiping and neglecting their holy duties. Now their sloppiness had nearly caused a major scandal for as everyone knew, if the eternal fire of Vesta was allowed to die out it would bring ruin to Rome. Pompeia fed the last of the sticks into the fire and stood up. Of course it didn't help that all the vestal virgins were bored out of their minds she thought. But duty was important and Pompeia always took her duties very seriously.

She was twenty four, with black curly hair that fell to her shoulders and large green eyes. She was dressed in the traditional robes of a vestal virgin, the female priestesses of Rome, a long head dress that draped over her head and shoulders and a Palla, a simple cloak fastened with a brooch. Opimia and Floronia were always complaining about their clothes. They were either old or unfashionable. They made the girls look like old women. But what did those two know. Pompeia didn't mind. For her the clothes were part of a noble and ancient female tradition. Women had no voice in the great affairs of Rome. Only a Vestal commanded respect. Men would listen to a vestal. Men would obey a vestal. That ancient female foothold in a decisively man's world had to be honoured. It had to be defended and Pompeia was proud to defend it.

The temple of Vesta, the goddess of the hearth, where the holy fire was kept burning was where she spent most of her time performing her daily routine. Against the wall stood the vases for collecting water from the sacred spring, kitchen equipment for preparing food used in rituals, the wills and testaments of various senators and in a locked chest, the Palladium, the ancient wooden statue of Pallas Athena, which Aeneas had brought to Rome from Troy and given to the city's founding fathers five hundred years ago.

As she stared absentmindedly at the holy fire she became aware of a boy waiting quietly at the entrance to the temple. He stood very still with his eyes down cast as if the sight of the holy temple and its priestesses was too much for him to bear. She strode towards him and recognised him as the cook's boy from her father's house.

"Well, what does my father want?" she demanded.

"My master asks you to come to his house at once," the boy replied. Then without another word he was off, disappearing into the crowd that was packed into the forum beyond the temple grounds.

Puzzled, Pompeia watched him go. She was not expected to visit her father's house that day. Something urgent must have come up. She glanced towards her matron who had witnessed the scene. The matron, a strict but fair lady nodded.

"You may go, but be back by nightfall."

Pompeia smiled happily to herself as she left the temple and stepped into the covered two wheeled carriage that was waiting for her. Her duties may be sacred but oh how she enjoyed being out in the city on her own with its bustling, exciting crowds, away from the stuffy formality of the temple. The outside world was a huge mystery waiting to be discovered she thought. In the city she could watch the people. She could study how they lived, how people dealt with each other, the conflicts, the passions, the emotions! The city was fascinating.

She knew the real world was far removed from her own sheltered existence. She had known no other life than that of a Vestal virgin. At the age of seven her father had put her forwards as a candidate. It was considered a great honour and many of the leading families of Rome had competed for her position. Little at the time had she realised how momentous a day that had been for her but, despite the constraints and boredom, she was proud of what she did and who she represented. The goddess Vesta stood for family, kindness and honour. Vesta was pure and through her purity she gave strength and unity to Rome. Pompeia had agreed to serve the goddess for a term of 30 years during which she was forbidden from marrying and having sexual relations. The punishment for being unchaste was to be buried alive beneath the ancient cattle market.

The carriage was pulled along by two Gallic slaves. Preceding her on foot was a Lictor, a young man dressed in a smart toga. The man shouted at the people in the road to make way for her. As they left the temple grounds she composed herself. It was all an act but it was what the people would expect from her.

What did father want? The last time they had met a furious row had ensued. She did not see him very often and his stubborn, old fashioned character had often caused friction between them but he was all the family she had now that her mother had died.

They turned into the forum and she glanced at the money lenders standing in front of their stalls shaking bags of coins to attract business. Further along the lawyers too were touting for work calling out the number of their court victories like gladiators confirming their fights. A young poor and dirty looking boy tried to reach inside her carriage to touch her but the Lictor angrily struck him with his cane and the carriage moved on.

"I will go through the Trigemina gate today," she announced.

Below the temple of Jupiter on the Capitoline Hill they turned left and headed west for the Tiber. The carriage rattled and jolted on the cobbled street. The smell of raw sewage rose from the drains below the road but Pompeia pretended not to notice. So much of public life was an act. Women were supposed to act in a certain way and in her time she had become an expert actress. Yet sometimes it was necessary for her to show her true feelings. She would go insane if she didn't.

Soon she heard the noise of cattle bellowing in their pens and the cries of the cattle merchants haggling with each other. They entered the cattle market, the forum Boarium and turned sharply southwards skirting the great city wall and ignoring the brand new Aemilian Bridge that spanned the Tiber. The Aemilian Bridge was the fastest route to her father's house on the Janiculum hill but Pompeia had something else in mind today. The three arches of the Trigemina gate loomed up and they clattered through the middle arch and out of the city of

Rome. Immediately beyond the walls they were beset by beggars, filthy looking men and children, some as young as five, who held up their hands and cried out pleading for a few coins or some bread. At the sight of her carriage and the Lictor however even the boldest of the filthy stinking humanity seemed to hesitate. Then they recognised her and cry of joy and reverence rose up.

"Stop," she ordered and her carriage came to an abrupt halt. From beneath her cloak she produced a purse and as the beggars crowded around her she proceeded to hand out money. They took it eagerly and many wept and others cried out blessings on her name. As they crowded around, her face was a mask of tight aristocratic detachment. It would have caused a scandal if she had pretended to converse with the beggars as an equal. The great Patrician families already looked dimly on her charity.

Her salary from the state was more than sufficient and from an early age she had made regular journeys down to the Trigemina gate in order to help the poor. She was her father's daughter alright. Over the years it seemed that she had developed something of a divine status amongst the down trodden, so much so that the issue of her conduct had even been raised in the Senate. They had been worried that she was becoming too political. Well let them talk. She didn't care what those rich, privileged senators thought of her. That had been the reason for the quarrel with her father. The last time she'd met him he had tried to tell her that it did matter what the Senate thought of her. How hypocritical of him she thought, after all his legal work defending the poor. The row had left him furious with her but part of his fury, she knew, was because he could not force her to do his will.

There were more beggars on the Sublicus Bridge, a little way further down river but as the carriage trundled westwards over the wooden bridge she did not stop. Ahead of her the towering ridge of the Janiculum rose steeply above the banks of the Tiber. Its slopes were covered in trees and giant rocks and among them she could see goats grazing peacefully on the sparse vegetation. The sunlight reflected playfully in the green water of the Tiber. Her father had once lived in Rome but had moved out to a comfortable, but more modest villa perched on the ridge of the great hill. It was to avoid the noise and smell of the city he had told her, but Pompeia thought it was because of the memories of her mother which had filled their old house. It hadn't been a bad investment either for from her father's terrace he had a fantastic view of the whole city of Rome with lay below, east of the Tiber. Those had been her happiest moments with him, sitting on that terrace, with a cool breeze in her hair and gazing down on the great metropolis. She should have visited him more often she thought, especially now that mama was gone and he was all alone up there. Maybe then they would not quarrel so much.

***

They sat together in silence in the dining room, he on the chair beside the wall with a grey cloak wrapped around his shoulders and she by the window which looked out over the terrace and garden. The flowers in their beds and pots were in full bloom and the whole place was lit up by colour and the scent of a dozen different perfumes. She could hear the soft humming of insects and the rustle of birds in the trees. The news of her father's sudden illness and the doctor's visit had shocked her beyond words.

"Papa," she said at last turning to him, "I think the time has come to start doing all those things you wished to do once. You still have time and your friends would be honoured by a visit." Numerius shook his head.

"I am not leaving Rome," he replied. "And you will tell no one about my condition. There is a war going on and the city will need me."

They were silent for a while longer and then his mood seemed to improve. He glanced at his daughter.

"Pompeia, I would like to give you my will for safe keeping in the temple."

She nodded lowering her eyes, "Of course, we have space."

"I will be dead within a few months," he said. Then he paused, "I am going to ask you to do something for me, a final request."

A tear appeared in her eyes and she nodded again. "Of course papa, I will pray to Vesta."

"Come Publius," Numerius raised his voice and the young freedman appeared. The young man looked worried but Numerius smiled at him. "I have not departed just yet," he chuckled. "Have you got it?"

In reply the freedman handed over a sealed scroll of parchment marked with the blood red seal of Numerius' signet ring.

"It is customary that a will should be written before several witnesses but I have not done so," Numerius said.

She took the scroll of parchment and stared at it.

"I ask only that you honour me. There is something that you need to know," Numerius said quietly, "It is recorded in my will," he pointed at the parchment, "but you should know of it only after I am gone. Promise me now that you shall honour my wish."

She looked up at her father and fought to hold back the tears in her eyes. There was a kind and infinitely compassionate expression on Numerius' face, but also a hint of something else, shame. Desperately she wanted to rush across the room and throw her arms around him but such a show of emotion would just have upset him.

"I promise on the holy name of Vesta," she whispered bringing her emotions back under control.

"Good then we are done", Numerius clapped his hands and a slave brought in a canter of wine. He offered Pompeia a cup but she declined it.

"Lady," Publius now spoke out, his boyish face a model of quiet resolution, "your father gave me my freedom, both of you have for many years treated me with every honour and decency a man could expect and I th…th…thank you for this and I would like you to know that I will always will be at your ser…vice as a friend, an ally and as …" the young man started to stutter and his voice faded away.

"As family," Numerius said finishing the sentence. "For that is what you are Publius. In my will I have adopted you as my son. My daughter here is a vestal and cannot continue the family name, yet the name must go on, it is my final duty as a father, so it may as well be you."

Publius' face turned a dark red. He stuttered again and fell to his knees and grasped his patron's hand.

"Alright, alright," Numerius said patting the man on his shoulder as the young freedman broke out into great sobs.

"Publius," Pompeia interrupted sharply, "The man who takes my father's name does not show weakness in front of others. We are a Patrician family, descended from the first founders of Rome and we are born to lead. The people will not look kindly or respectfully on a man who tries to win favour by pretending to be one of them. You must remember that."

As she spoke Pompeia caught a glimpse of approval in her father's face.

The boy rose quickly to his feet. His cheeks were still red but he managed to compose himself.

"I am s..sorry," he sniffed, "You are quiet right."

Then he hurried away.

Pompeia glanced out of the window and waited until Publius was gone.

Then she turned to her father.

"I like Publius, he is loyal and a good man," she said, "But are you sure that he is the best choice to become your son?"

Numerius raised his eyebrows and gave her a challenging look.

"He wants to become a lawyer," he replied, "It is a good profession. Publius will continue the work that I started. Our house will be known for our service to the law and to the people. That will be our reputation."

Pompeia nodded, she did not wish to argue with him today. Nothing she would say would change his mind anyway. It would do no good reminding her father that the families reputation had been irreparably damaged by what her uncle had done all those years ago. The murder of her grandfather would be what people would remember, not her father's service to law.

"I would like to have a walk in the garden and sit on your terrace," she said rising to her feet.

Father and daughter strolled to the edge of the paved terrace where a low hedge marked the boundary of the garden. Beyond, the hillside fell away steeply; a dry and parched wilderness of boulders and grew yellow scrubs. Tall trees provided the terrace with some shade and a cool westerly breeze was coming off the distant sea. Down below her the green Tiber snaked its way through the land disappearing off into the north. The city of Rome shimmered and glistened in the heat and she could pick out the individual monuments. They sat down on a garden seat and Numerius called for more wine.

"Mama would have loved it up here," she said.

"Maybe," he shrugged and took a gulp from his cup, "But she would have complained about the journey into the city and about being separated from her friends. You never did get on with her did you?"

The sudden question caught her by surprise. It was true. She had never been close to her mother. They had shared little in common and at times it had seemed to her that all they did was compete for Numerius' attention.

"Yes," she nodded, "She was so different. Was that why you sent me away to be a vestal?"

Numerius smiled and took her hand in his, "Vesta is lucky to have you as her priestess," he said with sudden warmth. "And I too am lucky to have you as a daughter."

Pompeia felt the warmth of his hand and it brought back a thousand memories.

"Why did you marry mama?" she asked suddenly.

Numerius raised his eyebrows. "A man needs a woman," he stopped himself sharply.

"It is alright," she said, "I understand the full nature of my vows to Vesta."

Numerius took a moment to study her.

"Well, I married Claudia for her money and family status. She was Fabius' niece after all."

"Why?" Pompeia asked.

"To honour my father," Numerius replied. "It was his wish."

"What about love?" Pompeia said.

Numerius turned his eyes to the ground.

"Marriage is a sacred vow and must never be broken", he said sternly. "The laws of our ancestors gave me the right to govern my wife in any way I like.

I did not rule her harshly or too kindly. You must understand that we had never seen each other before we were married. It was all arranged by the families".

"What about afterwards, did you love her?"

"I suppose in a certain way," Numerius hesitated, "But we were never really intimate." He glanced at her with a sad smile. "After you arrived we agreed to have no more physical relations with each other."

Pompeia was silent for a while. "I understand Papa," she said at last. "They say that I am married to Rome but sometimes I too find it a loveless relationship."

***

It was growing dark as her carriage made its way back to the temple. In her hand Pompeia held the sealed will that her father had given her. The news that he was dying had changed everything. She was no stranger to death but now that mortality had come so close, its touch had made her think about life and what really was important. There had been a reason why she had asked her father about her mother. Pompeia was in love.

She blushed as she remembered the last festival of Lupercalia, the Wolfs festival, that had been held in February and to Lucius Cantilius. No one knew about Cantilius. He had been one of the young handsome priests belonging to the college of the Luperci, a minor religious cult that worshipped the God Pan, and who clad in goatskins had run around the ancient walls of the Palatine hill lashing out at the crowds with their thongs. From the first moment she had seen him she could not take her eyes off him.

The festival and its sacrifice to the She Wolf who had suckled Romulus and Remus would purify the city and ensure its fertility. Women had lined the path along which the priests had run and had held out the palms of their hands, hoping to be lashed by the thongs and thus blessed with fertility. She knew it had been a stupid and highly dangerous thing to do but unable to resist her desire, she had done it anyway, and so disguised with a long cloak and hood she too had pushed her way to the front of the crowd and had held open her palms, for what was life worth without someone to share it with.

Chapter Nine – On the road to Rome

It was still dark when Titus slipped out of Canusium. He rode the same horse which had helped him escape from the battle eleven days earlier. In the days that had followed the shocking Roman defeat, Scipio, the Tribune had kept him busy. Titus had first been dispatched to the town of Venusia with a message for the Consul Varro. The sole surviving supreme war leader of the Roman people had found shelter in a simple house in the town and it was here that Titus had met him. Barely thirty men had escaped together with the Consul and Varro had looked exhausted and crushed. His face had the haunted look of a man who knew he had been responsible for Rome's worst ever defeat. A man like that would have no friends and his families name would be mud for all time but Titus had not felt sorry for the consul. The man's incompetence had caused the deaths of every single soldier in his company. If Varro's shame was too great to bear then he could always fall on his sword.

After reading Scipio's dispatch the consul had managed to collect himself sufficiently to give orders that all able-bodied men should follow him to Canusium. Titus had ridden back that same day, ahead of the troops with the news that the Consul was coming to take charge of the survivors. When Varro had finally arrived a force of around 10,000 men was being assembled, the pitiful remnants of an army that once had mustered 80,000.

And now Titus was off again on another errand. Idly he touched the leather case around his neck which contained the despatch, which the consul had ordered him to take to the Senate in

Rome. Don't stop for anything or anyone he had been told. Ride day and night. Speed is essential. The new orders had thrilled him. He was going to Rome! He was going home at last. He would be able to visit his mother and sister and reassure them that he was alive for news of the great disaster at Cannae must surely have reached the city by now. And there was something else.

Titus smiled to himself as he thought about the summons to Scipio's improvised HQ. The young officer had received him alone and before handing over the Consul's official dispatch had presented him with a private letter. It was an introduction, to be delivered to a retired lawyer in Rome, an acquaintance of Scipio's, and the letter formally asked the lawyer to agree to undertake Titus' education once the war was over. The man is not the best teacher, Scipio had added, but at least he won't mind teaching a Samnite. You will have to wait until the war is over I'm afraid but my reputation will not let you down.

Titus had not known what to say. Ever since his father had died he had decided that he would make something of himself. He had set his heart on rising above the station to which he had been born. It would not be easy, he knew that. He was not a Roman citizen, only a poor second class citizen, without the right to vote in the assemblies or stand for office and despite the boasts of the Romans that their institutions were fair and open to everyone, a strong racial prejudice against foreigners still existed amongst the leading Patrician classes. He had quickly realised that the key to success was education, but education cost a huge amount of time, which he did not have, and money, money which he would never likely possess. But now at last he had a chance, a huge chance and his smile grew and grew until it split his face from ear to ear.

Now as the dawn approached he rode carefully down the hill side heading northwest. He thought again of the conversation with Scipio. The officer had changed his mind about the reward, he didn't fully understand why, but it probably had something to do with publicity for Scipio had asked him to keep the matter private. That was how the rich and powerful acted he thought; they said one thing in public and another in private. It was the same with women he thought disapprovingly. To Titus, honesty and speaking the truth were virtues but he knew enough to know that if he wished to make something of himself he would have to have to learn to act a little, like the rich and powerful.

He glanced up at the towering hills whose peaks were becoming visible in the early morning light. The hills always reminded him of the place where he had been born. The peoples of Italy had been divided into lowlanders and highlanders since the dawn of the world. The Romans and their Latin kinsmen along with the Campanians in Capua and the Greek city states in the south had all been lowlanders, making their living from farming and trade. In the highlands however the Samnites had lived in small isolated villages' eaking out a living from their flocks of sheep and now and then raiding the lowlands when times were tough. The Romans were proud of their heritage and their nation but so too were the Samnites and war between lowlander and highlander had been bloody and continuous until a few generations earlier the iron will of Rome had finally endured and the proud Samnites had been forced into the domain of the growing Roman Empire, and so had become allies of the Senate and People of Rome.

Titus had however had a happy childhood in the mountains. He had learned the craft of the mountaineer and the herdsman. He had started work nearly as soon as he could walk for all hands were needed to help run the family business. There had been no time or money for such luxuries as education. His father had always scoffed at the idea of becoming a Roman citizen, but once he'd given his loyalty to Rome he had never wavered in his oath to the city or spoken against her.

***

For the first part of the morning he pushed his horse as fast as he dared. Titus loved horses. He had grown up with them in the high mountains and the beasts had been treated as part of the family. His boyhood home had been a mountain farm where his father had raised and traded horses. Then one terrible day a band of horse thieves had come and stolen the whole herd. His father had been away and Titus, still just a boy, had not been able to stop the thieves. The feeling of unfairness and powerlessness that he experienced that day still haunted him. Unable to raise fresh funds the business had collapsed and the family had been forced to move to Rome. It had been a hard decision to make but his father had said it was for the best. There was work in Rome for a skilled man and the future of Italy now lay in Rome the old man had told his family.

His father had found work in a blacksmith's and so Titus had become a blacksmiths apprentice. The crowded slums of Rome had been a huge change from the fresh mountain air and freedom of the high woods and lonely rocky crags but Titus had put his back into his work for the family needed to eat. Rome had been so unimaginably different, but the people in the slums had not judged his family or persecuted them for who they were or where they came from. They had given his father a chance to make a living and over time accepted the family as one of their own.

Then one day his father had been struck down in the street by a loose roof tile and the accident had killed him. It was not an uncommon occurrence. His father's death had come in the year that Hannibal had arrived in Italy and by the following year Titus had been conscripted. The elderly blacksmith for whom he and his father had worked had promised to look after his mother and sister but the man was old and Titus had worried what would happen if the man died or moved away. It had been nearly a year since he'd last seen or heard from his family.

***

It was just before noon when Titus spotted the smoke in the distance. He wiped the sweat from his brow. The smoke was drifting lazily to the east but he couldn't see the source of the fire for his view was blocked by a wooded ridge. He glanced back down the mountain track he'd been following but saw no one. Dismounting, he started up the path leading his horse by the reins. This part of the track was high up in the mountains and he'd seen very few people. When he reached the crest of the ridge and emerged from the trees he paused. A meadow with a stream lay before him and in the meadow, all alone, was a small farm. The farmhouse was on fire. As he stared at it, a section of the roof crashed inwards with a great roar. There was no sign of anyone. He tapped his fingers on his leg unsure for a moment of what to do. But his path led him directly past the burning building.

The roar of the flames grew louder as he approached but the breeze was blowing the smoke away from him and he had a good view. The first body lay beside the mountain path. It was a woman. She lay face down in the dirt, arms splayed apart. Blood had spilled out in a puddle beneath her chest and her fingers grasped at the soil as if she had been trying to drag herself along. Titus crouched down beside her and touched the body. It was still warm. He looked up anxiously. Whoever had killed her may still be close by. He glanced again at the farm. There was another body just beyond the porch. It was a child whose head had been bashed in.

Titus glanced up the track and then back the way he had come. This was none of his business. His orders were clear. Speed was essential and yet he hesitated. The scene brought back memories of the day that horse thieves had come to his farm and ruined the family business. On that day he had followed his instinct and had not resisted the thieves and because of that decision his family had escaped with their lives. But that had not happened here. Killing women and children was barbaric. What could these simple mountain folk possibly have done to deserve such a death? He stared at the burning farm and then slowly tied the horse's reins to the wooden farm fence and turned to face the flames. It was then that he noticed the dead oxen in the meadow. He frowned with growing curiosity. Why kill them?

Titus felt the heat on his face and kept a hand to his mouth to ward off the smoke. Carefully he skirted round to the side of the farm and as he did so he came across the third corpse, the body of a man. The smoke was thicker here and it billowed away blown by the breeze so that his view was partially obscured. The corpse had been decapitated and was stark naked. Even his shoes had been taken. Titus crouched down beside the body. Why take the man's clothes? He reached out and touched the corpse. It was still warm and the blood had not clotted. All of the farming family had been killed and very recently too.

As he rose to his feet he saw the man. The stranger was crouched over an odd looking machine with tripod wooden legs. As Titus caught sight of him the nose of the bow like machine swivelled and there was a sharp twanging noise. A bolt hurtled away into the distance. There was a dull thwack and one of the cows, a hundred paces away, keeled over onto the ground. Titus stood rooted to the spot. The man had large scars across his arm. Some distance away a horse stood tethered to a tree.

The man stiffened and straightened up as he caught sight of Titus. For a long second the two of them stared at each other. The stranger was old but tall, muscular and fit looking, with a clean shaven face and dressed in a plain farmer's tunic. In his hand he was holding another bolt ready to load into the machine. There was something menacing about him that made the hairs on Titus' neck stand up. The man was wearing the farmer's clothes. That was why the corpse was naked.

Without saying a word Titus turned and fled. He felt the heat from the burning farm on his face. The noise from the roaring fire drowned out all other sounds. His horse was where he had left it and he threw himself into the saddle risking a glance behind him. The stranger was running towards him. He had a sword in his hand. Titus dug his heels into the horse and the beast lurched forwards up the mountain path. He thundered up the track and after a few moments glanced back over his shoulder. With no hope of catching up the stranger had stopped and was standing in the middle of the path watching him with his hands on his hips.

Bandits, Titus thought darkly as he stared at the solitary figure. Titus hated bandits, they were nothing but scum. The countryside was full of them now that war had ravaged Italy for over two years and law and order were under pressure everywhere. But there was something odd about this one. For a start he appeared to be alone and what bandit had a machine like that man had? It looked like some kind of bolt thrower. Titus shook his head. Bandits didn't care who you were. The man had killed the farmers, simple decent people like himself. The scum should be thrown from the Tarpeian rock he thought spitting onto the ground before wheeling his horse around and galloping away up the track.

Chapter Ten – The house on the Palatine

Fabius' house was a mansion on the Palatine hill. The Palatine was the grandest and most desirable of all addresses in Rome. It was the hill on which the original city had been founded by Romulus some five hundred years before. It was the neighbourhood where wealthy aristocrats rubbed shoulders with new money. The streets were clean and free of rubbish; there were no towering apartment blocks, seedy brothels or cheap looking shops. If the rest of Rome locked its doors at night and hid its wealth away from stranger's eyes the Palatine chose to flaunt its wealth, its residents competing for attention and status. Their efforts showed in the elaborately decorated doors, the mosaic in the vestibules and the grandeur of the stone work. You were nobody in Rome if you didn't own a house on the Palatine.

From the street Fabius' house however looked surprisingly ordinary, with a stout plain wooden door set in a shallow vestibule. Numerius was shown into the atrium and found Fabius engaged in his morning prayers to the Lares, the household gods. Numerius gripped his walking stick tightly so that it would hide his trembling hand. That morning he had felt the attack of Malaria coming before it happened and he'd had time to lie down on a couch and prepare himself. But despite his preparations the fit had left him soaked in sweat and feeling weak and exhausted. The disease would return again and again and each time it would weaken him until eventually he would die. It was afternoon now and he did not feel much better despite the potions the doctor had given him. But he had to keep going for there was a new crisis and Fabius needed his help.

"They have asked to address the Senate," Fabius said as he slowly got up on his feet. "I fear that they will demand the impossible."

The old patricians face looked troubled. Numerius nodded. That morning when he was being seized by his fit, ten Roman noblemen, members of the senate who had been captured by Hannibal, had ridden into the city and had confirmed everyone's worst fears about the recent battle. The nobles had asked to plead their position before the Senate.

"There was a Carthaginian with them, a man called Carthalo who presumed to speak to us about peace," Fabius growled. "I made sure he was not allowed to enter the city."

"What of the nobles?" Numerius asked.

Fabius growled in disgust and his troubled face grew darker.

"The mother of one of these nobles came here this morning," he said, "She begged me to save her son. She begged me to have the state pay for his ransom and that of his colleagues."

"That would not be wise," Numerius shook his head.

"Oh," an inquisitive look appeared in Fabius's eyes. "Many senators feel just the opposite. Indeed, the whole city seems to be clamouring for the state to pay for their release. Why do you think differently?"

"It's a sign of weakness," Numerius replied. "These nobles have allowed themselves to be captured. They do not deserve to speak to the Senate as equals or demand anything from us."

"Even if it means that they will have to ride back to Hannibal to face death?"

"Yes," Numerius nodded.

There was a long pause as Fabius examined Numerius. Then he grunted.

"I agree with you," Fabius said. "That is what we must do but I fear that when it comes to a vote, the issue will be too close to too many hearts and that the wrong decision will be made. These nobles have families, important and wealthy people, they are using all their influence to help their kinsmen and if they succeed what message will that send to our soldiers. If you are rich you will be freed but if you are poor you will be forgotten. Morale will collapse. It must not happen. We must win that vote, Numerius."

"We will win it," Numerius said gripping his walking stick.

Fabius grumbled to himself. Then he gently patted Numerius on his shoulder. "The dictator has called the Senate to meet later today to decide the matter. He and a few others agree with me, but we are a minority and the gods know what sort of trouble

Metellus may cause us. Come I wish to show you something," Fabius said gently taking Numerius by the arm and leading him towards the dining room.

***

The dining room was a square space five or six yards in length and around its edges were several couches and tables. Fabius strode purposefully towards the furthest corner. Puzzled Numerius looked on as the old man bent down and kicked away the carpet that covered the floor.

"I discovered it only after I had bought this house last year," Fabius said placing his hands on his hips. Set within the smooth stone floor was a trap door with an iron handle.

"The previous owner was killed at Trebia and I never met the son who sold the house but it seems they liked their secrets," Fabius continued. "Here, you are younger than me, come and pull it up."

Numerius bent down and gripped the iron handle. The trap door came away much easier than he had expected. It swung up right on two iron hinges and Numerius peered down into the dark hole below. Steps had been cut into the rock and led away into the darkness.

"Where does it lead to?" he asked.

Fabius was busy lighting an oil lamp. "Follow me," he said as the lamp began to glow. Carefully the old man placed his feet on the stone steps and began to descend holding the lamp out before him. Numerius followed close behind. In the flickering light he could see that the stairs were just wide enough to allow one man to go up or down. Numerius placed his hands on the cool sharp rocky walls in order to steady himself. The stairwell was steep and seemed to twist away into the earth. Down and down they went for what seemed like a minute before he became aware that Fabius' lamp had stopped moving.

"Here we are," the old man said stepping out into a flat open space. He fumbled around on the wall for something and found it. A few moments later another oil lamp began to glow. Fabius repeated the process with another lamp on the opposite side and soon the flickering light filled the whole space. Numerius saw that he was standing in a large chamber, nine or ten yards in length and five or six across. Against the far wall someone had stacked a pile of old and dusty couches but apart from that the chamber was empty. He could smell the faint odour of raw sewage coming from somewhere. He looked up and saw that the chamber was cavernous, rising two or three yards above him to a rough ceiling of red volcanic rock. The rock turned the light from the lamps red, giving the whole chamber a hellish feel.

"Looks like it's the gateway to the underworld," Numerius muttered.

"You could say that," Fabius replied as he walked to one side of the chamber and checked something in the wall. Numerius saw what he had missed on his first inspection. There was another doorway into the chamber.

He took a step forwards to get a closer view. Fabius was checking the iron handle on a small stout looking wooden door. "More secrets," Numerius muttered.

"Yes, it leads to the Cloaca Maxima. That's why you can smell the shit,"Fabius said.

Numerius grunted in surprise. The Cloaca Maxima was one of Rome's greatest yet little known achievements. A vast man made underground sewage system that had helped to drain the marshy valleys between the hills of Rome. The Cloaca was already four hundred years old. It was an underground world where very few would venture.

"Gods, what were these people thinking when they built this place," he exclaimed.

"Have a look at this," Fabius said raising his oil lamp above his head.

Numerius moved closer to the wall and in the flickering light he saw the drawings etched into the rock. The artist who had created them had to have been an amateur for the drawings were crude. In one a man with a giant phallus was screwing a woman. In another there was a scene from an orgy and in another two women were going at it with each other. Fabius moved the lamp along the wall and Numerius saw that there were hundreds of drawings. He stopped beside a scene of a man riding in a chariot drawn by two panthers. The artist had done a better job here as if the drawing had been more important than the rest.

"It's Bacchus, the god of wine," Numerius exclaimed.

"Yes," Fabius replied with obvious distaste, "and this was the chamber where his followers would come to celebrate and revel in his name."

Numerius understood now. The cult of Bacchus was new to Rome but already it was viewed by many as a dangerous eastern sect that was undermining the traditional values of the Roman people. He glanced around the chamber trying to imagine the orgies and illicit sex, drinking and debauchery that would have occurred here in the name of Bacchus, the great liberator. Women of all social ranks were rumoured to come to such parties and to allow themselves to be taken care of by slaves. Nothing it seemed was taboo. It was well known that only women could be full members of the cult but slaves were known to have taken part too and in some circles it was rumoured that plots against the state were being devised by them. That was why the followers of the cult had to meet in secret. That was why they had dug a secret entrance from the sewers into this house.

"Can you imagine it," Fabius snorted, "Women being in control. It goes against the natural order of things. What will these women demand from us next, a say in government? It cannot be tolerated. The only people who have the right to lead Rome are those men who can trace their ancestry back to the founding of the city."

Fabius turned on Numerius and his face looked alarmed.

"This here," he pointed at the walls, "is what will become of us if we don't show that we are worthy to lead our city. If we made peace with Hannibal we will have lost our authority to govern and the natural order of things will be overthrown." He sighed,

"And then Rome will just become another inward looking, pleasure seeking town soon to be forgotten by history. That is not what our forefathers had in mind for us."

Numerius was still staring at the drawings on the wall. "Maybe it is so," he said at last, "but the women that I have known and love are strong minded creatures who share our love for our city." He glanced at Fabius. "I would not object to arming our women with swords and shields, if it was thought necessary and Hannibal was threatening to take Rome. Our women have more to lose than just their lives if they were captured."

Fabius gave Numerius a long quizzical look and then shook his head.

"I am sorry. You must miss Claudia your wife. I mourn for her too." He paused. "But you do have some strange thoughts in that head of yours," he said with a mocking smile, "and once they called me dim witted."

Chapter Eleven – In the interest of unity and the Republic

Rome was tense and nervous. It showed in the worried faces of the people and the lack of conversation in the street. Numerius could sense the mood as Fabius and he made there way on foot to the Senate house. The wailing of women in mourning was a continuous reminder of the great and terrible disaster that had struck the city. Yet there were signs too that the measures agreed upon by the Senate, just a few days ago, were being put into action. The city seemed calmer after the initial wild panic. There were no women on the streets and every man they came across was armed even though their equipment was often pathetic. In an alley, a line of men and boys were queuing patiently to sign up to a newly forming Legion. One of the Dictator's enrolment officers stood up from his seat and saluted as they passed by.

Fabius had decided to take the long way to the Senate House saying that he wished to gain a feel for the mood of the city. So they had turned south west and taken the street that passed by the Lupercal cave where Romulus and Remus were supposed to have been suckled by the She wolf. The cave where this was supposed to have happened had been turned into a shrine and all were admitted for a small fee. The street had continued past the fine aristocratic houses and the temple of Jupiter Victorious until it ended in a steep flight of stairs that led down to the valley floor below and the Capena gate just beyond. At the top of the stairs Fabius had paused.

"What do you think of our morale?" he muttered.

Numerius glanced in the direction of the Janiculum, across the Tiber to the west, hoping perhaps to catch a glimpse of his house.

"They have obeyed the law which is a good sign yet that doesn't stop them from worrying about the future," he said slowly. "These new troops we have seen, there are too many old men and boys. These soldiers are no match for Hannibal but perhaps they are enough to defend the walls. That's the best we can expect from them."

"Their morale Numerius?" Fabius pressed his question.

"They need some kind of re-assurance. A runaway horse would cause them to panic and bolt," Numerius shrugged.

Fabius glanced around them. Then without another word he began to descend the steps.

At the bottom of the stairs they entered the Appian Way, a wide street that followed the valley north eastwards between the Palatine and the Caelian hill.

From the valley floor the Palatine's steep cliffs of sheer rock looked formidable and lofty but the view was partially distorted by the newly built Insulae that had been erected against the cliffs, their ground floors occupied by shops and craftsmen. The Appian Way was busier than the Palatine and there was a continuous movement of carts, farm animals and people coming in from the Capena gate and the two old men had to watch out that they kept to the pavement. Traffic accidents were common as was the danger of being splattered by someone else's shit, emptied from a window in one of the apartment buildings above. They hurried along receiving the occasional inquisitive glance from the locals. As they approached the junction with the Sacred Way they were forced to slow their pace as the traffic began to grow congested.

Up ahead, beyond the intersection, in the street leading to the Esquiline hill a property developer had been busy raising two new Insulae. Work on the apartment buildings however seemed to have come to a halt and the wooden scaffolding and piles of building materials looked lost without their labourers. It was just as well Numerius thought as he glanced at the half finished three storey buildings. The men were needed in the army now.

They turned left into the Sacred Way and entered the forum.

***

The bad news hit them as soon as Fabius and Numerius entered the Senate house. Syracuse, the great Greek city in Sicily and an old Roman ally was being ravaged by a Carthaginian fleet. Cisalpine Gaul was in open revolt. The tribes of the Atellani and the Hirpini had just gone over to the enemy and there were unconfirmed reports that the former Greek cities of Tarentum, Crotona and Locri were wavering in their alliance to Rome. Fabius was at once besieged by anxious senators imploring him with various demands and inquiries and he was escorted to his seat on the front bench as Numerius faded into the ranks of onlookers hovering around the doorway. There was a growing sense of tension and outside in the open space of the Comitium a great crowd was gathering.

The dictator, Marcus Junius Pera who had only been appointed a few days earlier called the house to order. He had, he declared, this morning learned of the arrival of the ten noblemen taken prisoner at Cannae and had decided to allow them to plead their case before the Senate. The great hall fell silent as the nobles were called forth. They came threading their way through the crowd of onlookers in a single file, many of them bearded and still wearing their military uniforms. Their leader strode straight for the speaker's platform as if he had done this many times before.

Numerius had become conscious of the size of the crowd that was gathering behind him in the open space of the comitium and in the forum. The pressure of so many bodies was pushing him forwards onto the floor of the Senate and he struggled to keep his balance.

The leader of the prisoners began telling the Senate of how he and his fellows had not idly fallen into captivity, but had done all they could in a heroic last stand, which had finally been cut short through lack of water and the utter hopelessness of their situation. They had done no worse than the men who had fled to Canusium or who had died on the field. The speaker had gone on to argue that Rome had ransomed their prisoners before and that if they did so again they would find many thousands of eager, battle trained veterans who would be able to swell her armies. When the speaker finished a great cry of support rose from the people gathered outside. Numerius glanced around and saw many in the crowd were stretching out their arms towards the prisoners and crying out to the senators to give them back their children and their relations.

Numerius watched as Fabius bent forwards to consult the senator beside him. They spoke briefly and then both men nodded. It was clear from their calls and posturing that most senators were of the opinion that the prisoner's ransom should be paid and Numerius' throat had gone dry in trepidation as he watched Fabius' colleague stand up and walk towards the speaker's platform. Whatever the man had to say, his words would have to be powerful enough to sway the house and the people gathered outside. The senator, a man called Torquatus; a hard and mean looking character wasted no time. He tore into the prisoners claims that they had acted with as much honour as the men who had managed to escape or who had died at Cannae. He had proof he shouted angrily from men who were there that the nobles who were before the Senate today had retired on their camp and had wasted every chance to escape throughout the night that had followed. Others had urged them to escape and some six hundred men had indeed managed to slip away through the Carthaginian lines. However these Senators; loved and honoured as they may be, had chosen not to do so and in that way they had badly served their country for if they had escaped there would have been no need for a ransom and their arms would once again be at the disposal of the state. No Senators, Torquatus had cried, these men do not deserve our pity or our ransom or our respect. When he had offered to produce witnesses the Senate had finally fallen silent. It had been gutsy speech, made against the overwhelming feeling of the house but when it was over Numerius felt strangely relieved. At least someone had spoken up for honour.

Soon after the dictator had called for a vote and the atmosphere in the great hall had reached a fever pitch of tension for never before had the Senators been asked to consider a vote upon which the lives of so many of their fellow senators now depended. The vote had duly been taken. It had been close but with the tiniest of margins the ransom had been refused and the captured Senators ordered at once to return to Hannibal. On hearing the result the crowd outside the Senate house had broken out into a great cry of distress. So great was the noise that contrary to protocol the dictator had ordered the doors to the Senate house to be closed. Inside the house angry scenes had erupted with senators trading insults with each other and others seemingly ready for violence and it was only with difficulty that the dictator had managed to restore order.

Fabius was next to rise to his feet to address the issue of the Carthaginian envoy who had proposed peace talks. The house quietened down as the old man shuffled to the speaker's platform. In his mild and quiet voice he reminded the house that Rome had seen great disasters before and that none not even the great loss of Cannae could compare to the days when Brennus and his Barbarian hordes had sacked Rome a 170 years before. And yet after each defeat Rome and its people had managed to return stronger and more determined than ever and so it would be this time Fabius declared, but only, he warned, if the fathers of the people managed to stay united and firm in their purpose. There would be no more talk of peace he said. The city was still safe, there was no sign that Hannibal was marching on Rome and all the time, day and night, Rome was regrouping and forming new armies. The vast resources of Italy were still at her command and the Latin allies remained steadfast in their ancient loyalty to Rome. And even if most of southern Italy defected to Hannibal he was confident that Rome would endure even this terrible blow, for without victory he declared, there could be no survival. He ended his speech with a plea to all those gathered in the house to ask themselves what their fathers would have done and what their children would think of them if they now surrendered Rome's destiny.

It had been a stirring speech and Numerius felt a flood of emotion welding up. It was all a matter of morale now he realised. The city could be defended and the means were available for Rome to win the war but the great danger, the mortal threat, now lay not with Hannibal but with a collapse of morale. If the Roman people lost the stomach to continue the war, if they stopped enlisting in the Legions, if they stopped believing in victory, then all would be lost without a single battle having to be fought.

Before Fabius had managed to sit down Metellus, the secretary to the high priest was on his feet and demanding to be heard.

"Honourable members," he cried, "At our last meeting I spoke to you about neglect and unfaithfulness, both of which are most un Roman virtues. Since then the number of bad omens in the city has increased to such a level that I truly fear for our existence. A wolf was seen entering through the Capena gate in broad daylight and leaving again unmolested. Fiery rain has been reported in Ostia, cold water flows from hot springs and the sacred chickens in the temple of Concord have all died. I promised you a list of men whom the high priest declares have neglected to do their religious duties to the gods and I have it here!" he shouted holding up a scroll for all to see.

From the benches there was instant uproar. A few Senators stormed towards Metellus with raised fists and clashed with Metellus' supporters who had jumped up in his defence. Numerius ran his hand across his face in dismay as the dictator shouted for calm.

"What is this? Would you prevent me from doing my duty," Metellus' voice rose above the tumult. "All of you know that the high priest and the college of Augurs must interpret the will of the gods and this is what we have done, nothing more. This is the evidence that the auguries have given us. Why then do you dare to protest?"

Metellus strode across the floor; as around him his supporters fended off the verbal and physical threats of his opponents; and handed the scroll over to the dictator. "I trust that you will follow our advice," Metellus snarled before abruptly turning on his heel and returning to his seat.

***

The small back office in the Senate house was used mainly to store the house's administrative documents but today it served another function. In the centre of the room a table had been set up and around it sat nine men. Fabius was seated beside his old friend Pera the Dictator, a stern aristocratic white haired man of around sixty who now wielded supreme executive power for the next six months. Beside him sat his newly elected second in command Grachus, a younger military man with quick intelligent eyes. Numerius was flanked by the hard man of the group, the former lawyer Torquatus. On the other side of the table sat Metellus representing the high priest and beside him were the three leaders of the other main religious colleges, the augurs who interpreted the will of the gods, the Quindecemviri, the keepers of the Sybiline books and the Septemviri Epulones who were in charge of organising the religious festivals.

"You have read the list?" Metellus said looking at the Dictator.

"Yes we have," Pera replied casting a cautious look at the priest.

"Well then, what are you going to do?" Metellus' pig like eyes gleamed as he searched the faces of the men opposite him for clues to their intentions.

Fabius cleared his throat and placed his hands on the table. "We would like to propose something to you young man," he said carefully.

"You wish to bribe me," Metellus smiled, "But it won't work."

"That's not what some say," Torquatus interrupted.

Metellus shot him a dark withering look.

"No, it is not a bribe," Fabius replied holding up his hand to silence his colleague, "more of an understanding with you and your supporters and the high priest...in the interests of unity and the Republic."

"Go on," Metellus said.

Fabius glanced at the list of names that Metellus had handed them earlier.

"We cannot agree to have these men punished," he said looking up at Metellus. "There are too many important people on it. In particular there is mention of all the magistrates left in the city and several officials who are serving abroad. These men are doing important work in the defence of the city. There are also men on the list whom Pera wishes to appoint to army commands." Fabius paused. "But you are right. We need to show the proper respect to the gods. I have no doubt that something has gone wrong and that the gods are angered and have reminded us of their anger." Fabius lowered his eyes, "But perhaps it is not a matter of intentional neglect but one of clumsy execution of the sacred rituals which has left the gods confused by what we offer and desire. So..." Fabius took a deep breath, "I have asked Pera and Grachus to prepare the appropriate sacrifices with special care before they leave the city with their army. We are also going to have to elect a large number of new magistrates and senators to replace the men who have fallen at Cannae. We propose that you submit a list of candidates whom you would like to see in these positions and then..." Fabius leaned backwards, "we will have them elected."

The room fell silent. Metellus drummed his fingers on the table. Then he looked up with a contemptuous grin. "In times of great distress we must do everything we can of course," he replied. "My colleague here has therefore seen it necessary to consult the Sybiline books in the temple of Jupiter. Do you know what they told us? The books of destiny say this. They say that in the year of the consulship of Varro and Paullus, a Barbarian Gaul and a Greek will take up permanent residence on the Capitoline hill."

The government men looked at each other in horror all except Metellus who seemed to be enjoying their discomfort. The Sybiline books were hundreds of years old, written during the time of the kings and according to legend they contained the whole history of Rome, from start to end, recorded before it had even occurred.

"The Sybiline books are never wrong," Fabius grunted respectfully and there was a sudden wisdom in his eyes, "But their prophesy does not need to be fatal. If they say that a Gaul and a Greek will take up permanent residence on the Capitoline then let it be so. We shall make it a truth even though it is a most repugnant idea. We should have a Gaul and a Greek buried beneath the temple of Jupiter. In that way the prophecy in the books will be fulfilled and the Gods satisfied."

The men around the table were silent. Pera was the first to speak. His eyes lit up with sudden delight like a boy discovering the solution to a puzzle.

"It would be better to have two Gaul's and two Greeks, one man and one woman buried *alive*," he exclaimed, "for this will cover us from all angles if the books have made no distinction between the sexes or whether the people are to be alive or dead."

"Very good, these are our thoughts too," Metellus nodded looking slightly taken aback. "Yet the books have revealed more. They write that in this year the very purity of Rome has been contaminated and that to regain it, the ancient law of sacrifice must be carried out."

Metellus' face glowed with cruel delight. "The books say that the Vestal Virgins have been unfaithful in their vows to Vesta."

"You have proof of this?" Pera replied looking astonished.

"Cock," Torquatus said.

"You know my daughter is a Vestal," Numerius said rising to his feet.

Metellus glanced at Numerius and smiled. Then he rose to feet and his fellow priests rose with him.

"It is written in the Sybiline books, whom am I to contest them," Metellus shrugged glancing at Fabius, "but maybe the gods have decided to punish you for your failure to wait until our ambassador returned from Delphi. I will speak with our father, gentlemen but I think we will be able to agree to your offer," he paused, "On condition that this sacrifice is made."

Chapter Twelve – Secrets

All six vestal virgins clustered patiently around their matron in the small circular temple of Vesta as the old woman went through their individual schedules and tasks for the coming week. Pompeia stood with her hands clasped together. What a bore she thought. She really couldn't understand why the old matron had to stick so diligently to her weekly routine for all the girls were fully aware of what they had to do. Their routine, after all, had barely changed in over four hundred years.

At twenty-four Pompeia was the second oldest. Aurinia was the oldest at thirty-six, plump and strict, she liked to keep herself to herself. She only had another year to go before her vows to Vesta would be considered fulfilled and she would leave the temple. Then there were the two adolescent troublemakers, Floronia and Opimia, both seventeen and both from very wealthy families. The matron on several occasions had rebuked them for slackness in their duties. And then there was Julia, a shy twelve-year old. It was Julia's company that Pompeia enjoyed most she had taken on the task of teaching the youngster the routine and etiquette of the temple and the girl was a quick learner. Finally, there was tiny Musa, a girl of seven who had joined the Vestals only that year and who still wet her bed in the night.

The matron at last fell silent and as the girls dispersed to their allotted tasks Pompeia approached her.

"My father is ill, may I go to him," she asked.

The matron glanced at her with a stern eye. "Your father is lucky to have a daughter like you child," she said. "This is the third time this week you have asked permission to visit him."

Pompeia blushed. "He suffers from the bad air."

The matron stared at her. "I am sorry to hear that child. Go to him then," but as Pompeia turned to leave the old woman caught her by the elbow. "You do your duties with special care, I know," she said quietly, "I knew from the first moment when you came here that you would serve our mother well. Watch yourself now child, you are my dearest."

Pompeia strode down the temple steps. A carriage and a Lictor were waiting for her but she waved them away and proceeded into the forum on foot. The matron's words disturbed her. There was something in the old woman's tone, a warning. Did she know? She couldn't possibly know. She had taken every precaution and yet...

She did not look back. In the forum men stopped to stare at her and a few called-out greetings but she ignored them all. There were no women to be seen for they had been banned from the streets but the law did not apply to a Vestal who was carrying out her religious duties. At the northern end of the forum she turned in the direction of the old cattle market as if she were heading for the Tiber and her father's house on the Janiculum.

When she was half way down the street she glanced over her shoulder. The traffic was light and seeing nothing suspicious she slipped into an alley that led to a long flight of narrow stairs.

She paused and checked again to see if she was being followed but all seemed as it should. She started to climb the stairs. At the top she paused again to catch her breath. The walls that protected the great temple of Jupiter on the Capitoline towered above her and set within them was a wooden door. From a pocket, she produced a key, unlocked the door and passed on through into the temple complex.

The temple of Jupiter, with its massive white pillars and three inner sanctuaries dedicated to Jupiter, Juno his wife and Minerva his daughter rose up before her surrounded by an open paved space. A few priests were around but no one paid her any attention. Pompeia followed the outer walls until she came to a smaller building in the extreme south western corner of the complex. She slipped up the steps, through the tall stone pillars and into the darkness of the shrine. The air inside was cool in contrast to the burning sun outside. She checked again to see if she was being followed but there was nobody about. She turned quickly, feeling her heart thumping in her chest, and examined the room. A large altar stone stood in the middle of the room and beyond it was an inner sanctuary with a heavy curtain drawn across the entrance. She grasped the curtain and opened it slightly. Then she sighed with relief, she was alone.

She had been waiting for only a short while before he showed up. Lucius Cantilius was a handsome young man, with a wolfish charm and a strong well built body. He entered the shrine without paying her the slightest attention and knelt before the altar stone in prayer. Then when he was finished he rose to his feet and came over to her and they embraced.

"They have sent me to buy some more sacred chickens," he whispered running his hand fondly through her curls, "So I can't stay long."

Pompeia pressed her face into his chest.

"I missed you," she whispered.

He sighed and held her close and did not speak.

"We must not meet in these places Lucius," she said breaking apart, "It's too dangerous. Someone may see us."

He smiled showing a mouth of fine white teeth, "Don't worry; there is only an old priest who comes here in February."

He ran his finger down her cheeks until it came to a stop on her mouth.

"Once we are far away from Rome," he said, "We will be able to be together all the time. I nearly have all the money I need in order to support us. It won't be long now, I promise you."

She looked away.

"What is it?" he said running his finger down to her neck.

"Nothing," she said taking his hand in hers. "Let's talk about something else."

He leaned back against the walls of the shrine.

"Floronia and Opimia visit this shrine too, did you know that?" he said.

"No," she shook her head and felt the warmth of his body as she pressed herself against him. "Why do they come?"

"Probably because people pay them to ask Terminus to settle their land disputes in their favour, I don't know."

"That's horrible," she muttered, "They nearly allowed the fire to die out a few days ago."

Cantilius chuckled and was silent for a moment.

"You do still want to run away with me don't you?" he asked.

Pompeia closed her eyes and didn't answer and she heard Cantilius sigh.

"Talk to me," he whispered.

"I don't know what to do," she replied, "It's horrible for me to say this but it's like I have two loves, Cantilius, one is you and the other is my position as a Vestal and the promise I made to serve the goddess."

She felt him wrap his arms around her.

"You must choose," he said, "I know it's difficult, but you must choose Pompeia, you must decide what life you shall live.

Come away with me and I will make you a happy woman, I promise."

Gently she broke free from his embrace. "I know you will," she said firmly.

He stepped towards her and kissed her neck and she felt the kiss tingle all the way down her spine.

***

Pompeia hurried back to the house of the Vestals. Her mind seemed weighed down by a heavy burden. She wondered what advice her mother would have given her, but nothing came to mind, her mother and her would in all likelihood never have discussed the matter. Her mother had never been the type of person she had felt she could approach. It was dangerous what she was doing and deep down she felt guilty. She had not broken her vows of chastity but she was dangerously close. She just wished there was someone with whom she could talk to but there was no one. She could not say a word to anyone and it made her feel desperately lonely.

The house of the Vestals stood at the foot of the Palatine hill in the forum. It was here that all the Vestals lived whilst in the service. In front of the house was the small circular temple of Vesta where the eternal and sacred fire was tended day and night. Pompeia was in her quarters washing her hands when a slave came to tell her that she had a visitor. She quickly cleaned herself up and went downstairs into the long rectangular colonnaded garden of the house of vestals. It was Publius. He stood awkwardly at the main entrance to the house kicking the heels of his feet on the dry paving stones. He was carrying an old barbarian spear and wore a faded army uniform with dents in the armour. When he saw her he straightened up.

"Lady, it is so kind of you to s...see me," he stuttered. "I will not take up much of your time, I promise, but I must sp...speak with you about an urgent matter."

"Of course," she nodded gracefully, "I see that they have called you up for military service."

"Yes", he nodded, "That is w...why the matter is urgent."

She examined his equipment with a critical eye. "Well I am sure that we can provide you with better arms than these," she said. "If you are to take my fathers name then you must look the part. My father was a Tribune in the last war. I will see that you are provided for with a horse and new armour."

"I cannot ride," Publius stammered.

"Never mind then," she looked away. He started to speak but she raised her hand, "No not here, come we shall walk in my garden."

The two of them entered the long colonnaded garden. In the centre, which was open to the sky, a couple of fountains bubbled and gurgled and fine stone statues of long dead Vestal virgins adorned the grass.

"I grief for our father," Publius said wiping the sweat from his forehead, "and I am humbled by his generosity. It is my adoption that I would like to discuss with you."

Pompeia remained silent as they strode round the garden.
"I sense lady, that you have reservations about my adoption. So I have come to re-assure you that I intend to prove my self worthy of our father's name."

Pompeia folded her arms across her chest but did not reply as they made their way around the garden.

"When our father dies I will sell the house and the other properties," Publius went on. "There are s...some debts which must be s...settled you see and some properties make us no money at all. Then I shall buy our ancestral house here in Rome, the house that your father sold. In that house, where our family have lived for generations, I shall raise my own family. The house belongs to us and I shall restore the tradition."

Pompeia smiled.

"It is not that I dislike you Publius," she said slowly, "You are a good man and I know my father loves you but you must decide for yourself what life you will lead. You cannot just copy another man and hope you will find the same fortune. Every man is different and I worry that you just wish to be like my father. You must be your own man Publius."

Publius was silent as they continued their walk.

"There is more," he said at last, ignoring her comments. "I need a wife. I have a duty to continue the family line and produce an heir and with this war the matter has become urgent. So I will marry. I have selected two women," he said glancing at her, "they are freeborn, young and without scandal."

Pompeia nodded.

"Of course you must marry," she replied. "But is now really the right time? The city is in mourning."

It was clear from his reaction that he had not considered that.

"It must be now," Publius said nevertheless. He glanced up at her. "I would like you to help choose a wife for me."

She stared at him for a long moment deciding whether to laugh or not.

"Alright, do these ladies have names?" she asked.

Publius' face lit up in relief. "Yes," he said his voice growing in excitement, "I have arranged to visit their homes tomorrow. The first meeting is at dawn and the second two hours later." He beamed, "What father will refuse to marry his daughter into a family that has a Vestal as one of its members?"

"But do you not have any preference at all?" she inquired.

Publius shrugged, "I need a wife and an heir," he said simply.

***

The first house they visited was a modest building on the Aventine. The family matron had just lost three of her sons at Cannae and shrouded in her mourning clothes she had sat throughout the entire audience in sombre silence. The father of the family had not even showed up. He had taken to wine after the news of the loss of his boys. The girl Publius was hoping to marry was young barely seventeen and giggled nervously throughout. A pretty girl Pompeia thought but thick as a tree trunk.

The second home was a grander affair on the Caelian hill and the family had connections to the college of priests Publius told her. They were shown into an atrium and told to wait. When the girl finally came in she was accompanied by two lawyers, mean looking men. Publius was just about to greet her when the girl caught sight of Pompeia and froze.

"What is this, you bring a Vestal into my home!" the girl cried out.

Pompeia, used to being seen in public, stood her ground, her face a model of composure that could not be ruffled by any insult. Publius tried to speak but the girl had already turned to her advisers.

"I cannot be associated with one of them," she snapped. "This will not do. Tell them to leave at once."

"Have I offended you?" Pompeia said in a calm voice.

The girl turned to her and seemed to grow visibly upset clawing at her hair.

"You," she pointed her finger at Pompeia, "You Vestals are all whores, you have betrayed your vows and you are all going to die. Everyone knows what you horny bitches have been up to! Get out now. Get out of my house!"

Pompeia felt like someone had hit her in the face. She swayed on her feet, her mouth suddenly felt very dry and she tried to swallow. Then Publius was at her side leading her towards the entrance hall. The young freedman looked horrified and was muttering apologies, one after the other but Pompeia seemed only to hear half his words. They stepped out into the street and the door was slammed shut behind them.

"You had better take the first one," Pompeia stammered.

Chapter Thirteen – Homecoming

The college of cattle drivers had built their Columbaria on top of a small hill just outside the city. The low rectangular mud brick walls looked old and weather beaten. There was no roof. Grass and weeds had sprung up in the open central space and in the cracks between the bricks and the paving stones. Just beyond the wall a line of Cypress trees, stiff and silent like sentinels, provided some shade from the hot noon sun. Adonibaal checked to see if he was alone and satisfied that he was he strode across the last few yards and entered the narrow gap between the walls. The urns of the dead stood neatly in their pigeon holes. There were hundreds of them. Slowly he made his way along one side of the wall reading the brass plated inscriptions. Then suddenly he stopped and brushed the dust from one of the urns.

"Hello Flavia," he said.

Adonibaal gazed at the urn that contained the ashes of his bride. Slowly he got down on his knees. So this is where they have buried you he thought. He had been away for twenty four years. He knelt and looked at the urn. It was of a cheap design, cracked in places and the only thing identifying her was her name and the day on which she had died, scratched onto a brass plate. This was all that remained of her, that and a memory. There were no flowers or offerings but someone had left her a silver coin. He picked it up and held it between thumb and finger. The coin was old, very old. No one had been to the grave in years. He glanced at the urn next to hers. It was her father. He smiled sadly as he remembered the look on the man's face when he'd learned that his daughter was going to marry into the aristocratic Fabian clan. Old fool. Well at least the college of drivers, to which her father had belonged, had done its duty and ensured that she had received a proper burial and so could pass on into the afterlife.

That should have been my duty he thought.

He opened his hand and looked at the two tiny figurines. He had carved them onboard the ship that had taken him to Carthage, all those years ago. One image of Flavia; one for the daughter he had lost. After all the time that had passed he could still picture Flavia's face as clearly as if she was standing beside him now. She had been the only woman he had ever loved. The only woman he had ever wanted. He cocked his head. Yes if he listened carefully he could hear her voice and the way in which she laughed. She had understood him from the very first moment when they had met. Flavia and he had been meant for each other, they were soul mates.

Everything he had done had been for her. They had both been virgins. On the first night that they had spent together they had sworn an oath of loyalty and promised to wait for each other. He had given his word in the presence of the gods that he would never abandon her. She in return had told him she would never love another.

"Spirits of the departed," he whispered turning to look at the ground. "I honour you and wish you to know that I am loyal still and that our oath endures. Dearest Flavia, I was not here to say my farewell to you. Forgive me for this. You were strong and kept your promise. Fortune was not your friend but do not despair, for one day soon we shall be together again. I was and am your husband."

He placed the two figurines on top of the urn.

In his weaker moments, when he had despaired of the life he was living her memory had always come to guide him back to the light and given him the strength to continue.

Then his mood darkened as the memories came flooding back. They had never given him the chance to say goodbye to her. They had not allowed him to see her and his daughter being buried. He raised his face to the sky and stifled a cry of shame and anger. They had all been against him, thwarting his every move, striking at him with everything they had, his father wielding the law, Janus the whip and his brother, most painful of all, by breaking his word and betraying his confidence. He clenched his hand into a fist and pushed it into the soil. He had trusted Numerius but his brother had gone straight to his father, like a dog would go to its master and after that he'd lost Flavia and everything that mattered to him in life. He had trusted Numerius. He had loved him and had thought he'd known his mind. But his brother had left him to die like some sort of wounded beast. His brother had done nothing to help him. From his cell in his father's house he had begged Numerius for help but his brother had not come, he had not stood up for him and when his punishment was read out Numerius had remained silent. His brother's desertion had cut deep for Numerius had been his only real friend.

***

Adonibaal descended the hill with steady confident steps as he headed for the old salt road in the valley. The noon heat was already fading and the sun was getting low on the horizon. He had changed his appearance after he'd left Hannibal's camp. Gone was the beard, the ponytail and the foreign clothes. Instead he had become clean shaven and had his hair trimmed in the short Roman fashion. On the road to Rome he'd stumbled across a farm whose owner had been murdered. He'd guessed that bandits were to blame. The farmer however had been his size so he'd taken the dead man's clothes and changed into a plain sleeveless black tunic with a belt and a pair of sandals. Now if anyone looked at him they would see a simple shepherd or a farm labourer. Slung across his back he carried a large quiver into which he had placed "Centurion" and the dismantled parts of the Scorpio, the Roman army crossbow he'd found at Cannae. He'd dismantled the Scorpio in such a way that only a very close examination would reveal it for what it was. The Scorpio was a brilliant and inspired piece of engineering, a perfect snipers weapon. It could be operated by a single man and fired a bolt with terrible accuracy over a distance of a hundred yards. It had been designed for city sieges and was easy to carry and quickly assembled. The bolt from a Scorpion could even punch through armour although he doubted Fabius would be wearing any. It had however been some years since he had last used the weapon and being in a remote spot he had decided to test and hone his skill. That had been a mistake.

He thought again about the encounter with the boy. He had been angry with himself afterwards for his lapse of concentration. The boy had surprised him and then fled before he could decide what to do. Maybe the long years spent in the company of thousands of men in Hannibal's army had made him forget the demands of operating alone. The boy had seen his face and he had seen the weapon. He would think he'd killed the farming family and maybe he would report the matter to the local magistrate? Yet he had shrugged off his concerns. There were swarms of bandits operating in Italy now that Hannibal had crushed the Roman armies. The magistrates would have more important matters to concern themselves with and the boy knew nothing of real importance.

He stepped onto the old salt road. The road was nothing more than a dusty unpaved track. He paused to allow a wagon pulled by an ox to pass by. In the distance, he could see the walls of Rome. The great fortifications, for which Hannibal had such respect, made of giant blocks of yellowish stone, rose to a height of ten yards and snaked their way across the hills. For two hundred years now those walls had kept out all invaders. For two hundred year's they had made the citizens of Rome feel safe. He smiled. He was happy to be back he realised.

As he drew closer to the Colline gate the old salt road merged with another road and the traffic grew thicker. Workmen were repairing sections of the wall and the ditch in front. The dull rhythmic thud of their picks and spades at work seemed to sum up the sullen atmosphere of the workmen. So they still intend to fight he thought or at least someone intends to fight. He passed the shrine of Venus Erycina, the goddess of prostitutes and glanced up noticing suddenly that he was being watched by armed men on top of the gate house.

As he covered the last few yards a soldier stepped forwards to block his path. The man held up his hand for him to stop.

"State your business in the city?" the soldier demanded.

"I have come to help," Adonibaal muttered. "I heard that every man is needed."

"Isn't that the truth," the guard replied glancing curiously at the quiver. "Where are you from then?"

"Nowhere," Adonibaal replied, "I go where the grass is green and where my sheep take me."

The soldier glared at him trying to see if Adonibaal was making fun of him. "And where are your sheep now, old man?" the soldier said.

"Foreigners took the lot, three days walk south of here," Adonibaal grunted keeping his eyes on the ground. The guard suddenly looked uncomfortable. "Three days walk, you say?" He turned and glanced down the road apprehensively. "And they expect us to fight with boys and old men and useless weapons," he muttered. "How can we win?" As if conscious that he had said too much the guard waved him on.

Adonibaal was just about to pass under the gate when the guard reached forwards and pulled "Centurion" from out of the quiver. "What's this?" the soldier said in surprise staring at the weapon, "Looks foreign to me."

The guards stopped chattering and sauntered over to have a look at what their colleague had found.

"I found it," Adonibaal said sternly, "Its mine. They told me to come armed."

"That's a fine blade," one of the guards muttered enviously.

The soldier who held "Centurion" examined it intently turning it over in his hand. Then he shrugged and handed it back to Adonibaal with a grudging look.

"Alright, alright, old man, we're not thieves," he said.

***

Adonibaal entered Rome and as he did so he pulled the hood of his Palla over his head. It looked a little odd in the summer heat but the fear of being recognised worried him more. It had been twenty-four years, but he knew that people had a knack for recognising faces. He had grown up in the city and knew its streets like the back of his hand, yet just one casual chance encounter with someone who knew him would be a disaster.

His thoughts turned to Numerius. His younger brother would be an old man now. Maybe he was dead; maybe he had already long ago left the city. He'd heard nothing and knew nothing about his brother's whereabouts but there was always a chance that he had remained in Rome. He didn't like to be reminded of his brother because it normally put him in a bad mood, but now that he was in Rome and knowing he may come face to face with him at any moment, he felt a growing sense of curious excitement. From beneath his hood his eyes began to search the faces in the crowd.

His brother owed him. His brother had been the chief beneficiary of what he Adonibaal had done. Murdering his father had turned him into a fugitive and a traitor, a man whose name and memory were erased from history for all time. But Numerius; he had been free to continue his life. He would have inherited everything, the family estate, their title, his father's wealth and as head of the family he would be able to marry whom ever he liked. As eldest those things should have been mine Adonibaal thought. He'd trusted his brother, he'd loved him. They'd fought together, shared the pain and misery of a thousand beatings and humiliations and still his brother had betrayed him. Why? Why? Why? He'd being asking himself that question for the past twenty four years and had long ago given up believing he would ever know the answer. His brother had been the only man who'd known about his plans to marry Flavia but on that fateful night when he had murdered his father, Adonibaal had still been unable to accept that Numerius could really have betrayed him. Those doubts had saved his brother's life.

He took the street called Alta Semita, and headed towards the city centre. The Quirinal district in which he found himself was the most northerly hill in Rome and the Alta Semita, one of the oldest streets in the city. Modest houses lined the road, their front rooms turned into workshops, taverns and bars. He'd forgotten how noisy Rome could be. The sound of the city broke all around him. Blacksmiths at work, barking dogs, street vendors crying out for business, crying babies, the crunch of sandals and boots on the stones, the whinny of horses and a new sound he hadn't heard before, the wailing of women in mourning. Every man, even the boys seemed to be armed with a variety of weapons and he pulled "Centurion" from his quiver. It would do to blend in and act like all the men were doing.

He passed the tavern where he had first met Flavia as a young man. The owner was a stranger but the tavern had hardly changed and the sight of the old place brought back a hundred memories. He had finally come home and with that realisation he became aware of a new understanding; whatever happened now he would not be leaving the city again. He had come home for good. He would not run away a second time.

The Alta Semita was just another section of the ancient salt road which had existed before the city had been built. It ran straight towards the forum and on to the cattle market, the forum Boarium beside the Tiber, but he was not ready to enter the forum yet and he turned left at the first chance and then right into the Long road, the Vicus Longus.

Adonibaal turned his attention to the soldiers he saw in the street. Boys and old men the guard at the city gate had told him and the man was right Adonibaal thought. The Senate was scraping the bottom of the barrel. As he strode along, from beneath his hood he studied the soldiers he saw, observing the way in which they carried their weapons, the state of their armour and shields, the looks on their faces. Amateurs, he concluded. They would flee at the first sight of Maharbal's cavalry. But cavalry alone could not get past a wall like the one that surrounded Rome and he had to give them credit for one thing. They had not given up. Somehow they had found the courage, these old men and boys, the courage and strength to keep on fighting despite the hopelessness of their situation. He had to admire them for that. Hannibal was right. To win the war the city did not need to be occupied, they only had to break the morale of these amateurs.

Up ahead he could see the forum and he abruptly turned left into a side street. Immediately he found himself in another world. The Subura, the low lying valley squashed between three hills was the poorest and most dangerous neighbourhood in Rome. The street narrowed dramatically until it was barely a yard or so across. Tall Insulae, some five stories high, their balconies nearly touching each other across the narrow street, lined both sides of the alley. A couple of children without shoes ran past, brushing against his legs and a one armed beggar sat on a door step holding out his hand in miserable silence. Stinking rubbish lay in heaps and water stains on the walls marked the places where the gutters had crumbled.

Adonibaal headed deeper into the tangle of narrow alleys and crumbling apartment blocks. A woman's voice called out a warning and he had just enough time to step into a culvert as a bucket of piss and shit landed on the paving stones close by. He didn't look up as he hurried on. The smell in the Subura was what most shocked visitors, that and the rampant poverty and malnourishment. The valley in which the neighbourhood was situated had once been a swamp until the kings had constructed the great drain, the Cloaca Maxima which now carried all the cities effluence down into the Tiber. The Cloaca however ran directly through the Subura and on hot days the smell seeped out and lacking the cool winds that people enjoyed on the hill tops, it lingered.

Adonibaal knew his way around and soon he emerged from the squalid slums and made his way to the junction of the Appian and the Sacred Way. As he approached the junction he noticed the half finished Insulae that lined the street on his left. Piles of building material had been left behind together with the scaffolding used by the workers. He halted, glanced up at the building sight and then back along the street ahead of him. The junction where the Sacred Way turned right towards the Forum was only twenty or thirty paces away. He grunted thoughtfully and continued on down the street.

The Appian Way took him in a south westerly direction, skirting the Palatine hill to his right and the Capena gate and the city walls to his left. At the start of another street he paused and gazed up at the Aventine hill which was his destination. He felt his heart thumping in his chest. Up till now he had not been afraid, he had been in control, but now the most dangerous part of his mission was approaching, the only time where he would be at the mercy of the unknown, where he had to put his life and trust in the hands of strangers. Oh how he hated not being in control. It scared him like nothing else.

He climbed the steps towards the main street on the Aventine, the Clivus Publicus and paused to study his surroundings. The Aventine was considered to be a new neighbourhood in Rome and apart from the temple of Diane, people joked, there was no real reason to go there unless you wanted to learn a foreign language. The Aventine was the district where all the foreigners lived because the housing was cheap. The people were highly multi-cultural, mainly poor Latin farmers from the country to the south of Rome and Samnites and Etruscans from the mountains who had flocked to Rome in search of jobs, food and security. Yet the city had also been swollen by recent refugees from the north since Hannibal's invasion of Italy and Adonibaal could hear a multitude of different languages being spoken in the streets. He drew his hood closer over his head. If Rome was on the look out for spies, this would be where they would be looking.

As he made his way towards the temple of Diane he felt a cool wind on his face. He glanced up. The sun was beginning to set on the horizon. He would have to hurry. On the tiled roof tops birds sat in long rows watching him. He was approaching the temple of Diane, the huntress goddess, when there was a sudden commotion. Someone screamed and there was a scuffle in the street a few yards ahead of him. Adonibaal fingers tightened around "Centurion". Up ahead the crowd parted and three men burst towards him. They were dragging another young man along by his arms. The man's legs kicked at the paving stones in a vein attempt to escape. Adonibaal stepped aside as the men passed by with their screaming prisoner.

"Another bloody runaway slave who thought the goddess would protect him," a man next to Adonibaal muttered shaking his head.

Adonibaal glanced towards the great temple of Diane with its bright white stone steps, soaring pillars, sloped roof and huge porticoes on either side. The building dwarfed everything around it. The goddess Diane was not even a Roman goddess but a Latin deity. Her presence on the Aventine explained why so many Latin settlers had come to live here. He smiled as he remembered his tutor telling him the story of how Rome's crafty elders had used the great temple to bind the Latin tribes into a political and religious bond with Rome that they would never dare break. The temple was a symbol of the eternal unity between the Roman and Latin people. A bronze statue of Diane gleamed at the entrance to the temple and beneath it someone had left an offering of food.

"Bloody runaways," the man next to Adonibaal continued, "Always causing trouble. If it isn't the slaves then it's the women, coming to the temple to offer the huntress their leftovers they do, and here is I who have to clean it up after them. No consideration whatsoever. And then there are the funeral societies, now there's a spectacle to cheer up a hard working man."

Adonibaal turned on the man, "Do you know where I can find Demetrius the Macedonian," he said.

Chapter Fourteen – The Subura

Titus was covered in dust. It was smeared across his face. It had gotten into his nose, ears and hair and under his finger nails and it made him cough. His throat was parched. For two days now he had ridden without hardly any rest. He desperately yearned for a wash and for a proper bed on which to sleep. Now he finally mounted the steps up to the senate house, taking two stairs at a time, oblivious to the spectacle that he made.

"Despatch from the consul Varro!" he cried in a loud voice.

He reached the senate door just as a cluster of senators rushed out to meet him.

"Despatch from the consul," Titus panted holding out the tightly wrapped scroll with a straight arm.

"You have come from Cannae?" one of the senators exclaimed. Titus nodded.

"Then Varro lives!" another cried.

The group of senators parted to allow another man through. This senator was old and the others seemed to treat him some respect.

"I will take that son," the man said, "My name is Quintus Fabius Maximus. I will see that it is read to the Senate."

Titus dipped his head in acknowledgment. When he looked up again the gaggle of senators were already streaming back into the house and he was left alone. His task accomplished he washed his face in a public fountain and drank till his stomach was full. Then with renewed vigour and mounting excitement he hurried through the forum and turned left into the Argiletum, the street of the booksellers, which in turn led into the heart of the Subura. Some men avoided the Subura like they did the plague but for Titus it was home and he knew the people, the customs and every twist and bend of the neighbourhood. As he pushed his way deeper into the maze of narrow alleys, the grin on his face grew wider and wider and then suddenly he was there. He tilted his neck to look up at the crumbling tenement block that was home. In the front room on the ground floor someone was working, hammering on a piece of metal. The dull metallic ringing noise was suddenly interrupted by a yelp of pain and a string of oaths. Titus sighed with relief as he recognised the voice.

He stepped through the leather curtain that hung across the doorway and immediately felt the heat from the small furnace. In a corner beside the furnace, a fat sweating man, stripped to the waist was labouring over a work bench on which lay a white hot piece of metal. The man looked up quickly as Titus entered.

"Well if it isn't young Titus, returned from the wars!" the fat man exclaimed and there was no mistaking the genuine surprise and delight in his voice. A big smile appeared on the man's face.

"You look well Frontinus," Titus beamed.

Frontinus laid down his tools. He looked around fifty with chubby drooping cheeks and a dash of thinning hair that still clung on around his ears and the back of head. Sweat and dark soot stains covered his big fat hairy chest. He laughed and a moment later Titus was embraced by a mountain of sweaty, wobbly flesh.

"We thought you were dead," Frontinus said as he let go of Titus, "the news has been terrible, everyone knows someone who was killed."

Titus shrugged and smiled. "Well I survived and now I am here," he said.

"Have you come back for your old job?" Frontinus laughed and slapped Titus on the back nearly knocking the young man off his feet.

"Working for you," Titus grinned, "You taught me too well. I would rather set up my own business and give you a run for your money."

Frontinus' eyes twinkled in delight. "Ha!" he snorted, "A year in the army and he's already got an attitude. But seriously, the job is yours if you want it. I could do with the help. Business is crazy. Everyone is demanding weapons. I am working day and night. The neighbours have started to complain about the noise…"

Titus was glancing towards the stairs that led to the higher floors in the tower block and Frontinus' voice rambled to a halt.

"Is my mother here?" Titus asked.

"Of course," Frontinus' face grew serious, "Stupid me, talking about myself again. You had better go and see her. She has been worried sick about you all week."

Titus nodded but as he was about to ascend the stairs Frontinus caught him by the arm. "Titus", he said with a sudden tightness in his voice, "She is up there and so are the jugs of wine. She is drinking herself to death. You had better have a word with her. She doesn't take any notice of me and she's behind on the rent. Milo has been patient with her but it won't last, you know what he is like."

"Right," Titus said as the smile faded from his face.

***

His mother did not stop crying for half an hour. The two of them sat at the wooden table in the one room apartment. Titus was silent, his hands folded together on the table. The room was sparsely decorated, a couple of sleeping mats, the old table, two chairs, the urn containing his father's ashes and a few clothes. On the wall, in a little alcove, was a small statue of Venus. He stared at the pottery on the floor. All the jugs were empty but the stale smell of wine still lingered. He was home.

"You have been drinking again mother," he said at last.

She lifted her head, her hair was dishevelled and her hollow cheeks were streaked with tears.

"I am so glad you have come home," she whimpered, "Promise me that you will not leave again. I don't know what I will do without you."

Titus looked away, "I am still with the army," he replied, "I must follow orders. I have sworn an oath of duty to the officers."

His mother's eyes lit up. "And what about your family," she cried, "Don't you have a duty to us also? Or do you not care? Do you like seeing me beg from Milo every time I need something?"

"That's not fair," he replied unable to look her in the face. He reached down into his tunic pocket and placed a small bag of coins on the table. "It's all that I have got," he muttered. "But you must promise me that the drinking will end."

He was rewarded by a sharp slap in the face. His mother's eyes blazed.

"How dare you tell me what to do?" she cried, "I raised you and looked after you and your sister. You are the man in this family now. It is your duty to put bread on the table! If you can't do that, what kind of a man are you!"

Titus felt his cheek burn and it was not all from the slap.

"Where is Aelia?" he replied trying desperately to change the subject.

His mother seemed to regain her composure. She swept her hair behind her head and wiped her eyes.

"Your sister is out," she replied firmly, "she doesn't tell me where she goes or whom she sees. The child is impossible."

"They have told me that women are forbidden from going out," Titus said.

His mother shrugged and scooped up the bag of coins. "You know what she is like, thirteen summers and she thinks she knows everything. She disguises herself as a boy."

"Where does she go?" Titus said with growing alarm.

"I don't know," his mother replied wearily, "Maybe she has become a prostitute; she never seems to be hungry."

Titus leaned back in his chair in dismay. It was his mother's turn to avert her gaze. Then she stood up and came around the table and placed her arms around her son's neck.

"I am glad you are here," she muttered.

***

Frontinus scooped the water from the bowl using both hands and splashed it over his face. Then he reached for a rag and wiped his neck, arched his back and allowed himself a long contented sigh.

"How long can you stay?" he asked glancing at Titus who stood leaning against the wall fidgeting with his fingers. Above the table in the workshop a single oil lamp cast a dim reddish light around the room.

"I am at the disposal of the Senate," Titus replied, "I must report to them at dawn. They will tell me then if they have another despatch for me. My mother doesn't want me to go but I have orders."

"I know. Not much time eh," Frontinus sighed. "Terrible business, war," Frontinus shook his head, "I was at Telamon when we slaughtered the Gauls. That was a bloody day. It is strange how fortune governs men. Some men die in battle, some live, some lose a leg or an arm, some become famous and some like I," he raised his eyebrows, "are lucky to grow rich. Yeah Fortune must love my fat arse but tomorrow I shall go to the Temple of Diane and donate some money to the members of the college of blacksmiths who have suffered loss in this war. That is right and proper."

"Come and have a look at this?" Titus said with sudden eagerness in his voice. He had sat down and was staring at a tightly rolled scroll that he had placed onto the table.

Frontinus drifted across the room and frowned.

"What have you got there?"

Titus looked up triumphantly. "It's a letter. See the seal mark in wax? That belongs to Scipio of the Cornelii. I saved his life during the battle and he gave me this as a reward."

"You saved a Patrician's life at Cannae?" Frontinus looked impressed.

"I did," Titus nodded solemnly, "and in return he has promised to have someone give me an education."

The triumphant tone in Titus' voice made Frontinus smile. He picked up the scroll and examined it carefully, rolling it between his fingers.

"Gives a name and an address here," he said slowly, "one Numerius Fabius Vibulani. Whose he then?"

Titus shrugged. "I suppose he is the man whom I am supposed to give the letter to. Maybe he will teach me."

Titus looked up at Frontinus with sudden excitement. "You can read, can't you? Shall we open the letter and see what it says?" Frontinus studied the scroll for a second longer and then placed it back onto the table and shook his head.

"No, it is sealed for a purpose. Only the man to whom it is intended should have the privilege of opening it up."

Titus nodded disappointed, "I shall have to wait of course until the war is over, that is what Scipio told me, but I can wait."

Frontinus placed a hand on Titus' shoulder and sighed. "I know how much this means to you," he said kindly, "but the war may last for a long time yet. Prepare yourself that Titus."

Titus nodded, touching the letter with gentle reverence, "I know but this is the only chance that I will probably ever get. A learned man is treated with respect. An educated man has opportunities. I will finally have the means to look after my family and buy them proper clothes and food." Titus looked up at Frontinus and there was a sudden passion in his eyes and voice. "I will be able to walk down the street and men will be able to say, there goes Titus, a man who has done well for himself and his family."

Frontinus chuckled and sat down opposite Titus. "Your father would be proud of you and he would be proud of you even without an education."

"So you don't believe that I can do it," the seriousness in Titus' voice caught Frontinus off guard and he waved his hand in a gesture of dismissal. "Forget what I said," he muttered knowing there was no point in arguing with Titus, "a tired old man's words."

Titus grunted and looked down at the scroll on the table. "If I have time I shall deliver the letter to this Numerius' house tomorrow." Titus looked up at Frontinus, "If for any reason I cannot do it, will you bring the letter to the man's house?"

Frontinus nodded. "I will," he said.

Titus placed his hand on the fat blacksmith's arm. "I will better myself and my family," he said and there was no mistaking the determination in his voice, "and when I do, I shall not forget old friends and favours."

Frontinus opened his mouth to reply but was interrupted by a sudden loud banging on the door outside.

"Open up in there," a voice cried.

Titus drew his sword but Frontinus raised a cautionary hand. The fat man suddenly looked nervous. No one in their right mind walked the streets of the Subura at night. At night the Subura was owned by the thieves and muggers who lurked in doorways and alleys and who would kill for the price of a cup of wine. Only those with nothing to fear went out at night.

"Whose there?" Frontinus growled knowing the answer already.

"Who the fuck do you think it is?" came the reply.

The blacksmith gestured urgently for Titus to sheath his sword. Then he unbolted the door and stepped back. The street outside was pitch black and for a moment Titus could see nothing. Then a man, completely bald, stepped into the room, followed by two enormous thugs who had to duck through the doorway. The bald man looked around 40 although he was actually only 30, with green tattoos up both arms and a hard drinking, tough looking face from which two crazy bulging eyes took in everything in the room. A menacing atmosphere seemed to follow the man into the workshop.

"What can I do for you Milo?" Frontinus said.

Milo did not answer as he looked around the workshop. Then his large fish eyes caught sight of Titus.

"Well...well," Milo muttered in surprise, "what have we here. Titus the Samnite has dared to show his face again. Still playing at being a soldier? I heard that Hannibal gave your lot a kick up the arse."

"I thought Hannibal was your enemy too?" Titus retorted.

Milo chuckled and slowly shook his head, "Doesn't concern me soldier boy. Rome will be the same with or without Hannibal. Some men no doubt will lose everything if he comes here but it's not going to affect me. The rich and powerful will always need a man like me to keep order in places where they don't dare to go themselves."

Milo took a step towards Titus, examining him from top to bottom as if he was a new species of animal. Then with a speed that caught everyone by surprise he slapped him hard in the face. Titus winced and rocked backwards on his feet but he had the good sense not to react. To strike back would be to invite death. He'd lived in the Subura long enough to know the law of its streets. Milo was that law, he was the judge, jury and executioner and in the Subura life was cheaper than fresh meat. From the corner of his eye Titus caught Frontinus shake his head in warning. Mastering his shock, Titus did the only thing he could do; he turned his eyes sullenly back to the man who had hit him.

"That's for showing me disrespect," Milo grinned. Then he slapped Titus again with the back of his hand, "And that's for leaving the neighbourhood without my permission."

"He was drafted, what could he do?" Frontinus protested.

"Silence old man!" Milo shouted without taking his eyes of Titus. Titus felt his lip beginning to swell up and a trickle of blood on his chin.

"Yes, just like your father," Milo grinned again, "He too was a proud independent man, but at least he had some sense about him. You would do well to remember that." He poked Titus playfully in his stomach. "Whilst you were away playing at being a hero I looked after your mum and sis. Did you a favour, did you know that? Life is hard here in the Subura; I look after my own, your father understood that boy. Now you can thank me."

The thugs behind him laughed as if on cue.

"Thank you Milo for looking after my family," Titus muttered blushing at the humiliation.

Milo grinned and looked around at his men. "See, everyone loves me." His words were followed by more sycophantic laughter. "Especially that sister of yours," Milo turned to look at Titus again, "She's got a fine pair of tits on her these days. Tell her that I will call on her soon."

Titus made no reply as the thugs laughed again.

"As for you, Frontinus," Milo said suddenly changing the subject and turning to the blacksmith, "What the fuck do you think I am here for?"

Frontinus nodded and shuffled over to a strong box which he unlocked using a key that hung around his neck. From it he took a bag of coins and placed it on the work bench. "This month's dues," he muttered.

"Very good," Milo said gesturing for one of the thugs to retrieve the money. There was a broad smile on his face. "You can now rest assured that your business will flourish and prosper under my protection. The college of poets is grateful for your contribution."

Milo winked at Titus and was turning to leave when something caught his eye. It was the leather despatch case that hung around Titus' neck. Milo frowned and pointed at the case.

"What is that?" he demanded.

Titus shook his head and made no reply. Angrily Milo stepped across the room and yanked the case from Titus' neck. The leather strap broke as he did so and a single tightly rolled scroll tumbled onto the table.

"Well, well, what have we here," Milo said picking up the letter with sudden interest. "What's this then Titus, state secrets? You can't even read."

Titus felt his legs start to tremble but he said nothing. Milo frowned as he read the name on the letter. "I know that man," he hissed suddenly, "he's an arse," what business are you conducting with him?" There was a sudden viciousness in Milo's voice.

"It's none of your business, give it back," Titus growled suddenly finding his voice. He lunged for the letter but Milo was quicker and closed his fist around it.

"I will ask you one more time, after that the pain will begin," he hissed.

"Titus is going to be educated," Frontinus suddenly interrupted.

"Now give it back to him Milo, this doesn't involve you."

Milo opened his mouth in surprise, looked from Frontinus to Titus and then closed his mouth without saying anything.

"Educated," he blurted at last, "and how did you manage that?"

"He saved a Patrician's life at Cannae," Frontinus said stepping in between Milo and Titus and folding his arms across his chest. Milo grunted in surprise and for a moment his eyes seemed to roll about in their sockets. Then he shook his head, turned towards the furnace and threw the letter into the fire.

"No, there will be no education for you Titus," he said, "It's time you understood who you are and where you belong. Your place is with me and the people of the Subura."

Titus emitted a strangled cry as he stared at the letter burning away in the fire. He tried to move towards Milo but Frontinus blocked his path, holding him in a bear hug. Then as Milo and his thugs exited the room laughing, tears began to roll down his cheeks.

***

Titus lay on his mattress unable to sleep. It had taken Frontinus a long time to calm him down but now he was calm. Milo and his gang of armed slaves had governed the Subura for as long as he could remember. They were part of everyday life. They kept order in the streets and alleys through a mixture of intimidation, free hand outs, employment and powerful connections to the Senate. The college of poets was supposed to be exactly that but all knew it had been set up as a legal cover for Milo's activities. Everyone knew that Milo was not a man to be crossed. Those that did simply disappeared. If someone had vanished, no one would ever ask questions. Milo knew everything that went on in the neighbourhood. His informants were everywhere. He took what he wanted, tolerated no rivals and lived beyond any law.

Titus' father had warned him long ago about Milo. Do not join him son, whatever he tries to offer you. Milo will lead you into ruin, it's his way. The greater your ruin, the greater is his hold over you. So Titus had learned to avoid trouble, to take the occasional threats, bribes and humiliations in his stride and so to ensure that his family survived, for that was all that really mattered. But now, with the burning of his letter of introduction and the possibility of getting a replacement slim or non existent, something had changed. Milo was looking to recruit him and make him into another of his thugs. That would be his future if he joined Milo and Titus knew that he could not go on refusing the man without incurring consequences. Sure he himself could hide in the army but what of his mother and sister? They would be left to Milo's mercy. He'd thought of trying to leave but where would they go? They had no money and no connections and Italy was being convulsed by war. Education was his way out of the slums. That was his best chance and Milo knew it too. Titus closed his eyes. He had to hold onto that dream and find a way.

Chapter Fifteen – Plotting Murder

Demetrius was a short shifty looking character with a long grey beard.

"Who are you?" he said as Adonibaal stood on the doorstep to his house.

Adonibaal stared at the small Macedonian.

"Philip would like to know if you received the statue of Gasoteris."

For a moment Demetrius looked perplexed. Then a little colour shot into his cheeks and he glanced around to see if there was anyone within earshot.

"It arrived on the summer equinox," he replied, "Would you like to see it?"

Their eyes locked and the bond of trust was sealed.

"I would," Adonibaal replied stepping into the house."

Demetrius closed the door behind him and locked it. Then he leaned against the wood and studied his guest.

"Gisgo has sent you?" he whispered.

Adonibaal nodded. The house was a simple building, a workman's dwelling. They stood in the front room which was filled with hundreds of stone and bronze statues of all shapes and sizes. A doorway at the back led to another room in which he could hear a woman singing quietly to herself. The smell of fish soup was overpowering. The residence had none of the grandeur of the rich houses that Adonibaal remembered from his youth.

"Your trade is in statues?" Adonibaal asked.

"As you can see," Demetrius spread his arms out wide.

"What about the woman?"

"She is my wife, you can trust her," the Macedonian said hastily. He poured the contents of a jug into two cups. As he did so Adonibaal noticed that the man's hand trembled with the effort.

"Thank the gods that you have come," he muttered. "What's your name? No don't tell me your name, I don't want to know."

He handed one of the cups to Adonibaal and tried to smile.

"It's about time that they sent a replacement," Demetrius said. "I have been here for two years. The Romans have eyes in the back of their heads. Do you know what that does to a man's nerves? I can't wait to return to Pella. I have served my king well. Yes I have," he muttered to himself.

Adonibaal placed his bowl of soup back on the table without touching it.

"I am not your replacement," he said.

The Macedonian stopped eating and stared at him. Then he sighed deeply and lowered his eyes.

"So what do you want from me?" the disappointment in the man's voice was clear, "a hiding place, money?"

Suddenly there was a new hope in the man's voice.

"How long will it be before Hannibal comes? Is he on his way? Does Gisgo have any messages for me?"

Adonibaal felt a growing sense of disappointment. Demetrius looked worn out. The strain of being a Carthaginian spy in Rome was clearly showing. Damn you Gisgo he thought. Damn you to hell. Gisgo had told him that the man would be able to help him. He'd reassured him that Demetrius was the best of the best, a master spy with a long record of success. The Macedonian had survived longer than any other spy. It was all rubbish. Demetrius had even forgotten to ask him for the final security check. He could not rely on this man. It was only a matter of time before he gave himself away.

"I need some information," Adonibaal muttered.

"Yes of course," Demetrius nodded, "whatever you need. The Romans are very active. Just a few weeks ago they crucified twentyfive slaves in the field of Mars. They were accused of plotting against the state. I think they are watching me too." He glanced nervously at the door. "I must let you know that I am

164

planning to leave soon. When Hannibal comes my work here will be done."

Demetrius did his best to answer Adonibaal's questions. When he could think of nothing more to ask Adonibaal rose to his feet. At least the spy had not been a complete waste of time he thought. His answers had given him a good understanding of the mood and disposition of the city, the senate and most crucially the whereabouts of the senate leaders. He glanced casually at the spy trying to see if the man had guessed the purpose of his mission but it was difficult to tell as Demetrius would not look him in the eye.

As he stood up, the Macedonian spy rose with him and stretched out his arm in greeting.

"I wish you luck with whatever you have come to do," Demetrius smiled, relieved no doubt that the stranger was leaving.

Adonibaal embraced the man and as he did so the thought of killing him crossed his mind. It would make sense. No loose ends, no one who could give him away. For a moment as they embraced he was tempted. With one twist of his hands he could break the man's neck. It would be over in a second. He held the embrace as he sensed Demetrius trying to break apart. But then he would also have to kill the woman in the back room and the man whom he had asked directions from. Both of them may recognise him. It would all become rather complicated. As he let go, Demetrius stumbled backwards with sudden fear in his eyes.

"If you plan to kill me," he muttered quietly. "Let the woman live. She is not involved in any of this."

Adonibaal's eyes glinted darkly and for a long moment he didn't move. Then without a word he turned towards the door.

"Wait," Demetrius said holding up his hand. A bead of sweat ran down his cheek and he eyed Adonibaal nervously. "We are on the same side after all," he tried to smile, "Please," he said handing over a sealed scroll, "My report, will you give it to Gisgo?"

Adonibaal took the scroll and slid it into his tunic.

"So Gisgo has plans has he?"

There was a searching inquisitive tone in the spy's voice that instantly put Adonibaal on guard.

"Hannibal is coming," he said solemnly, "I have been sent to discover the state of the defences around the city. I am leaving tomorrow." He paused as his contempt for the Macedonian spy grew. "Gisgo told me that you are to be rewarded."

And with that he stepped out into the street.

***

It was getting dark as Adonibaal entered the Subura. The shop keepers were closing their stalls and people were disappearing from the streets. He found an apartment block and rented a room from the janitor. It was on the 4th floor. The janitor, a fat unwashed man with a belly that protruded over his belt stood in the door way as Adonibaal inspected the dwelling.

"You want it?" the man coughed.

The apartment was a single room with a solitary window overlooking an alley. There was a strong smell of old wine, urine and vomit.

"For a week," Adonibaal said tossing the man a couple of copper coins.

"No whores!" the janitor grumbled, "This is a respectable building and you shit in the bucket provided. Milo's orders!"

When he was alone Adonibaal placed the Scorpion on the floor and crossed to the window. There was not much to see in the alley below. In the apartment, across from him a man and a woman were shouting at each other. He judged the distance between their open window and his and grunted with satisfaction. He had an escape route if he needed to get out in a hurry.

That night he didn't sleep much. The domestic argument across the alley went on and on and in the apartment, next door someone had started to play on a flute. He lay on the straw mattress which was the only furniture in the room and stared at the ceiling. In his early years as a fugitive he had often thought about taking revenge on his brother. The thought had kept him warm at night and focussed during the day but as the years had passed it had given way to a growing desire to return to the place and time where his life had broken off. Gisgo had played him well but then Gisgo had a knack for knowing what people wanted. He stared at the cracks in the ceiling. He was happy to be home he thought but his happiness was matched by anger and the memories of dark painful days from the past. He was not going to be pushed out again. He had come home to stay. They would just have to make room for him. He allowed himself a smile. It would be a fine thing to once again be able to stroll down the Sacred Way in the forum and hear people speak your name with respect like they used to do. It would be a fine moment when he took his seat in the Senate like his father had done before him. But these things would only happen if he managed to kill Fabius. Once the old Senate leader was dead and Hannibal ruled in Rome, Adonibaal would be free from the intolerable life he had been forced to live.

He tried to picture his brother's face. What cause had he given Numerius to hate him so much? Had they not been brothers united by a common enemy, had they not shared the pain and suffering from the same tyrant, had they not been best friends? Had they not gone to war together? The only explanation he could think of was that Numerius had grown greedy and envious and had made a deal so that he would inherit everything, but there was something unsatisfactory about the explanation.

He thought about Fabius and tried to picture his face. Fabius had been an awkward uncle like figure when Adonibaal had been growing up. There had been little warmth and friendship between them despite the close family links; the older man annoyed by the boy's energy, bravado and lack of traditional respect and Adonibaal by the fact that Fabius always sided with his father. In a way it had been a clash between generations, rebellious youth and energy against age and experience.

He'd worried that Fabius may have left Rome but Demetrius had confirmed that he was indeed still in the city and had also told him where Fabius lived. In the darkened room Adonibaal allowed himself a triumphant smile. In a few days the cold calculating aristocrat would be dead and the news of his death would be the signal for Hannibal's advance on Rome to begin.

He was woken by the janitor moving up the stairs and shouting out the hour of the day. Leaving the Scorpion behind in his room he made his way up the Palatine hill and found Fabius' house exactly as Demetrius had described it. In an alcove across the street he crouched down and busied himself with his foot pretending to be massaging it whilst watching the front door hoping to get a glimpse of his target, but he was to be disappointed. Demetrius had told him that the Senate would be meeting first thing tomorrow morning. Fabius if he was at home could therefore take two possible routes to the Senate House. Adonibaal glanced northwards up the street and limped off until the road ended in a steep staircase that led downwards towards the Forum Boarium. This was the quickest and most direct route that Fabius could take to the senate house he thought as he descended the steps. He was about half way down the hill when he paused. To his right a house had been built onto the slope and a short and narrow entry shielded by bushes led to the door. Adonibaal nodded in satisfaction. This would be his first possible killing point. He glanced back up the stairs from which he had just come. It was a secluded enough spot and there was a good escape route into the cattle market but the Scorpion would be useless here. If the attempt was to be made here then it would have to be done with Centurion. It would have to be a stabbing followed by a wild flight down the stairs. Then he would have to lose any pursuers in the market. He lingered for a moment thinking it through and then began to retrace his steps.

***

He found the second killing point in the half-finished apartment buildings which he had first noticed the previous day on his journey to the Aventine. If Fabius were to take the long route to the Senate house he would have to pass down the Appian Way until he came to the cross roads where he would turn left into the Sacred Way, which led to the forum. Adonibaal paused beside the half completed building site and glanced up. All work seemed to have stopped. The place was deserted. There wasn't even a guard to keep an eye on the piles of building material dumped all over the place. He slipped through the doorway on the first floor and entered a dark damp room. His eyes adjusted to the darkness and he paused to listen but heard nothing. There was a stairway in the corner and he went up it, past the second floor and emerged into the sunlight on the third. The walls of the third floor were mostly complete but there was no roof. He moved to the western side of the building and found what he was looking for, a window. It was a square shape set in the stone wall and when he looked through it he saw the Appian Way and the cross roads stretching out before him. Satisfied he got down on his haunches to observe the traffic on the street. It was maybe thirty yards to the busy cross roads, an easy range for the Scorpion. He grunted in approval as he noticed the traffic slowed down as it approached the cross roads. It was the perfect killing ground for the sniper weapon. Again he lingered watching the traffic and thinking the action through from start to finish. He would have to bring the Scorpion in during the night and install it beside the window. The weapon would have to be abandoned once his mission was completed. That didn't matter. He ran through the different scenarios in his mind. What if Fabius were to be carried in a litter or a carriage? The sniper weapon would be useless then. Were there other routes to the Senate house he'd not thought about? He shrugged off the doubts. Plans would always change. He was used to that and it didn't bother him. He would get his man, he always did.

He left the window and explored the rest of the third floor and frowned in slight disappointment. The stairway seemed to be the only way in and out of the building. It was a ten yard drop to the ground, too high to jump without the risk of injury. He went down the stairs and examined the ground floor. At the back a doorway led to a small courtyard surrounded by a high wall. In the centre of the courtyard was a well. He peered down it and saw that it was deep. A bucket attached to a rope lay beside the hole. He looked at the wall and felt a growing disappointment. There would be no escape that way. That left only the front door through which he'd come in. It was not ideal for he would emerge just yards from the execution site and people may see him. Still it would have to do. No plan was ever perfect. He made his decision. The assassination would take place tomorrow at first light.

***

It was late that morning when Adonibaal returned to his room in the crumbling apartment block in the Subura. The janitor was gambling with another man, throwing dice, as he came in. The two men glanced at him curiously but it was the curiosity of bored men. One of them tried to say something but Adonibaal was already half way up the stairs and the man closed his mouth.

In his room Adonibaal checked the various parts of the Scorpion and satisfied that all was well he unsheathed Centurion and began to sharpen the blade. There was nothing else to do but wait now until it grew dark. The hours passed by slowly and as they did it seemed to grow hotter in his room. He stared at the wall, fighting the boredom and the tension that was starting to build up inside him. After another hour had past he got to his feet and began to pace around swinging Centurion at imaginary enemies.

Something was nagging at him and it wouldn't go away. Since he had returned to Rome he had felt a growing curiosity to see his old house. It had been so long ago since he'd left. The more he thought about it the more irresistible became the urge to go and have a look. Finally he could resist no more and sliding Centurion into its scabbard he left the room. There was no sign of the janitor or his friend as he left the building.

The wailing of women in mourning was everywhere as he made his way along the familiar streets of the Caelian hill. The Caelian was a well to do district, maybe not as grand as the

Palatine, but a good neighbourhood where many Equestrians, members of the second order of aristocrats had made their homes. The sight of so many familiar places brought forth another torrent of memories from his youth. Every building, street, bar and shop had its own significance but as he wandered along Adonibaal felt indifferent to it all. The thought of seeing the old house drove him on. By rights it should have been his house. It should have been the house in which he'd raised his children. It should have been the house in which he would have received guests, family and friends. But he had no children, no guests and no friends. He had no place to call his own. His life had been wasted on death, misery, hatred and loneliness. That was all he had achieved.

When he finally turned into the street in which he'd been born he paused in the middle of the road. His eyes wondered along the row of houses until they came to rest on his old home. It was still there. The door had been newly painted but from the outside it looked just like he remembered. He knew then why he had come. He had really been hoping to get a glimpse of his brother. Perhaps, now that he was so close, he needed to see him, to know the truth of why he'd betrayed him. He needed to know before he died.

The house had been built the year after the Gaul's had sacked Rome and was nearly one hundred and seventy five years old. The Vibulani had owned it all that time, a proud record, the ancestral seat of an ancient patrician family. He remembered the faces of his long dead forefathers, whose death masks had adorned the library in a long chronological line, perched in their alcoves in the wall looking down on the living. As young boys he and Numerius had always treated the library with respect bordering on awe. He'd been taught the names and deeds of all his forefathers until he knew them by heart. One wrong name or misquoted deed would have earned him a beating. He may have fought his father at every opportunity but not when it came to the masks in the library. They had truly been awesome and from a very young age he'd vowed that he would be like his forefathers, that his deeds would equal theirs and that he would make them proud.

He smiled but there was bitterness in his eyes.

What, he thought now, would they make of him? What would all those masks make of a man who had betrayed his own country? A man who had murdered his own father? There would be no forgiveness for that in the afterlife but he was not seeking forgiveness. He had come to make them all famous, famous beyond their wildest dreams.

Just as he was about to turn away the door to his old house opened.

Adonibaal froze in dismay. A man appeared, laughed and waved to someone inside before starting to walk down the street towards him. It was Janus, his father's old slave, the man who had been used to beat him for all those years. The slave who had aspired to become better than him!

Adonibaal recognised him immediately. Janus had put on weight and his hair had turned grey but it was still the same despicable servant who had locked him away on his father's orders all those years ago. The same man who had taken such delight in his downfall.

What was he still doing in the old house? Adonibaal faded into the shadows of an alley as Janus past by just a few yards away. The slave was singing happily to himself. A short sword hung from his belt and he was tossing a small bag from hand to hand. Janus was in a good mood and Adonibaal had to keep his wits about him as he followed on behind. The slave stopped frequently to chat with people in the street and as he did so Adonibaal felt his anger grow. The man was being treated with respect. Everyone seemed to know him. Eventually Janus entered a bar and, all alone, installed himself at a table. The bar front was open to the street and one could see straight through to the back room, where a staircase led to an upper floor. Adonibaal sat down across the road in another bar and watched the slave from beneath the hood of his Palla. The day wore on and Janus seemed to be getting himself drunk. His nose and cheeks grew pinker with each cup of wine. Then suddenly two women appeared, prostitutes by the look of their clothing, and joined him at his table. The slave laughed as the two women began to shower him with attention. It was not long before the three of them got up, with arms around each other, and swayed uncertainly towards the stairs at the back of the bar.

As they disappeared up the stairs Adonibaal rose from his seat and crossed the street. He went straight up the stairs. There was a small landing at the top with three doorways. He could hear Janus laughing to his right. A brown leather apron had been hung across the doorway suspended from hooks in the wall. Adonibaal pushed it aside and stepped into the room. Janus was on his back on the bed and the two girls half dressed were standing over him. The girls screamed as he appeared. Centurion slid noiselessly from its scabbard and the cold steel glinted in the sunlight.

"Get out!" Adonibaal said in a calm voice. The girls fled banging into each other in their haste. Janus was rising to his feet but Adonibaal stepped forward and the sharp point of Centurion hovered over the slave's throat forcing him back onto the bed.

"What do you want? Money, I have money?" Janus screeched.

Then his mouth fell open and he stared at Adonibaal.

"I know you," he said, "But it can't be. It's you. It's you Caeso!"

Down below in the bar Adonibaal could hear the women shouting.

"Yes Janus it is me," he said calmly, "Do you remember what you did to me all those years ago?"

"I was…I was just doing what your father had ordered me to do," the man stammered.

"Why do you still live in my father's house?"

Janus looked utterly bewildered, his pink face streaked with a sudden outbreak of sweat. "I…I own it now," he whispered. "Your father, in his will, he made me a freedman and gave me the house."

Adonibaal stared at Janus in utter disbelief and dismay. Surely it couldn't be true. But the man was not lying. He could see it in his eyes. Someone was coming up the stairs behind him.

"Is my brother still alive? Is he in Rome?"

"He is," Janus stammered. "He's got a house on the Janiculum."

Adonibaal felt his heart pounding away.

"I will give you my house," the freedman suddenly blurted out.

Adonibaal ignored the man's desperate pleas.

"A long time ago I tried to kill you," he muttered, "but you were lucky then and were not in your room. Your luck has just run out. Time to die Janus," he said as Centurion punched into the freedman's throat. Blood spurted out onto the bed and wall and Janus gurgled, his eyes bulging, staring at Adonibaal. The Mercenary did not look at him again. He knew the wound was enough to kill. He turned and strode from the room. A man, the bar owner stood on the landing gaping at him in astonishment. Adonibaal stepped forwards, grasped the man's neck with his left hand and pulled him onto Centurion's bloody steel. The sword slid into the man's stomach. There was a stifled cry of pain. Then Adonibaal flung the body to the floor without another glance and went down the stairs. He strode straight through the bar, past the two prostitutes who were stunned into silence, past the open-mouthed drinkers and out into the street.

Chapter Sixteen – Death on the streets of Rome

Numerius was having a bad morning. The sweats and shivers had persisted longer than usual and had left him drained and exhausted until he could hardly stand. Yet something else alarmed him more. His daughter's life was in danger and it was the fear for her safety which made him get off the couch and call for his cloak. He remembered the smile on Metellus' face when the priest had accused the vestals of being unchaste. Oh how much he had wanted to wipe that smile from that face forever. They had no evidence. Everyone understood that but the priests didn't need evidence. Numerius knew his history. He had read about it when studying to become a lawyer. There were precedents for the priest's behaviour. When Rome had been threatened with catastrophe in the past, a vestal had always been sacrificed to appease the anger of the gods and reassure an anxious population. It was a tradition, one of the many which the priests had; an extreme measure to be taken in extreme times and no legal authority could stop it.

Well the gods be damned he thought and so too the law. He was not going to allow some ambitious priest to murder his daughter. Fabius was the key. After the back room meeting in the Senate house, all had agreed that the business with the Vestals had probably been meant as a warning to them, not to interfere again in the affairs of the priests. Metellus had craftily avoided attacking Fabius directly and instead it seemed, he had chosen to make his point on him, Numerius, one of Fabius' close allies. It had been a callous, calculated act of political power. What would Fabius, the old family friend do now Numerius thought? Surely he would not allow this to happen?

Surely the old man would honour their long friendship? Numerius had resolved to go and petition him at once.

Publius came running holding his master's cloak. He looked worried and nervous. The incident in the house of the woman he'd been hoping to marry had been a crushing blow to his self confidence. He couldn't understand her behaviour, and as always with matters which he couldn't understand, he blamed himself. He had blamed himself until Numerius had told him about Metellus and what the priests were forcing the government to do. Then at last he had understood and as he did so he had startled himself. Publius had grown angry.

His master was in a foul mood as Publius hastily draped the cloak over his shoulders.

"Damned superstitious fools," Numerius grumbled. "Where are my sandals?"

Publius placed them at his patron's feet and stepped back.

"The people are fickle," Numerius snapped. "I will remind them of this family's long history of service, duty and sacrifice for the Senate and People of Rome. My daughter is not going to die because some idiot somewhere has failed to properly do his religious duties. They will have to come and get her over my dead body. What madness!"

He glared at Publius challenging him to reply but Publius wisely kept quiet.

"Bring a knife," Numerius growled.

He strode towards the door. Once outside he set such a pace that Publius, who had gone back into the house to fetch the weapon, had to run to catch him up. The two of them did not speak again as they descended the Janiculum hill towards the Tiber. It was early in the morning and there was a fresh cool breeze blowing in from the sea. Pompeia would be alright Numerius knew. She would not be easily rattled. He'd sent a slave to the house of the Vestals to demand that she come to his home whilst the crisis lasted. But his daughter did not always choose to obey him and he wasn't sure she would come. Of course it would be far safer for her at his home but he did not have the legal right to force a Vestal to do what he pleased.

"Unfaithful to her vows!" he cried suddenly. What a load of nonsense. His daughter would never do anything to compromise her sacred promise. He was certain of that.

***

They caught up with Fabius just as the old man was preparing to set off for the Senate House. One of the agenda points in the morning's meeting of the Senate was to decide on whether to approve the back room agreement that had been struck with Metellus. Fabius was standing in his atrium, already fully dressed in an expensive looking white toga. He lowered the letter he'd been reading and scowled at Numerius and Publius as they were shown in.

"Now I don't want to hear anything more about this Vestal business!" he cried. "We have discussed it Numerius. It must be done in order for us to maintain our unity and the common cause."

"My daughter is a Vestal!" Numerius cried out, "You would think differently if your daughter was involved."

"I will not listen to this anymore. There is nothing more that I can do."

Fabius handed the letter to a slave and marched past them towards the door. Numerius followed Fabius out onto the street with Publius discreetly a few steps behind.

"There is no proof these vestals have broken their vows," Numerius said catching up with Fabius in the street. "It is pure superstition. The rashness of the Consuls, their poor judgement and skill are to blame for our defeat. Not six girls who haven't harmed a soul. The consuls and the consuls alone should take the blame for what has happened."

Fabius stopped and there was anger in his eyes.

"Do not smear the highest office in the Republic with such accusations! Have you no respect for our institutions."

"Tell me that I am wrong," Numerius grasped the old man's arm.

Fabius stared at the hand that gripped his arm. Then he looked up at Numerius with a mixture of anger and compassion and then finally he sighed and laid a hand on Numerius' shoulder. "There are six vestals," he said, "One will be sacrificed, we will take the eldest, your daughter will be spared."

Fabius started to walk down the street but Numerius kept level with him.

"But you can't guarantee that," Numerius snapped, "The high priest is in charge of the vestals. It will be his right to decide who is to die. You must not vote for this Fabius, I beg you."

The two men kept up the heated argument as they strode down the street followed by Publius a few steps behind. They were oblivious to the big hooded man who watched them from across the street.

***

The traffic on the Appian Way was relatively light. A patrol of armed men in single file crunched along beside them on the opposite pavement. In the street a couple of carts loaded high with lumber creaked and rumbled on their wooden wheels. The farmer leading them cracked his whip at the oxen and shouted at them. In the opposite direction, coming from the cross roads where the Appian ran into the Sacred Way, a litter carried by four slaves, one at each corner, was approaching. The curtains around the litter prevented anyone from seeing who was inside.

The two arguing men ahead of Publius were approaching the cross roads when Numerius suddenly staggered and vomited.

"What's the matter?" Fabius blurted out taking a step back in surprise. Numerius was bent double as he vomited again. Then Publius was at his side holding his former master around the shoulder.

"He's ill," Publius replied, "Don't you know."

Fabius seemed taken aback by the direct and challenging tone in the young freedman's voice but he said nothing.

"I am alright Publius," Numerius muttered raising himself up. The young freedman let go of his shoulder and moved to stand between Numerius and Fabius, turning his back on the senator. There was a hint of aggression in Publius' movement which surprised both men. He's angry about the way Pompeia is being treated Numerius thought with sudden insight. From the corner of his eye a small movement caught his attention. Then with a dull zipping thwack something buried itself into Publius' chest. The freedman's eyes bulged and he gasped and staggered under the impact. Blood trickled from his mouth. He stared at Numerius in confusion and then his eyes rolled crazily in their sockets and he collapsed to the ground like a rag doll. Someone screamed. Numerius was conscious of movement all around him. Two of the slaves carrying the litter dropped it sending their companions lurching sideways into the road and the screaming occupant rolling out onto the street.

Reacting on instinct he threw himself at Fabius bringing the old man down and knocking the wind out of him. It was not a second too late. There was another zip and an iron tipped bolt smashed into the ground just where they had been standing a moment ago. The impact sent sparks flying into the air. More men were shouting. Numerius didn't think. Half standing, half crawling he barged Fabius into the relative shelter of a doorway which was just a couple of yards away. On the other side of the road the patrol stood staring at him, frozen in their tracks alongside a wall.

"Keep down!" he screamed as Fabius tried to get to his feet. In the street he heard someone cry out his name. He turned. It was Publius. The young freedman lay stretched out on the ground, blood soaking through his tunic and tricking down the sides of his mouth. He had raised an arm and was trying to crawl towards Numerius but he couldn't move.

Numerius' earlier weakness had vanished. Adrenaline pumped into his veins. He wrenched his eyes away from Publius and stared wildly up the street trying to see who was shooting at them. Beyond the cross roads people had flung themselves onto the ground or were running away. One of oxen pulling the lumber cart stood stupidly, unmoving in the middle of the cross roads. The farmer had disappeared.

Numerius eyes wildly searched the houses and shops up ahead. There was nothing. He could see nothing suspicious. Then a sudden movement in a window of a building site caught his eye. He blinked and stared. A face from a window was staring straight back at him.

"He's in that building! Get him. Get him!" he screamed pointing towards the building site beyond the intersection. The soldiers across the road stared at him dumbly.

"Do as he says you fool's!" Fabius cried.

The old man's words seemed to wake the men up. Led by their officer they stormed forwards, raising their shields as they swarmed up the road. A voice was calling out to Numerius again. It was Publius. The young freedman stared at him, just a few yards away, his hand still raised, graspingly towards him. Then the light in the young man's eyes faded and his head and arm fell to the ground and he was still.

"Gods," Fabius groaned, "Why would they want to kill him?"

Numerius stared at Publius' body, his face distraught.

"It was not him they are after," he hissed, "It was you."

***

Adonibaal stared at the scene in utter shock. He had missed the target, twice! Move, he had to move, get away his brain told him but he was rooted to the spot. He had not anticipated the sudden move by the slave who had put his body in the way of the target. The man could not possibly have known what was about to happen. It was a fluke. The Gods had intervened he thought struggling with growing panic. Up till then everything had gone according to plan. He'd assembled the Scorpion during the night, placed it in position. Then he'd hurried off to watch Fabius' house. The shock of seeing Numerius so close by had momentarily thrown him off balance. He had not been expecting him and he had definitely not expected to see him in Fabius' company. His brother had looked frail and older than he'd imagined. Well it made sense, he thought bitterly, for him to side with Fabius. The sight of Numerius and Fabius together had just inflamed his hatred for his brother and for a moment he had seriously considered shooting Numerius but that was not his job today and he was a professional. The target was all that mattered. Focus on the job. Focus on the kill.

And now it had all gone horribly wrong.

He heard his brother shouting. Incredibly the man had spotted him. He had to get away. He wrenched himself onto his feet and dived for the stairs. In the street a group of soldiers were storming towards him. He reached the first floor just as the first soldiers closed in on the main doorway. No escape that way. He darted out the back and into the courtyard. The wall that surrounded it was too high to climb. Panic was swiftly taking control of him. Desperately he searched for a way out. There was none. He slid Centurion from its scabbard and turned to face the doorway from which the soldiers would appear at any moment. Better a noble death than to be taken alive. Then he noticed the well. The sound of hob nails on paving stones and the excited cries of men were very close now. Without thinking he jumped into the well. All went dark. His elbows scraped and jarred along the damp walls and his arms flailed wildly. Then suddenly he was wedged fast. The well had narrowed until his body had jammed. A shower of small stones and dust clattered onto his head. His shoulders rested against the stone walls and his feet were submerged in water. He fought to control his panic and looked upwards to the hole of light. How far had he come? He tried to calculate the distance, maybe ten yards or so, it was difficult to say. Was it enough? Then he heard voices above him. A head suddenly poked over the edge of the well and stared downwards, straight at him. Adonibaal froze, held his breath and boldly stared right back at the man.

"Have you got him?" he heard a voice cry out.

"No," someone closer by answered, "What about the top floor?"

The head disappeared.

"He's gone," another voice cried out, "Must have got over the wall. Get some men to check the houses on the other side, quickly now."

***

It was night. Using his hands, knees and feet Adonibaal clambered up the stone walls of the well. He was lucky, damn lucky! The well was old and must have existed well before the building site had been erected. Many of the stones that formed the wall's, were not smooth but disjointed and uneven which allowed him to gain a grip for his hands and ledges for his feet. He poked his head carefully over the rim and paused to listen but could hear nothing. He raised himself on his forearms and rolled out onto the ground breathing in the cool air. In the night sky the moon was the only source of light. For a moment he lay there catching his breath. Then he got to his feet and slipped silently into the abandoned building site. Would they have left a guard? He was tempted to go and see if the Scorpion was still in its place but decided against it. Of course they would have taken it. He struggled with a depressing thought. He had failed! Now the Romans would be alerted to his presence and intentions. What a fucking nightmare! Still he'd escaped and if they thought he was going to give up and run, then they were in for a surprise. He always got his man! The most urgent priority now was to hide and plan another attack. Suddenly he felt exhausted. How long had it been since he'd last eaten?

Slipping out of the building site he glanced at the cross roads where his botched assassination attempt had taken place. In the faint moonlight he saw that all traces of what had happened, that morning, had been cleaned up. He turned away and set off back to the Subura. The streets were completely deserted for no sane man went out at night in Rome. Without any form of lighting, the alleys and streets looked sinister. He crept along through the darkened alleys pausing now and then as he heard whispers, rattling and felt the movement of things in the darkness, but no one approached him.

He halted at a corner of an alley and leaned against a wall watching the building where he was staying. Nothing moved, nothing looked out of the ordinary and yet... Would they have begun to search all the hostels? It was a possibility. He'd left nothing behind in the room but he'd have to return. It would look suspicious if he'd paid for a week only to vanish after two nights. That kind of suspicion might get reported to the authorities.

He approached the apartment block and gently rang the door bell. A few moments later he heard a shuffling sound behind the door and then a gruff voice that sounded like it had just been woken up.

"Who's there?"

"Room eight," Adonibaal replied glancing over his shoulder down the darkened alley. Something was moving back there.

He'd half expected to have to argue with the janitor but to his surprise the man unlocked the door without a word. Adonibaal stepped inside. The janitor glanced at him casually and then hastened to lock the door, sliding the inner panel into a groove in the ground and then fastening both ends of the cross bolt into hollows, sunk in the doorposts.

"Can't be too careful, what with all these thieves," the man muttered, returning to the chair in his tiny cabin inside the entry hall. Adonibaal nodded and headed for the stairs. Oil lamps hanging from hooks on the wall cast a flickering shadowy light across the hall. He was half way up when it suddenly struck him how oddly casual the janitor had been. The guest rules he'd seen printed on a pamphlet in his room had clearly stated that guests were to return to their rooms before nightfall. And yet the man had just allowed him back in without a word of complaint. He frowned as he reached his landing. The janitor had not said a word. Suddenly he grew alarmed. Something was not right. But it was too late. As he moved towards the door of his room, a man stepped out of the shadows, blocking his way and folding his arms across his chest. It was hard to see his face in the shadows.

From the corner of his eye Adonibaal sensed more movement behind him and to each side. Shapes appeared from the shadows. Centurion slid noiselessly from its scabbard and the steel glinted into the glow from the oil lamps. The big man who blocked his way chuckled.

"No need for that eh," he said opening his palms wide to show that he was unarmed. "There is no need for both of us to die." The man took a step closer and Adonibaal saw that he was bald. A hard but intelligent looking face appeared from the shadows. "You killed my man," the stranger said, "Now why did you have to do that?"

"What are you talking about?" Adonibaal said. There were three of them behind him. Not have a go heroes but trained men by the way they had spaced themselves out. He could send one of them down the stairs but the other two were going to be tricky.

"A man called Janus, you killed him yesterday," the stranger said.

"What's he to you?" Adonibaal said raising Centurion.

The man shook his head and laughed softly. "You are not from around here are you stranger? My name is Milo, I own the Subura, I own the people and I know everything that goes on in these alleys. Janus worked for me. He was an informant, gave me lots of juicy gossip about the rich and famous. Now I have lost my man. It's not good for business."

Adonibaal stood very still.

"So what's that to me?" he growled.

Milo arched his eyebrows. The man seemed to be in complete control of the situation and it surprised and unsettled Adonibaal. He was used to seeing fear on men's faces. This Milo was different. He was not afraid.

"Janus was a piece of shit," Milo said, "but he did what was required from him. You on the other hand; you are good with a blade, a man like you, you are hired to kill, you do kill, that's what you do for a living."

Milo took another step forwards. He was now so close that Adonibaal could smell the faint whiff of perfume on the man's clothes.

"That's far enough," he snapped.

Milo stopped.

"Tell me who you are working for? Was it Julius' gang on the Aventine? Priscus perhaps…?"

Adonibaal stared at Milo as his mind raced. "Out of town," he muttered.

Milo frowned, "I can understand the job on Janus but that one you did today on the Appian, who was the target and why?"

The hallway fell silent. Adonibaal looked at Milo and then a smile appeared on his face, a smile of pride.

"Quintus Fabius Maximus," he said quietly, "he was the target."

191

Milo's eyes twinkled in the flickering light. For a long moment, no one spoke.

Then Milo nodded. "You know what," he said, "I think he is speaking the truth. That takes balls stranger, Fabius fucking Maximus indeed. What's he done to deserve death then?"
"I can't tell you," Adonibaal replied.

Milo grunted and there was sudden gleam in his eyes. "You know what lads," he said quietly, "I think we have caught ourselves a baby killing, Baal worshipper from across the sea."

"You a Carthaginian?" a voice whined behind him.

Adonibaal said nothing.

Then Milo smiled again. "Of course he's one of them Quintus. Who else would want to kill Fabius?" Milo laughed softly. "But don't worry stranger, you are safe with us. When Hannibal enters Rome, I am going to be the first man to greet him and show him the sights and you will be there with me as proof of my good intentions."

Chapter Seventeen - The fugitive

The men in white togas who stood around the oak table in Fabius' atrium were arguing angrily with each other. The house was filled with their voices. A gaggle of armed men lounged near to the entrance hall. They looked bored. The slaves hurried nervously in and out with plates of food and drink. The men, Fabius, Grachus, Torquatus and a few that Numerius didn't know, were discussing the assassination attempt. The disagreement seemed to revolve around what measures to take in response. Torquatus, the government's attack dog was arguing for martial law but Grachus and a few others were against the idea. The dictator, Pera had been unable to attend.

Fabius at last raised his voice.

"Gentlemen," he said with a sardonic smile, "I am touched by your concern for my welfare, but truly we have more important things to discuss. Let's not be distracted by this vain attempt on my life. Hannibal and his army are the main threat. We must decide on how to confront him."

The table fell silent. Torquatus shook his head whilst Grachus looked down at the floor.

"We can't just leave a mad man to roam around the city," one of the other senators said.

"I will find him," a voice said.

The senators turned to look at Numerius. Fabius opened his mouth to speak but Numerius spoke first.

"I will lead the investigation. Fabius is right, Hannibal is the main threat. We must concentrate on him."

"And why should the investigation be given to you?" a senator said, "What experience have you in such matters?"

"The assassin killed my son. That is why I will lead this investigation."

Numerius didn't care what they thought. His grief was hidden behind a mask of stoicism. That was the way he always dealt with grief. But he had watched Publius be murdered before his own eyes. There had been nothing he could have done to prevent it but still he felt responsible. He'd never asked the freedman if he had wanted to come with him on that fateful walk to the Senate house. He had just expected it, as if the man were still a slave, and Publius, loyal Publius had simply followed him and gone to his death. He was going to find the man who had killed him.

"Alright," Fabius said, "The investigation is yours. Report your findings to me as soon as possible."

Fabius glanced around the table but there were no dissenters.

***

After the meeting had broken up Numerius was preparing to leave when Fabius came to see him. The old man took him to one side and there was a warmth and grace in his manner that Numerius had never seen before.

"I never thanked you, old friend, for what you did this morning," Fabius said gripping Numerius by the shoulder. "I grieve for your son. He was a good man, and he served a good father. He knew that; so don't feel bitter at his loss, Numerius, it was still a noble, if unfortunate way in which to go and meet the gods."

Numerius nodded.

"He said you were ill?" Fabius inquired.

"Yes, I suppose I should have told you earlier but I did not wish to be a burden at this time. It's Malaria."

Fabius nodded and his hand tightened its grip on Numerius' shoulder.

"This is bad news indeed," he muttered. Then he smiled sadly.

"It seems lightening does touch the same spot twice after all. I knew your father all his life and I see much of him in you. Don't let what happened between him and Caeso blind you. Your father was a hard man but he was so for a reason. You know what I am talking about. " Fabius nodded solemnly. "He would have approved of everthing you have done. He is proud of you." Fabius paused and looked away.

"You have served me with great distinction, just like your father," he declared. "I have not forgotten. I will make sure that the people will know about the sacrifices you and your kinsmen have made for Rome. I shall pray for you and for your son."

Fabius paused again searching for the right words.

"The vote was taken and passed in the Senate," he said at last. "We have our agreement with the priests. It is good news for the Republic. The matter is now closed but I will try and delay Metellus and his desire for blood. With some good fortune we will manage to see off Hannibal and the city will come back to its senses. I will do everything I can to protect Pompeia." He looked up. "Find this killer for me, Numerius."

***

The funeral pyre roared and crackled casting dancing, devilish shadows across the garden terrace. It was night. Sparks shot upwards only to die as swiftly as they had appeared. Numerius stood a few paces from the fire, his body stiff and motionless, his head bowed and veiled. He was dressed in a white toga. The first stars had appeared and on the fire clothed in white linen, Publius' body burned. Numerius was speaking to himself and as he spoke, in a clear steady voice his slaves shrank back from him in fright.

"Janus and Jupiter, and Mars our Sire, ye guardian spirits of Rome, and ye the spirits of the mighty dead, thou too Bellona, and thou Quirinus, and all ye gods, both young and old, I beseech you to give me vengeance and strike my enemy with terror, dread and death."

Numerius raised his head and looked upon the burning corpse. "Herewith I devote to the infernal powers, myself, my enemies and all who are on their side, for my son, Publius, may his name never be forgotten."

When he was finished the only sound on the terrace of his house, high up on the Janiculum was the roar of the fire as the flames greedily consumed the corpse.

In his library he closed the door behind him and paused to gaze at the masks that sat in their alcoves along the wall. The silent polished and frozen faces gleamed in the torch light, staring back at him. They were the death masks of his ancestors. He had taken them with him from the old house when he had sold the property. The library was his room. No one, not even Pompeia was allowed to enter. The room was an exact replica of his father's library and he had spent many long hours here preparing his cases and indulging his love of words. Along the three remaining walls there were shelves containing manuscripts, books and notes on his legal cases and in a corner a desk with a single chair. He stared at the masks as if challenging them to speak.

Numerius had not realised how much Publius had meant to him until the man was gone. Somehow he'd always expected his son to be there, to look after him, the house and his daughter and the family name. Such was the orderly way of life, the way it ought to have been, the way he had planned.

The loss had left him numb. They'd all gone now, his family, all apart from Pompeia. He was dying but death did not frighten him. Death made a life whole and meaningful. There was a part of him which yearned for it now. There was little left him in this world. He'd been faithful to his father, to his clients and to Rome. He had done his duty in war and in peace and now when it all seemed to be coming to an end, when he should have felt a sense of achievement; he only felt the sharpness of grief. The gods were punishing him. Fortune had turned against him and he didn't know why.

He stared at the masks. The spirits of his forefathers beckoned to him. Sometimes he thought he could see them, amongst the shadows of the trees in his garden, waiting for him. Soon he knew his death mask would join the long line of his forefathers in their neat alcoves. It would not be long now. But before that day came he would avenge his son's murder. He would hold death at arms length until justice was done. It would be his last case.

In his funeral oration, he had offered his own spirit to the gods of the underworld together with that of the man who had killed Publius. The gods would hold him to that promise. The greedy gods, in their fine, rich temples would not be able to refuse such a great offer; of that Numerius was sure.

***

The following day he set to work. There was much to do and he was conscious that he didn't have much time. To help him in his investigation he was given a unit from the Triumviri Nocturni, the privately operated and funded fire brigade of Rome. In addition to their duty as fire watchers; fire being a constant danger in the city, the Triumviri Nocturni, as their name suggested, were also the night time police force and were tasked with maintaining public order and the capture of criminals. The unit's HQ was in the Capena gate house, built into the Servian walls.

The twenty firemen were slaves but at least they were proud of their profession Numerius thought. He had them lined up in a row for an inspection. The men's equipment, ladders, buckets, rope, saws and pick axes was stashed in a separate store room and apart from that their only weapons were sticks. None of them had ever been involved in a man hunt and some of them looked far too old and frail for the active duty that was demanded from them. But they would have to do he thought.

He sent them off into the city in pairs with orders to search all the hostels and guest houses. It was a routine precaution and he did not expect it to produce any results, yet it still needed to be done. The city gates which had already been closely watched had been closed immediately after the failed assassination. Only persons with special permission were being allowed to leave. Numerius sat alone at the table where the firemen usually ate their dinner, his head clasped in his hands, trying to think. He felt tired and weak. He should have been resting but yesterday's events kept playing through his mind. He heard the bolt slamming into Publius. He remembered the look of shock on the freedman's face. He saw the assassins head in the window. He'd been too far away to make out any specific features. How had the killer managed to escape?

The problem he knew was that he had hardly anything to go on. He'd been unable to give his firemen a description of whom they were looking for. He wasn't even certain if the assassin was acting alone or whether the man was still in Rome. Nevertheless he would keep going; that much he did know. He wiped his forehead with the back of his hand. He'd been quick to demand the job but now that he was in charge, he didn't really know what to do. How did one find a fugitive in a city of two hundred thousand people?

The Scorpion had been the only clue left behind. He frowned. The Scorpion was a military weapon. It was a rare to find one. Such specialised weapons belonged to the army, they were not something you could just pick up at the local carpenter for a few coins and learn to use effectively within a few days. The assassin or assassins had carefully prepared the attack. They had chosen a good killing spot, with an escape route. That would have required some planning and experience. The more he thought about it the more convinced he became. This was not a random attack. The whole thing looked like the work of a professional.

"A hired man," Numerius said suddenly looking up.

He stood up and began to pace around the room and as he did so his eyes suddenly widened.

"Carthaginians," he whispered.

***

Numerius was pacing up and down when he became conscious of the man standing in the doorway to the fire station. He stopped. The man was tall with a receding hairline and looked to be in his mid thirties. He wore a grey tunic, carried a small leather case slung over his shoulder and wore a faded army focale, around his neck.

"Who are you?" Numerius said bluntly, annoyed at the intrusion.

"The name is Nicomedes of Syracuse," the man replied. "Fabius thought you might need me. I am at your service, Sir."

Numerius grunted. "How can you help me?"

Nicomedes stepped into the fire station and glanced around disapprovingly. He was carrying a walking stick which he prodded into the ground. Apart from that he was unarmed. "I am a doctor," he replied.

"I don't need a doctor."

"Fabius seems to think you do. He told me not to leave your side, Sir."

Numerius stared at the visitor. It was just the sort of thing Fabius would do; saddle him with a baby sitter.

"Syracuse," Numerius savoured the name. "Alright," he snapped, "If you insist on staying, then stay. Maybe you can help me after all. What do you know about Punic spies in Rome?"

Nicomedes looked a little uncertain. "I thought they were all rounded up when the war began, two years ago?"

Numerius placed his hands firmly on the table.

"Yes maybe," he said, "What about sympathisers? Who else would support the Punic cause?"

Nicomedes arched his eyebrows. "Well Sir, I am a Greek and we Greeks are the hereditary enemies of Carthage but some of my countrymen, especially in the Southern cities of Italy, may not share our loathing of the sea people. They may hate Rome even more."

"Who else...?" Numerius asked.

"Gaul's and Macedonians," the doctor replied with a nod.

Numerius stared at the table deep in thought. When at last he looked up at the doctor there was a grim, determined look on his face.

"If you are really here to help me, doctor, then go back to Fabius and get him to give you a list from the Censor. I want to know the names of all registered Gauls and Macedonians living in the city and I want that list right away."

Nicomedes looked perplexed. Then he sighed.

"And here was I thinking you were a dying man," he muttered. He turned for the door. "What do you need it for anyway?"

"I'm going to round them all up," Numerius said.

***

The arrests started before dawn the next morning. At the fire station which he had turned into his HQ, Numerius had assembled his motley crew of firemen and explained his plan. The slaves, excited by their new role, had taken to it with gusto. Doors had been kicked down, voices raised and suspects dragged from their beds. Most had come quietly, too shocked or surprised to offer any resistance and only twice the firemen had to resort to violence. With his list finally exhausted Numerius called the captain of the firemen to him.

"Take them to the Tullianum," he ordered.

Nicomedes frowned and watched the prisoners being marched away.

"What are you going to do them?" he asked.

"You don't want to know," Numerius grunted. "Perhaps it's best if you don't join me this afternoon."

"You are going to torture them?"

"Perhaps, yes."

Nicomedes sighed. "Well in that case you are going to need a doctor."

The Tullianum, the oldest prison in Rome had been built into the north east side of the Capitoline hill facing the Senate house. The building had originally been intended as a cistern for a spring but now the lower hold served as the room to hold prisoners. The arrested men were flung into the dirty crowded lower chamber and the iron grates above their heads were closed.

Numerius insisted on personally interrogating each detainee. The interrogation room grew hot and sweaty. Afternoon turned into evening, evening into night. It was the threat of torture that finally provided the breakthrough. One of the prisoners, a Macedonian, seeing the torture instruments laid out broke down and confessed. He'd spied for Hannibal for over two years but he knew nothing about the attack on Fabius. He claimed he'd been forced into spying for Hannibal. The man had thrown himself upon Numerius' mercy, pleading and crying for clemency. He had a wife and children. It was when the prisoner had started to talk about the spy who'd come to visit him, only a few days before, that Numerius' ears pricked up. The Macedonian had been able to give him a description. A curious thought started to grow in Numerius' mind as he listened. But the Macedonian's story seemed to end in disappointment. The spy had only come to inspect the walls and had already left the city, days ago.

"You shall live," Numerius said when the weeping prisoner had finally stopped talking. He beckoned to the captain of his firemen, "Cut off his hands instead and kick him out of the nearest gate."

The prisoner screamed in a high pitched voice as the soldiers grabbed his arms and began to drag him from the room.

"I can be useful to you, mercy, please, don't harm me!" the man squealed.

Numerius held up his hand for the guards to stop.

"How can you be useful to me?" he demanded.

"Please Sir, do not harm me," the miserable man was sobbing now. Then with an effort he wiped his eyes with his hand and began to speak.

Once the man was gone Numerius raised his eyebrows and glanced at Nicomedes. The doctor shrugged. He had not said a word throughout all the interrogations.

"I think we are done for today," Numerius said wearily. "Keep the prisoners in for tonight and then release the innocent ones at dawn."

Numerius shivered suddenly. The room had turned cold. He gasped. He knew the sign. The malaria was about to take him. He tried to rise to his feet but the room seemed to be in a spin. He felt the shivers spasm through his whole body and then he was falling. He felt someone catch him and then a calm voice was speaking.

"Easy now, easy Sir, I've got you."

***

It was mid morning before Numerius woke. He lay on a couch in the fire station HQ to which they had carried him. The malaria attack had left him weak and thirsty and drenched in sweat. Nicomedes had arrived at dawn and gave him a bitter tasting potion. It hadn't seemed to help but Nicomedes had said it would. For a while he remained in bed, gathering his strength and thinking about the strange conversation with the Punic spy he'd caught. Then he forced himself up onto his feet. He was wasting time.

"Capua has gone over to Hannibal," Nicomedes announced as he packed away his doctors instruments.

"Oh no," Numerius muttered closing his eyes. "Fabius was so sure that they would remain loyal, the traitorous swine."

"I think Syracuse may join them," Nicomedes said apprehensively.

"That would be a true disaster," Numerius replied reaching for his cloak and sandals. "But it won't happen as long as Hiero remains in charge. He has been a friend of Rome since I was born."

"Hhhhhmmm," Nicomedes stroked his chin, "There are rumours that one of his sons may force Hiero from power. If that happens then the party that favours Carthage will gain a foot in the door."

The doctor stood up. "If that happens, Sir, I hope you will not think any less of me. Syracuse is my home town but I have sworn to serve the Fabian house."

Numerius made no reply and continued to dress himself. Then when he was done he turned to Nicomedes.

"Of course," he said, "These are difficult times for all but Rome will win in the end. It is our destiny, Nicomedes. Nothing will stop us."
"Thank you Sir," the Greek bowed gracefully. "Fabius also has a message for you," the doctor said. "He told me that you might want to know that your father's freedman was murdered a few days ago."

Numerius whirled round and stared at the doctor.

"Janus?"

Nicomedes nodded. "Apparently he was killed in broad day light by a single man in a tavern on the Caelian. A dozen witnesses and some prostitutes all saw it. The tavern owner was also murdered."

"Who would want to kill Janus?" Numerius frowned as he spoke. "Have they caught the killer?"

Nicomedes shook his head, "They haven't, the man escaped. But we did get a good description of him."

Numerius felt his heart begin to pound with excitement.
"It matches the description of that new spy the Macedonian told us about yesterday," the doctor said with a triumphant smile.

***

Something was bothering Numerius as he made his way through the city. Instinct drove him onwards. He passed through the forum and turned into the Argiletum, the street of the booksellers. He hardly noticed the horde of pawn brokers who bustled around him. A thought had taken hold of him and it wouldn't let go. Images of the assassin flashed through his mind. He remembered the Macedonian spy's words and now Janus was dead. Could it all be a coincidence or were all these things connected somehow? He passed through the Subura and for once didn't notice the stink and poverty. At the city gate he was pleased to see that his orders were being carried out and that extra soldiers had been posted to the walls. He identified himself to the guards and passed under the gate and out of the city. It was a warm beautiful evening and he could hear the crickets in the grass. He turned to look at the sun setting over his home on the distant Janiculum.

The summit of the hill was rocky and barren apart from a line of Cypress trees. He approached with some caution but found to his relief that he was alone. The earth was dry and parched. He entered the low brick building and shuffled past the long lines of urns of the dead. It had been a very long time since he'd last been here. He stopped as he found what he was looking for. Slowly he got down on his knees. Her ashes were still there. She was still in the same resting place he'd arranged for her all those years ago. He sighed as he saw the coin he'd left her. Then he got down on his knees and bowed his head in sombre prayer.

"To the spirits of the departed," he muttered, "Honour to you Flavia and happiness too. I wish you to know that I have kept my promise. Many years have passed but you are still always in my thoughts and prayers. Sleep well and prosper, my love."

He raised his head and glanced at the urn. Their love affair had been brief but intense. It had started one night when he had sneaked out of his father's house and joined his friends in a binge of drinking and partying. He had noticed her right away. She had been different to all the other girls who were so quick to sell their virtue to a rich man and his promises. Flavia had spirit and courage. He had fallen in love. He had wanted to marry her but then one fateful night, he had introduced her to his brother. Caeso had in all likelihood never known about his brother's feelings. But then he had never asked either. He had just taken her from him, taken his girl and Flavia had decided that she liked Caeso more. She had never told him why but it had been the wrong decision. It had broken his heart.

He looked away. Those days were long gone now and he had moved on. But he still remembered that day she had died. He had been there. There had been complications during the birth and she had lost too much blood. She hadn't understood why Caeso had not come. She had kept calling out his brother's name, over and over again. He had tried to explain but she had been too weak to understand and then, as the life had seeped out of her, she had made him promise that he would look after her baby. He sighed. He should have come more often to honour her he knew, but it had been difficult during the long years in which he'd been married. But at least he'd kept the promise he'd made her all those years ago.

He was about to touch the urn when his fingers froze in mid air. Someone had left two small figurines on the top of the urn. Gently he lifted them up and examined them. It had been done recently for there was no dust on them. Then his eyes widened as he finally understood. His instinct had been right. His hunch was correct.

"So you have returned brother," he whispered.

Chapter Eighteen – The loss of innocence

Pompeia stood on the banks of the Tiber watching the river traffic. Her long hair fluttered in the cool breeze. On the river, a couple of barges were heading downstream to Ostia and the sea beyond. They were piled high with timber. It was noon and the august sun burned down on her. A small group of beggars had gathered in a rough semi circle behind her. They sat without speaking on the ground like a class of children waiting for their teacher to speak.

Pompeia ignored them. In her hands, she held a sieve. She had quickly understood the implications of what that horrible woman, Publius' intended wife, had said to her. The priests were preparing to sacrifice a Vestal. She had never believed it possible. As a young girl, newly acquainted with the order, the older girls had tried to frighten her with stories of innocent Vestals being sacrificed to appease angry gods. But they had just been stories, now it looked like it was happening for real.

The horror of what was about to happen had left her dazed. How was this possible? A vestal had not been buried alive for many generations. What wrong had they done? The rumours of unchastely were just lies, terrible lies spread around the city for reasons she didn't understand. With no one in which to confide she had again asked herself what her mother would have done. But her mother, as far as she could remember, had never made a decision in her life. Her mother had never set an example for her to follow. No, she was on her own. She had to follow her own example. She felt her stomach churning as she thought again about how important this decision was going to be for the rest of her life.

She glanced down the Tiber at the river traffic. The shock of what that horrible woman had told her had made her come to a decision. It was time to choose as Cantilius had said. She fought back a tear. Cantilius, poor Cantilius would he understand? Would he accept that she had chosen to remain and serve the goddess? She struggled to contain her emotions. She would stay, she resolved and defend her sisters and the goddess and their good names. That was what was most important. If she ran away now, she would not be able to live with herself. It was a tough decision but the right one and now that it was made, she felt a strange sense of relief.

She glanced down at the green water of the Tiber which lapped at her feet. She didn't have much time left. Her father had tried to reassure her that she would not be picked but she hadn't believed him. He could not guarantee her safety however he much wanted too, nor could Fabius. Once the priests had started to rouse the public there would be no going back. Of the six Vestals, she was the obvious choice. Musa and Julia were too young, too innocent, Floronia and Opimia had very powerful family connections which would protect them and no one, in their wildest dreams, could ever be convinced that Aurinia had been unfaithful.

There was just one thing left to do. She would give them a miracle. She raised her eyes to the sky and muttered a prayer to Vesta. Behind her the beggars stirred. She bent down and swept the sieve into the green water and raised it with both hands. There was a gasp from her audience. The sieve did not leak. The greenish river water swayed and then settled yet not a drop leaked through the holes.

Calmly Pompeia rose, turned and began to walk towards the Trigemina gate holding the sieve before her. People stopped to stare at her. A murmur grew amongst the crowd as the beggars began to follow. The procession, with Pompeia at its head swept through the gate and into the cattle market and still not a drop of water leaked from the sieve. As she turned into the street leading to the forum the farmers and merchants fell to their knees and men called out her name. Pompeia's face was a mask of detached composure, as if she was the only person in the street and the crowds around her just imaginary people. She held her head high and looked straight ahead of her, oblivious to the sensation she was causing and as she walked, people scrambled to get out of her way.

The procession swept into the forum and as she passed the Senate house and the Curia, the senators piled out of the building to watch her. The money lenders, lawyers, merchants and bankers too stopped what they were doing and rushed to get a glimpse of her. The crowds gasped as they saw the water being carried in the sieve. Pompeia continued up the Sacred Way until she approached the temple of Vesta. Here a hastily assembled group of priests belonging to the order of Aruspices blocked her way. The priests clad in their long scarlet and purple robes with hoods over their heads linked arms and barred the road shouting at her to turn back. But if they had thought that their presence was going to stop her, they had not reckoned on the wrath of the horde of beggars whom had following her. With a loud angry and rebellious cry the mob stormed forwards and the thin line of priests vanished under a wave of angry and unwashed bodies. The crowd that remained lining the street cried out in delight, and through the chaos Pompeia passed on, as if nothing and nobody could touch her. At the steps to the temple of Vesta, another crowd had gathered around the matron and the remaining Vestals. All the girls were there, staring at her in awe and trepidation.

Pompeia stopped before the matron and bowed.

"I bring Vesta the sacred water. Will you receive it, gracious mother?" she said.

The matron seemed unable to speak. Then a tear appeared in her eye and she nodded.

"Fairest Pompeia, Vesta will accept this gift," she replied. Then she moved to embrace Pompeia and as she did so the crowds cheered.

"Oh child," the matron whispered in her ear, "What have you done?"

***

It was evening when they finally came for her. Pompeia was in her apartment with Julia and the matron when the doors to her rooms were flung open. Metellus and a company of his priests marched in, their boots crunching on the fine mosaic floor. Metellus looked furious. He half ran towards her and when the Matron tried to intervene he roughly pushed her to the floor.

Julia cried out in fear but Pompeia placed a reassuring hand on the young girl's shoulders. Metellus face was a dark red, his eyes flashing, his chest heaving.

"Leave us," he bellowed at Julia and the Matron.

Then only he and Pompeia remained together with one of the priests who stood guard by the door.

"You do not scare me," Pompeia said calmly standing her ground. She had known Metellus ever since she had joined the order of Vestals. He'd been a young boy then training to become an Augur. She had always known him to be a bully, a man who was easily angered when he did not get his way. He owed his advancement up the religious hierarchy solely due to his ruthless determination to carry out his master's wishes.

"You were always a stuck-up bitch," he retorted.

"Does it please you to bully us Vestals? Do you think that Vesta will look kindly upon your contempt for us?"

The two of them stared at each other; she calm and composed; he furious and aggressive. She could not show any weakness Pompeia thought. A man like Metellus thrived on finding and exploiting weakness. She had seen him so often reducing priests to pitiful shaking wrecks with just words.

He slapped her hard across her face. She gasped at the sudden searing pain but then raised her head defiantly once more. He slapped her again but this time she just laughed.

"What's this? Have you no respect woman?" he shouted.

"I shall not be bullied by a liar," she hissed.

He raised his hand to slap her again but then thought better of it.

"No you are wrong," he said with a great effort.

Pompeia felt a sudden shiver of unease. Metellus was not only feared for his bullying, he was feared for his cunning and deviousness.

"I am not the liar, but you are," he said. "You see I know all about your tricks," there was a hint of triumph in his voice now. "The people may think you performed a miracle out there but you do not deceive me. I know that you filled the holes of that sieve with glue. What did you do with the sieve by the way, disappeared has it?"

He laughed softly to himself as if challenging her to deny it.

"The Vestals are faithful to their vows," she said. "You wish to murder an innocent woman. I cannot allow you to do this."

"No decision has been made on which Vestal will be sacrificed," he said, "So maybe you should think about being a little nicer to me," he chided.

"What for?"

"Because our holy father has given me authority to decide which Vestal will be sacrificed," he cried.

"I will not let you kill any of my sisters," she hissed and with a move that surprised him, it was her turn to slap him across the face.

He staggered backwards caught by surprise but then recovered and launched a flurry of blows at her head. Pompeia shielded herself as best as she could but it didn't stop her from crying out in pain.

"Really, do you think you can stop me?" he cried mocking her words. He paused stepping back and breathing heavily. Pompeia lifted her hands protecting her head. She felt a cheek swelling up into a bruise. She stared at Metellus with teary eyes, yet they were not tears of pain or fear but of determination.

"The decision has already been made in the Senate," Metellus shouted. "I too have made my decision. I had another in mind before you tried to pull off that trick today, but now that you have proved yourself to be so stubborn, it will be you who will be buried alive beneath the cattle market."

"I have done nothing wrong," she whispered, "The people will not believe you. You are a monster. You do not serve the gods. You only serve yourself."

Spit flew from Metellus' mouth as he interrupted her.

"You should not believe that your pious little miracle will bring the people onto your side. The crowd is fickle."

But she shook her head. "The people will believe their eyes. They will believe in my miracle. They will think you offend the gods if you dare to sacrifice one of us. There will be rioting."

When Metellus spoke it was not the answer she had been expecting.

"Oh don't count on your admirers to set you free," he cried, "They will believe me when I tell them about Cantilius, the young priest whom you have been fucking."

Pompeia opened her mouth and closed it again in shock.

"How did I know?" Metellus crowed triumphantly, "Well if you really want to know, Cantilius came to me. He told me everything, everything about you and your trysts in the temple of Jupiter."

"It's a lie," she responded weakly.

"Oh is it," he glared, "Let's ask Cantilius himself shall we."

Metellus nodded at his priest. The door was opened and after a short pause Cantillius was dragged into the room. Pompeia gasped. The young man's face was badly bruised and one of his eyes was swollen up. He seemed hardly able to stand on his feet.

"Is this the Vestal whom you fucked?" Metellus' sharp coarse voice cut through the room.

Cantilius' head lolled from side to side and Metellus shook him and repeated the question.

"Yes, this is the woman. She seduced me in the temple. She told me she wanted to have a baby," Cantilius whispered hoarsely.

Tears rolled down Pompeia's cheeks as she stared at Cantilius, They had tortured him. She reached out towards him with her hand and called out his name but he just stood there as if he had lost his hearing, his head resting on his chin.

"Get out," Metellus snapped and without a further word or glance Cantilius was dragged from the room.

"You tortured him, he has done nothing wrong," she hissed.

Metellus smirked. "I did nothing," he declared, "As I said he came to me with his confession. Maybe he'd realised the trouble he'd gotten himself into. You vestals are going to wash away the sins of Rome with your blood. The people know that it has to be so. You have no friends now. No one is going to speak up for you now."

Pompeia knew then that Metellus was speaking the truth. There was no one now whom she could turn to for support.

"I did not break my vows to Vesta," she glared at him in desperation. "Not even with Cantilius, whatever he may have told you. The doctors can prove that I am still a virgin."

Metellus looked down at her with a mixture of disgust and pleasure.

"Ah yes," he said, "I have wanted to do this for a long time."

With a speed that took Pompeia by surprise he pushed her back onto the couch. She cried out and tried to fight back but he was stronger. Her arms were pinned down and her dress was ripped away. She felt his stinking breath on her face. Pompeia screamed

"You are not going to be a virgin for much longer," Metellus laughed.

***

They sat together, alone, in Numerius' garden on the Janiculum overlooking the city of Rome. It was morning. Pompeia was clothed in the traditional robes of a priestess of Vesta. Her head was partially veiled and an angry purple bruise lit up her face but there was quiet dignity in her voice as she spoke. Numerius was staring into the distance, dark circles hung under his eyes and he was unshaven. Now and then he coughed.

She glanced again at her father. He seemed to have aged rapidly in the past couple of days. It was unbelievable how quickly his world was collapsing around him she thought. In the space of a few weeks he had contracted Malaria, had lost his adopted son and now his daughter had been raped. Fortune had abandoned him and she wondered how he was coping and how long he could last.

When she had first come to him and told him what Metellus had done Numerius had reacted like she had expected. Without uttering a word, he had risen from his chair and strode to where his armour and weapons were stored. Only after she had shouted at him had she managed to get him to sit down again. His face was ashen and his hands had trembled. You are a lawyer. Think it through to the end she had told him. What use was violence against such powerful men? She would not allow him to place his own life in danger for her. What had been done could not be undone. In the final reckoning it would be her word against theirs and they would not lose, they could not afford to lose. No, she had said with growing strength and purpose in her voice, the only thing that she could do was to keep on showing them that she was not afraid. She would continue, as before and act with as much dignity as she could muster. The priests would not be allowed to poke scorn at her. She would show them. She would endure the torment they had inflicted upon her and she would win the people, she would win the people to her cause.

Only then had Numerius spoken. He'd told her of his love for her as a little girl and of his pride on seeing her enter the order of Vestals. He'd told her about the sorrow of seeing her move out of the house and the way in which he had recorded her progress and the special care in which she undertook her duties. He'd had such faith and confidence in her. Then his voice had changed and grown warm and friendly like she remembered from when she was still a child. Nothing had changed he'd told her. She did not need to ask him for forgiveness for what she had with Cantilius. He could see now that his love and faith had been justified. Metellus was wrong if he'd thought she had no friends, and upon saying that, tears had finally sprung into her eyes.

He'd gone on to tell her that her fate was not yet decided. She should stay with him in his house. He would send for a few trusted men he knew, who would guard her night and day. If the priests came for her then he'd arrange for her to slip away to Ostia. There would be a ship waiting there which would take her to Marsillia where he had friends and where she would be safe. He would be damned if they took her. There would be violence then he warned but she had refused all his offers of help. She must show them that she was not afraid. She had done nothing wrong. Vesta would not allow her to be punished for something she had not done. The goddess would protect her.

Her reply had sent Numerius into a sullen silence.

"If you stay in Rome, there is another matter that will concern you," he said suddenly.

She looked at him without understanding.

"Did you love Publius?" he said gruffly.

"He was a brother to me," she nodded solemnly drying her face.

"I know who killed him," Numerius said, "The target was Fabius. Publius got in the way by accident. He was just in the wrong place at the wrong time."

"Who did it?"

"My brother, Caeso," Numerius replied raising his eyebrows. He glanced at her as if to read her reactions.

"Uncle Caeso!" she looked at him in surprise. She'd never met her uncle and knew very little about him apart from what everyone else knew, that he had murdered her grandfather. Her father had not liked to talk about uncle Caeso.

"I thought he was dead," she muttered.

"No, he has returned to kill Fabius. I think he is working for the Carthaginians."

"Do you know where he is?"

Numerius shook his head. "We are searching for him all over the city. I think someone may be protecting him. We've found nothing."

"Oh papa," she muttered as the realisation slowly sunk in. Pompeia stared at her father trying to gage his thoughts but the old man's face was unreadable.

She had never really thought much about her uncle, he was a man without a face, and his name had rarely been mentioned.

He'd been a taboo and yet now it seemed he had come back to haunt the family once more. History was repeating itself. The man had managed to kill two of her kin. When was this nightmare going to end?

"This will all end with me", Numerius said as if reading her mind.

She glanced at Numerius but he avoided her with a strange guilty look and suddenly she sensed there was something else. She understood that he would wish to protect her from the priests. But there was something else. She could not fully place it but there was something he was not telling her. It was as if he was trying to protect her from something. Perhaps that was why he was so keen to send her away to Massalia?

Chapter Nineteen – The right and proper thing to do

The following morning Titus rose at dawn. He'd hardly slept and when he had, his sleep had been disturbed by violent flashbacks to Cannae and he'd woken with a start, his body drenched in sweat. Ever since the battle he had felt alone. He had longed to be able to talk to someone about what he'd witnessed but only the men whom had participated in the battle could possibly understand the sheer terror and emotions of that day.

He found Frontinus as usual in his workshop on the ground floor.

"Numerius Fabius Vibulani," Titus said pronouncing the names with delegate care. "I am going to go to his house today."

Frontinus grunted and raised his hammer to strike at a white-hot piece of metal. "Without an official introduction they will throw you out onto the street," he said. "You are wasting your time.

The Patricians won't speak to you."

"Nevertheless I have to try," Titus said stubbornly.

Frontinus sighed and struck the metal with several hammer blows that rang out around the workshop.

"Suit yourself then," he grumbled. "But if you want my advice. Take your family Titus and return to the mountains, leave Rome. Milo has his eye on you and he won't give up until he has what he wants. You can't beat him."

"I will not run from him," and there was something in Titus' voice that made Frontinus look up, "I will not leave Rome and forgo what was promised me. I will convince this Numerius that I speak the truth."

There was stubbornness about the way Titus looked that made Frontinus smile.

"You look just like your father," the blacksmith said, "But even if this Numerius agrees to educate you, what about Milo? He won't leave you alone and you have a family to consider. Run to the mountains boy, it is sound advice."

Titus folded his arms across his chest.

"If I run now, I will run for the rest of my life," he muttered.

Frontinus sighed once more and fretted with a dirty cloth. It was clear that he was not happy with Titus' decision.

"There is a rumour going around the city," Frontinus said carefully, "that the survivors from Cannae are being sent to serve in Sicily for an indefinite period as punishment for their disgrace on the battlefield. If you stay in Rome, they will send you away Titus. It could be years before you are allowed to return and what will happen to your mother and sister in the meantime. Take them back to the mountains. You will have a life there at least."

Titus lowered his head and stared at the floor, deep in thought and the workshop fell silent. Then at last he looked up.

"The magistrates are not allowing anyone to leave the city," he said, "The mountains are filled with bandits and lawlessness. I have seen it for myself. I will speak with this Numerius and when Milo comes I shall stand up to him in the best way that I can. I may be just one man, but I was born free and I will not live my life like a slave. I have seen death and I have seen hell and I have survived them both and I will do so again."

Frontinus straightened up and nodded and there was a sudden respect on the older man's face.

"So you have Titus, so you have. You are not a boy anymore. Forgive me, I spoke hastily," Frontinus replied.

Titus glanced towards the doorway. "If I can educate myself, I can improve the position of myself and my family. If I can do this, all my ancestors will benefit."

Frontinus nodded solemnly.

"That is right and proper," he muttered. "If Hannibal comes to Rome I shall go to the walls and fight him. No Punic child killer shall enter my house as long as I live. That too is right and proper."

***

It was early evening and the day's heat was gradually losing its intensity. Titus and Frontinus sat on the large door stone outside the workshop enjoying the cool breeze. Titus was recounting his meeting with Numerius. He looked slightly disappointed.

"So he said that he would think about it," Frontinus interrupted.

Titus nodded. "The man is ill," he muttered, "he didn't admit it but I could see it in his face. He's got marsh fever."

"Go on," Frontinus said.

"Well they wouldn't let me meet him at first. He's got an office down near the Capena gate where the firemen are based. But I refused to leave and Scipio's name eventually got me into the room with him."

Titus took a deep breath. "He seemed surprised at first, then distracted and also a bit annoyed. I suppose with the war and how things are going people don't have much time to think about anything else. He didn't like it that I couldn't show him a letter of introduction. Nearly threw me out of the room at that point. He's a bit old fashioned, lectured me on Roman virtues and manners as if I was his son and then he questioned me aggressively on how I had come to know Scipio but I think by the end he was convinced that I was speaking the truth."

Frontinus scratched his chin. "A man with marsh fever isn't going to make a very good teacher, even if he agrees to do it," he sighed.

"We shall see," Titus shrugged, "But I was promised this reward and I shall have it."

"Fair and proper," Frontinus grunted approvingly. "So he didn't mind teaching a Samnite then? That does surprise me a little.

These Patricians like to keep to their own class you know."

"He never even mentioned it."

"Fair and proper," Frontinus frowned.

Titus suddenly looked thoughtful, "I don't know why I said it, a hunch I suppose, but remember when Milo burnt my letter he also claimed to know Numerius, he called him an arse, so I thought I would mention Milo's name to Numerius and he knew him alright." Titus leaned forwards with a triumphant smile.

"Numerius was a lawyer and has tried to prosecute Milo on numerous occasions. He would love nothing more than to bring Milo down. There is no love lost between those two, that's certain."

Frontinus' eyes widened in delight, "An ally," he muttered.

Titus nodded, "Maybe, if he doesn't die too soon. Numerius said he would send a messenger to Scipio to confirm my story. The last I know was that Scipio was at Venusia but he could be anywhere by now. It will take time before I have my reply. I will have to sit tight."

"How does the Scipio family know Numerius?" Frontinus looked puzzled.

"I don't know," Titus shrugged, "does it matter?"

Frontinus looked down at his blistered hands.

"I don't know how much time you are going to have," he said.

"Have you heard the latest news? Capua has gone over to Hannibal. Those fucking Campanians have proved themselves to be as reliable as the Gaul's. They are the second largest city in Italy. We protected them for over a hundred years and this is how they repay us. The scum have no honour."

"I am not surprised," Titus muttered, "At Cannae," he paused and frowned, "Hannibal's cavalry were terrifying. We were defeated by their cavalry, our men couldn't match them. They were superb riders."

Frontinus grunted something unintelligible. Titus looked up at the evening sky where the first stars were appearing.

"But I don't think Hannibal will come to Rome," he said.

Frontinus looked up sharply, "Why do you say that?"

Titus smiled, "Because cavalry alone cannot take a fortified city."

Frontinus stared at him and then he too grinned.

230

"You should do the rounds on the walls and tell the soldiers, they all believe Hannibal will be here within days. They are as nervous as young maidens on their wedding night."

The two of them laughed at that and the laughter eased some of the tension.

"Maybe you are right," Frontinus said slowly, "but I can't see how we can win the war by just hiding behind walls and fortifications. No Roman army will dare to face Hannibal in open contest now, not after Cannae. If what you say is true about the Carthaginian cavalry then it would be foolish to fight them in a pitched battle. Still I have faith in Fabius, if there is a man who knows what we must do, then it will be him. He will find a solution. Do you know what they call him now? The Shield of Rome."

"I heard that someone tried to kill him," Titus said, "Seems they killed the wrong man instead."

Frontinus nodded gravely, "Lucky for us they missed, Fabius has put up notices in the forum offering a reward for the assassins capture. But I reckon they will have fled the city by now."

Just then Aelia, Titus sister rounded the corner of the alley and strode straight past them into the building without saying a word. Her right eye was covered in an enormous dark, angry bruise. Titus rose to his feet and called out to her but she did not reply. Leaving Frontinus on the door step he went after her and found her sitting on the stairs. She had covered her head with her hands and her body shook and trembled as she sobbed.

"What happened?" he said laying an arm across her shoulders. Angrily she shook him off. "Don't touch me!"

"Who did this to you?"

She sobbed quietly and refused to answer. Titus repeated the question.

Again she refused to answer. Then Titus took her hands and forced them away from her face. In the flickering light from the oil lamps he could see that the bruise was huge and her lip had been split.

"I will ask you one final time, who did this to you?" he cried.

Defiantly she stared at him through teary eyes. "Who do you think you are, my father? Leave me alone!"

"I am the head of this family now and you will obey me. I can let you go if you don't."

She stared at him defiantly. "But you wouldn't?"

"Will you tell me?" there was something menacing in his voice that seemed to surprise both of them.

She sniffed and looked away and the threat seemed to work.

"Promise me you won't do anything stupid," she snuffled.

"I won't."

"My boyfriend," she said reluctantly, "Marcus, Servilia's son."

"Marcus, the illegitimate son of Servilia, the whore?" there was disgust in Titus' voice. "That's your boyfriend?"

"You see, I shouldn't have said anything," she cried.

"You have done it with him?"

She blushed and looked away and Titus groaned in dismay. Then he was off storming out of the workshop and into the darkened alley with clenched fists. He was closely followed by his sister who cried out for him to stop.

Titus found his sister's boyfriend sitting in the parlour of the local whore house. The boy was only fourteen and a full head shorter than Titus. He looked up with alarm as Titus came for him. Titus grabbed him by the throat and lifted him boldly from his seat and dragged him out through the doorway in front of the astonished customers. The boy screamed. In the dirty stinking alleyway Titus began to pummel him with blow after blow until the boys cries turned to sobs and he curled up like a baby.

"Don't you ever touch my sister again," Titus shouted furiously spitting on the bloodied and crying boy at his feet.

Aelia stood a few paces away shouting at him to stop but he turned on her and there was something in his eyes that cut her off in mid sentence.

"And you," he pointed a finger at her; "You will learn to behave like a proper Roman woman. If father could see you now he would have you beaten and locked up. How dare you bring such disgrace upon your family."

She stared at him in complete surprise and he could see she was scared now. Then she whirled round on her heels and fled.

"What?" Titus growled as a customer poked his head from the door way.

***

It was near noon the following day when Milo stepped into the workshop. Titus had been helping Frontinus with his work.

"Outside," Milo growled gesturing to Frontinus. The blacksmith laid down his tools, wiped his hands and without a word left the workshop glancing at Titus as he went out.

"I received a complaint about you," Milo said turning on Titus.

"One of my whores, Servilia, claims you beat up her son, in fact you nearly killed him."

"He beat my sister," Titus said folding his arms across his chest.

"I should have killed him for such disrespect."

234

"Ha!" Milo exclaimed with sudden amusement, "Yes I know about that. He's a little shit that Marcus, just like his mother. Always screwing around with someone they shouldn't be."

Milo strolled casually around the large heavy work bench. "But you put me in a difficult position Titus. Justice must be done. If you had a grievance you should have come to me. I would have sorted it out."

"Then sort it out."

"Look at me when I am talking to you," Milo snapped and reluctantly Titus raised his eyes and looked up. "Here is what I shall do," Milo said fixing his bulging eyes on Titus, "Marcus the shit will not touch your sister again. But in exchange for my protection you will come and work for me."

"I already have a job here," Titus lied.

Milo' face darkened.

"Well this workshop and everything in it could burn down and then you would be unemployed. Frontinus would be bankrupt and your mother would be without a roof and it would be your fault."

Milo paused. "You are not still harbouring dreams of becoming an educated man are you, a Plebeian wearing Patricians clothing?"

"That doesn't concern you," Titus retorted.

"Everything that happens in this neighbourhood concerns me," Milo's fish eyes flashed angrily, "I own this place and I own you."

"Go screw yourself," the words leapt from Titus' mouth before he could stop himself.

Milo grunted in surprise and for a moment the master of the Subura was at a loss to what to do but his recovery was fast and furious.

"Listen you little shit," he said grasping Titus by the throat and pushing him back hard against the wall, "When I say I want something done, I am obeyed. You have until the count of three to agree or else I am going upstairs and I am going to cut your bitch of a mother's throat."

Titus stared back at Milo but made no attempt to fight back. Milo began to count, taking his time with each number but he was interrupted when he was just about to say three.

"Let go of my son," a woman's hoarse voice said suddenly. Titus' mother was standing on the stairs. She gestured at Titus.

"Do as he asks Titus, for your family's sake," she commanded.

Slowly Milo's face split into a grin and he released his grip.

"I thought you were the head of your family," he said mockingly, "but it seems I was wrong. So we are agreed then," he smiled.

Titus scowled.

Milo's eyes seemed to pop out of their sockets and there was no doubting the menace in his voice. "If you defy me again you are a dead man," he hissed. Then with an effort the smile returned.

"Come to my home tonight, I need you to do something for me."

***

Titus had never been to Milo's house but he knew where it was. It was a place where few liked to go and Titus approached the building reluctantly. He was still fuming and humiliated at being forced to do something he didn't want to do. His mother had berated him for his foolishness in challenging Milo; she had even slapped him in the face afterwards but what hurt the most was that she had said that Milo was right. Aspirations of an education were just dream's, she had chided him. It was time, she had told him, that he learnt his place in society and joined the class to which he belonged. Her words had stung like a whip. He had felt betrayed, but he had taken comfort from knowing that she was wrong. His mother didn't understand, she didn't understand his ambition and what drove that ambition, but one day she would.

Milo's home was in the very heart of the Subura. He owned an entire four storey apartment block. From the outside, the building looked like any other run down tenement in the neighbourhood. A few thugs lounged around the arched double doors and Titus recognised them as Milo's men. He stepped inside and instantly he seemed to have entered a different world. Gone was the stink of the alleys, the smell of rotting garbage and rubbish, the crumbled masonry, dust and drip of broken drains and the bundles of human misery leaning against the alley walls. Instead Titus eyes widened in surprise at the luxury that surrounded him. Sweet perfume filled the room and a slave was fanning the air with a sail made of goat skin. Rich carpets from the east lay on the floors, statues of gods he'd didn't know adorned the alcoves in the walls and numerous oil lamps bathed the corridors and rooms in bright, colourful light. Milo's place was fit for a consul he thought. He'd never seen such a beautifully decorated home. The man even had running water and from somewhere in the house he could smell the delicious scent of fresh bread.

It seemed as if a party was just getting underway. Music was coming from down one of the corridors and he could hear high pitched female laughter. Richly dressed men and women, decked out with fine jewellery pushed past him speaking in loud excited voices and sipping wine. Some had painted their faces in vivid colours, red, yellow, blue; others wore outrageous costumes, impersonating the gods, yet others were clad like barbarians with blond hair and bear skins. Titus blushed at the sight but none of the guests seemed to take notice of him. He was shown into a small waiting room just off the main corridor and told to wait.

It was not long before Milo showed up. Titus stood up and nearly laughed when Milo came in for the boss of the Subura was dressed like the god Zeus, with a crown on his head, thick makeup around his eyes and a wooden trident in his hand.

Milo however seemed oblivious to the hilarity he had caused.

"Hhhhmmmm," he frowned as he examined Titus, "Are those the best clothes you have got. You look like you are homeless."

"They will think he's a slave, we don't have many in that category tonight," one of Milo's men smirked.

Milo laughed. "Very well, give him some perfume."

"So what do you want me to do?" Titus said trying his hardest not to laugh at the way Milo was dressed. The man looked like an idiot.

"Just do what they tell you to do," Milo said mysteriously.

Milo disappeared. The thug in the doorway gestured for Titus to follow him. The music grew louder as they entered the main corridor into the building. They turned left and Titus found himself standing on a circular balcony looking down at a hall. A wooden balustrade prevented him from falling off the edge. As he looked down into the hall his eyes opened wide.

In the hall below richly decorated couches and mattresses covered the stone paved floor and writhing upon them was a mass of naked women and men having sex. A band of three musicians were providing the music but their efforts could not mask the groaning, screaming and grunting mass of humanity. Titus stared at them, unable to look away. The naked bodies reminded him of snakes writhing in a snake pit. He felt his cheeks blushing furiously. A couple of ladies, old enough to be his mother and dressed up to look like barbarian women with blond hair were leaning on the balustrade a few yards away. They caught his eye and smiled.

Then someone was at his side. He looked up. It was Milo. The man grinned and laid an arm around Titus' shoulder.

"Quite a view eh," he said, "So what do you think?"

"Think of what?" Titus muttered.

"Have you never seen an orgy before?"

"No," Titus muttered. "I didn't know that Rome had so many prostitutes and that you could afford them all."

Milo laughed. Then he leaned in close and placed his mouth close to Titus' ear.

"Oh you have much to learn boy," he said, "It's not the women who are the prostitutes, it's the men."

Titus took a step back and stared at Milo in confusion.

"You see those two ladies," Milo said gesturing at the two who had earlier caught Titus' eye, "Wives of senators". Milo nodded towards a young woman riding on top of a man whilst another woman licked her breasts, "That's the daughter of an ex consul."
Titus said nothing.

"You see they like to come here to show their independence," Milo said quietly, "I provide them with the goods, complete discretion and in return they make sure that nothing bad happens to me. A good deal eh."

"It's a bacchanalian orgy," Titus said quietly.

"Yes some may call it that," Milo replied, "I just call it good business."

"So what am I doing here?"

Milo looked amused. "As I said," he replied, "You are here to do what they want you to do, understood."

Titus felt a spark of panic as Milo left him. Suddenly it was all clear. He was to be a male prostitute. He glanced down at the writhing mass of people. Without looking up he sensed one of the women further along on the balcony coming towards him.

"Look at me," she commanded.

Titus did as she had asked. The woman studied him carefully.

"How old are you?" she asked.

"Seventeen," he replied.

"Are you a slave?" she inquired with a smile.

"No, freeborn," Titus said with a note of defiance in his voice.

The woman chuckled, "I didn't think you were a slave, Milo may try and sell you as one but he doesn't fool me. Have you a drink?"

She snapped her fingers before Titus could answer and a few moments later a slave pressed a glass of wine into his hand.

"Drink it," she commanded, "you will feel better."

Titus took a long deep gulp.

"A nice shy freeborn virgin," the woman smiled again. "Well what you think of him?" she called to her friend who had remained where she was.

"Are you a virgin?" the other woman said glancing at Titus.

"Answer her," the woman beside him ordered taking hold of Titus' chin and running her fingers along his jawbone.

"If it pleases you," Titus muttered.

The woman's eyes sparkled. She was silent for a moment. "I think I will have this one," she announced.

Titus could smell her deep, rich perfume as she drew him closer. She leaned back against the wall and undid her dress.

She was stark naked underneath.

"Do it to me with your tongue first," she ordered huskily.

Titus stared at her flat stomach and gentle curves and the triangle of dark pubic hair. Then he got down on his knees. He had never done something like this before and as he fumbled around he could feel her impatience. Yet soon he seemed to be doing the right thing for he could feel her beginning to shake and quiver. It seemed an age before she suddenly grabbed his head, groaned and arched her back, thrusting her pelvis deep into his face.

"Good boy," she gasped panting for breath, "Now you may fuck me."

***

The orgy seemed to go on all night but the doors to the building had been bolted and no one was being allowed out. Titus found himself a place in the guard's room where Milo's thugs were drinking themselves silly. They were too drunk to notice him. He sat sipping wine and brooding on what had just happened to him. He had done as the woman had asked but his inexperience had finally caught up and she had angrily dismissed him when he had come inside her. He had not known that was forbidden. Stupid bitch, he thought as he silently cursed the whole party. If Milo punished him for this it would be intolerable. He took another sip of wine as he remembered the dark awkward fumble with a neighbour's daughter to whom he had lost his virginity a couple of years earlier. That experience had been nothing compared to this. He'd fucked a senator's wife and the thought brought a cheeky smile to his face.

He drained his glass and then suddenly froze in horror. Standing in the doorway to the guard room with its long wine stained table and gaggle of loud drunken thugs was a tall sober looking man. He had a glass in his hand and creeping up his arm was a long white scar. Titus knew he had seen the man's face before. Then he remembered. The burning farm on the road to Rome! It was the same man who had murdered those farmers. Without thinking he ducked and pretended to fiddle with his sandals. What was the man doing here of all places? Had he been recognised? But when Titus cautiously raised his head the man had vanished.

Chapter Twenty – Fortune smiles on the brave

Adonibaal had been surprised by the reaction of Milo and his men. The thugs who had cornered him on the landing of the apartment building could so easily have killed him or turned him over to the authorities yet they hadn't. He was not a particularly religious man but that night he had muttered a prayer to Jupiter for his good fortune. He'd known instantly that the only choice he had, was to go along with whatever this Milo wanted. The opportunity to escape, he knew, would come eventually if he remained patient. They had taken Centurion from him; as a precaution Milo had told him. Afterwards he'd been taken to Milo's house. They had not let him leave which had suited him just fine for the authorities would surely be hunting him by now. It made sense to stay off the streets.

The first few days he'd sat around doing nothing. The thugs whom he'd shared dinner with had ignored him and that was fine too. He'd realised that he had never considered what to do if the initial assassination attempt failed. He always got his man but he should have made a contingency plan. The truth was that he'd been too complacent. Now he needed some time to plan his next move and he was lucky to have Milo's protection. During the long hours of boredom, he'd considered what had gone wrong. But from whatever angle he looked at it, he always came back to the same conclusion, he had failed because of a fluke. He'd just had some bad luck.

He had thought about Janus and how good it had felt to kill him. From a very early time, when the brothers had started to hate their father, Janus had tried to squeeze into the gap opening up

245

between father and sons. The slave had made no secret of his ambition to replace the brothers as their father's son through adoption and it had caused great bitterness. Adonibaal had always thought it unlikely that Janus would be given an inheritance but the man's confession that he'd been given the house had stunned him. How could 175 years of Patrician tradition just be handed to a man of no rank or achievement? Had his father truly gone mad? He had frowned, suddenly unsure of himself. But if Janus had been left the house in his father's will, then for what had his brother betrayed him?

During the evening of the second night the mood in the apartment building had suddenly changed. A special party was being planned and Adonibaal had been told that he was going to take part in it. He had no idea what they were talking about. He was told to wash and had been giving an old soldiers tunic, complete with a wooden sword and a pot of perfume. The perfume baffled him but he did as he was told.

***

The woman would just not stop talking. The two of them sat on the ground with their backs against the wall, resting. He'd fucked her twice, once with her on top and once from behind and she had screamed every time she had come but now she just wanted to talk. All around them the orgy continued but Adonibaal was not looking at the writhing, moaning mass of bodies. He was staring at the opposite wall thinking of how he could get away from this woman. Her name was Marcella and her husband was a tax collector, away on business in Corsica. She was plain looking, in her late thirties but he'd got the impression that she was rather a lonely, sad character who was really just looking for someone to talk to. Yet every time he'd tried to leave she had pulled him back and made him stay. He'd noticed that she had no interest in any of the other males or women in the hall. Her words droned on and on and he closed his eyes. Then suddenly his ears pricked up. "What did you say?" he blurted out opening his eyes.

"I was saying," she repeated, "That there is a tunnel that leads from the sewers to the house. Pay attention soldier when I am talking to you," she chided him. "Now the tunnel leads to a room which the owners of the house had specially built for our Bacchanalian rites. I went there once for such a party. The owners made us leave through the tunnel and I got home stinking of shit." She laughed in a high pitched annoying voice. "Still better that way than if we had entered through the sewers. It wouldn't have been much of a party then would it."

"You mentioned a name?" Adonibaal said.

"Yes," she said triumphantly, "and do you know who owns that house now. Quintus Fabius Maximus. If only that old puritan knew what had gone on under his bed," she laughed again and gulped down the last of her wine.

Adonibaal was fully alert now.

"Could you show me how to get into that tunnel?" he asked.

She looked at him with a big smile, "Of course, but there are no parties there anymore, my darling Centurion."

Adonibaal smiled and placed another glass of wine in her hand.

247

"You can take me home if you like," he whispered in her ear, "I will be there just for you, no one else. Do with me what you like."

At the same time his hand wondered down to her naked thighs.

She giggled and he could see she was worn out and drunk. "Well that sounds like a nice idea", she murmured, "but my husband…"

"He won't return for a week", he said finishing the sentence for her.

She rolled her eyes and sighed as his fingers entered her. "Take me home, you big brute", she gasped.

***

Milo's thugs were drunk as Adonibaal stopped in the doorway of the guard room. He glanced casually at their leader.

"Where is Milo?" he asked him.

The man shrugged but said nothing. Around the boisterous table most of the men were too pissed to notice him. One the men tucked away in a corner bent down to undo his sandals. Adonibaal turned away. Fuck them he thought. He didn't need them anymore. Marcella had given him another way in. It was time to leave but he wasn't leaving without Centurion. He'd already found out where the weapons were stored. The weapons room was on the second floor. He reached it with a few strides. Someone was having a sex in a room next door. He could hear the banging of a bed post against the wall. The thug on duty in the weapons room never saw him coming. Adonibaal smashed his fist into the man's face sending him flying backwards onto the floor. With another blow the man was unconscious. It was over in less than a couple of seconds.

Adonibaal glanced at the array of weapons on the shelves. Then he snatched Centurion from the pile and examined the blade. The sword was undamaged and he smiled as if he'd been reunited with an old friend. He always felt naked without Centurion.

He tucked Centurion under his tunic and went back down stairs and found Marcella where he had left her. A drunken naked man was slobbering over her trying to get her to wake up. Adonibaal lifted him off her and flung him into a corner as if he was a sack of flour. Then he slipped his arm under Marcella's armpits and got her up upon her feet. Quickly he closed her toga and slipped on her shoes. The naked man in the corner was groaning, his hand holding his head from which blood was oozing onto the wall.

Marcella could walk but she was very drunk and he had to support her most of the way. He'd noticed that the main doors had been bolted, so he took her back upstairs to the first floor. The thug who guarded the weapons was still out cold on the floor but the banging of the bedpost had subsided. Adonibaal steered them towards the first-floor window, flung open the shutters and poked his head outside. It was pitch black and he could see nothing. Behind him he could hear a door opening.

Quickly he lifted her up in his arms. She weighed nothing and then he jumped. They hit the alley with a thud and he heard her gasp but he managed to get his body to soften the blow and she didn't seem to wake from her stupor. He grimaced as he rose to his feet. He could hear the dull noise of the party coming from behind the closed door, then a shout of alarm. They must have found the thug on the floor.

Quickly he vanished down the dark alley carrying Marcella. She had flung her arms around his neck and rested her head on his shoulder, babbling incoherently to herself. There was no moon tonight and he had trouble trying to orientate but eventually he found his way out of the maze of alleys. There was no sound of pursuit.

She had told him that she lived in a house on the Caelian. He had to waken her in order to get her to show her which house was hers. Eventually she managed to find it. By this time Adonibaal was covered in sweat and his arms felt limp and heavy. She giggled as he laid her down on a couch. The house was a modest affair which reflected the woman's status in society; just a few rooms clustered around a tiny atrium and no garden or slaves. They weren't rich enough to afford slaves she muttered. For a while he stayed with her until he was certain she was asleep. Then quietly he rose and examined his surroundings with the aid of a small oil lamp. The house was perfect and so was his cover he thought turning to glance at the woman.

***

She slept until the sun was already well established in the sky. Adonibaal dozed in a chair at her side. He was still clad in the old army tunic that Milo had given him for the party. When she did finally wake he could see that her mood had changed. She glanced at him uncertainly and then blushed with sudden embarrassment.

"How did I get home," she muttered.

"I brought you home," Adonibaal replied. "Don't you remember?"

"Yes I remember." As she rolled out of bed she refused to look at him. She fumbled nervously with her clothes. Adonibaal watched in silence.

"You may leave," she said when she was dressed.

"Last night," Adonibaal said ignoring her, "you mentioned something about a tunnel leading from the sewers into a house that is now owned by Quintus Fabius Maximus. Can you show me how to find the entrance?"

"Did you not hear me, I said you may leave," she said angrily. Adonibaal rose slowly to his feet.

"I am sorry. I can't leave without knowing how to get to that tunnel."

She stared at him with growing fury. "I shall tell Milo about your behaviour," she hissed, "He will have your balls cut off. Now get out, slave."

But Adonibaal shook his head and when she made for the doorway he moved to block her. She stared at him in disbelief.

"I have to know how to get to that tunnel," he said sharply.

She backed away from him and suddenly she looked afraid.

"What are you going to do to me?" her lower lip quivered. "My husband, he will be back soon, he will be here shortly."

"He won't be back for a week," Adonibaal folded his arms across his chest. "Just tell me how to get to this tunnel and I will leave."

She continued to back away from him, desperately glancing around the room for an escape route but there was none.

"I...I remember we exited the sewers not far from the house. There was an inspection shaft with a ladder," she stared at him confused. "Why do you want to know? It happened years ago."

"Is that all that you can remember?" Adonibaal sounded disappointed.

She nodded. Adonibaal stared at her for a long moment. Then he turned towards the main house door.

"Gods, you are that assassin who tried to kill Fabius," Marcella suddenly gasped raising a hand to her mouth. "That's why you want to know about the tunnel."

Adonibaal froze in his tracks. He had his back turned to her and she did not see the sudden coldness in his eyes.

***

Titus heard the shout of alarm from the floor above. A few moments later a red-faced Milo came running down the stairs. The makeup around his eyes was smudged and his usual cool had gone. He looked agitated.

"Get up. He's done a runner." Milo yelled at the startled thugs in the guard room. "Quintus is out cold on the floor. The bastard must have returned for his sword! Get out and find him!"

For a moment, none of the thugs were able to react but when Milo lashed out at one of them with his foot and sent him tumbling to the ground, the room erupted into a frenzy of activity.

"What's going on?" Titus cried as most of the thugs dashed up the stairs to collect their weapons.

"The Carthaginian has escaped," one of the guards replied carelessly. "Fuck knows how he did it. The main door is still bolted."

"What does he look like?"

"Big, tall bastard with a scar across his arm, you will know him when you see him," the thug yelled over his shoulder.

Titus was left standing in the guard room together with those men who were too drunk to walk or those that could not be woken.

He stared at the men running around in the corridor and suddenly he began to understand and as the realisation grew Titus felt his chest constrict with growing excitement until he could hardly breathe. He had found a way out. He had something on Milo that even the feared boss of the Subura would be unable to explain away.

They didn't find the Carthaginian as Titus knew they wouldn't. He'd gone out with the rest of the search parties because that was expected of him, but his mind was already thinking about what to do next. At dawn the dispirited men returned to Milo's home. The boss of the Subura had looked flustered. How can he have just vanished he yelled. He's got to be somewhere, tear down the whole city if you have to, but find him!

They had all gone out again at dawn but this time Titus had peeled away from the gang. He'd made his way towards the forum. On a white washed wall along the Sacred Way he found what he was looking for. He stared at the public notice feeling a little foolish.

"What does it say?" he called to a passer-by gesturing at the poster. The man glanced up at the notice.

"All persons who have any information regarding the brutal and unprovoked attack on Quintus Fabius Maximus report to the HQ of the Triumviri Nocturni beside the Capena Gate. A reward will be given."

The man glanced at Titus, "Do you know who did it boy?"

"Yes," Titus replied staring at the notice.

Chapter Twenty-one – Allies

Titus stood waiting for the man at the base of a statue of Mercury in the forum. He was alone and it was around noon. The forum seemed subdued and many of the traders who would normally pack the open spaces had once again decided to stay away. Rumours had been swirling around the city all day that Carthaginian horsemen had been sighted riding north on the Appian Way. There had been a small riot at one of the city's gates as a mob had been prevented from leaving. The soldiers had used their swords and the riot had left three people dead.

Titus glanced at the few market stalls which had opened and were doing a brisk trade. There was no sign of the man. A few yards away a lawyer was touting for business in a loud irritating voice. Titus glanced anxiously down the Sacred Way and wondered for the umpteenth time whether the man would come.

He was shaking the dust from his sandals when he sensed the movement.

It took them less than a second to surround him and as they did so he caught a flash of sunlight reflecting from a knife. Startled he looked up and stared straight into Milo's face.

"Well, well," Milo muttered, "waiting for someone, were we? You didn't think I was foolish enough to let you go."

"Have you found the spy you were protecting?" Titus retorted.

Milo's face had lost some of its usual colour and he was in a bad mood.

"You should have learned to keep your big mouth shut boy. You may think you have something to bargain with but you have nothing. No proof, no witnesses, no spy, no nothing and now you are coming with me," he said gripping Titus by the arm, "I'm going to keep you safe until I have decided what to do with you."

Titus shook off Milo's hand and took a step backwards. In response Milo's men jostled him and he saw they were armed.

"What about my family? What are you going to do them?"

Milo shook his head and caught Titus by the arm again. "Don't make me do this the hard way. They will join you when I've found out where they are hiding and it won't take me long to find them. Now start walking."

From somewhere within the forum someone blew a whistle in two short sharp bursts. A moment later came the noise of running feet. Milo and his men looked around in alarm. From behind one of the market stalls an old man dressed in a white toga appeared and started walking towards them with long confident strides.

"Seize those men!" he cried.

Within seconds the noise of running feet had turned into the shapes of armed soldiers who appeared from every direction.

The soldiers carrying their large oval shields advanced on the group.

"Tricked," Milo gasped. He and his men turned to flee but it was too late. They were surrounded by a wall of shields and spears.

"Surrender Milo," Titus cried pulling a sword from where it had been hidden in his clothes. The trap had worked.

"Never," Milo hissed, "You won't get away with this you little shit...," but his words petered out as a spear point prodded painfully into his back. For a moment Titus expected Milo to fight but it was not to be.

"Alright, alright," Milo said in a loud voice raising his hands,

"Give up your weapons lads, we don't have a quarrel with the army."

The man in the white toga pushed his way through the line of soldiers.

"Hello Milo," the old man said cheerfully.

"You," Milo's bulging eyes grew larger as he recognised his captor, "I should have known that you were behind this outrage."

"Chain him and have the rest of this scum flogged for public disorder offences," the old man ordered. Two soldiers stepped forwards, grabbed Milo by his arms and twisted them around his back. The boss of the Subura yelped with the sudden pain. Then his face darkened.

"Watch your back from now on old man," he snarled. "You are not going to get away with this; not this time."

"Don't you want to know the charges against you?" the old man replied.

"I have no interest in listening to your lies."

"Treason for a start, aiding an enemy spy during war time, I could think of a few other charges but that one should be sufficient to get you strangled."

Milo spat onto the ground before the man's feet.

"You had better release me right away," he sneered. "I have friends in high places. They are going to walk all over you, like flies over shit, when they hear about this."

"Oh I don't think so," the old man shook his head and took a step towards Milo. "I don't give a shit about your friends in high places Milo, you and I are going to have a talk today and maybe then I will let you live." The old man nodded to the soldiers.

"Have this piece of shit thrown into the Tullianum."

***

As he followed the prisoner and the soldiers to the city jail Numerius had some time to reflect on an extraordinary development. It had all started a few days back when a young brash man had pushed his way into his office at the Capena gate and demanded to speak to him. The boy had claimed to have been responsible for saving the Tribune Scipio's life at Cannae but could offer no proof. Then he had made his sensational claim. Scipio had promised to have him educated and had asked Numerius to do it. There had been a letter of introduction but it had been lost. He'd wanted to throw the boy out onto the street there and then, but his years as a lawyer had taught Numerius how to know when someone was lying or telling the truth. What had struck him right away about the youth was his sense of purpose and with growing interest he had realised the boy was speaking the truth. Scipio, the young Patrician had been a client of his, one of the few occasions when he had defended his own class. He must have impressed the young lord more than he had expected if the man was prepared to recommend him. The complement had cheered him up and he'd told the boy he would consider the matter.

The issue would have rested there if the same boy had not barged into his office again that morning. Nicomedes had tried to stop the brash youth but Titus had just walked straight in and stood at his desk. The boy had looked excited and unaware of the potential offense his impetuous behaviour may have caused.

If Numerius had considered rebuking the youth the thought died as soon as Titus had opened his mouth.

"I have seen the man you are looking for," Titus blurted out.

His words had taken Numerius by surprise but he had recovered quickly.

"What did he look like?" he said.

Titus had described Adonibaal and as he did so Numerius knew the boy had indeed seen his brother.

"Where?" the question had shot from his mouth and he had risen to his feet.

"That's difficult Sir," Titus had replied, "But I have an idea."

Titus had then told him everything. The boy was doing this to make sure he got his education Numerius thought. He was touched by the youth's ambition. It was unusual. Most men would have been happy with a few coins as a reward but not this fellow. As a lawyer Numerius had seen the squalor and poverty in which most Romans lived. He'd gained an insight into the lives of the ordinary people and he'd understood the simple things they desired and respected. But this youth was different and as Titus continued to speak Numerius had begun to like him. Yes, it would be worth helping this young man he thought.

The boy's story had however ended in disappointment. Titus had run into Caeso on the road to Rome where he'd seen him using the Scorpion. Then by sheer chance they'd met again at Milo's house. The boy had a sharp mind. He'd compared the assassin's description that Numerius had put out across the city with the man he'd run into and had figured out that the man was involved in the assassination attempt on Fabius. But then the trail had grown cold for Caeso had vanished.

"You and I shall make a good team," Numerius had said with a smile. "Come here is what we shall do."

Now Numerius glanced at his prisoner and smiled in satisfaction. He had often clashed with Milo when he had defended his clients against the boss of the Subura. They knew each other well and had learned to hate each other. Milo however had proved to be a resourceful opponent, with powerful friends and despite Numerius' skill he had rarely been allowed to win against the boss. Milo had developed an untouchable reputation but Numerius had never given up trying and now Titus had given him the chance to nail his old enemy once and for all. Titus had done well, very well indeed. It was brave to stand up to the boss of the Subura.

Fabius and the Senate would be interested in what had occurred. Milo's involvement with a Carthaginian spy would make it difficult for his supporters to defend him but they would still try he knew. There were powerful people with vested interests in keeping Milo in his position. He had seen them often enough at his trials. But the fact that the gangs of the Subura were openly colluding with the enemy would worry the Senate more. Milo's involvement explained how Caeso had managed to remain hidden for so long and if Milo was preparing to change his allegiance, how many more people out there were thinking the same thing. It did not bode well. The Senate should have had the whole neighbourhood cleared out he thought but he knew they would never agree to such drastic action.

As for his next move, Numerius thought, it was time to get down to business. Titus had urged him to march straight into the Subura and arrest Milo but that plan would not have worked. Numerius knew the Subura. The neighbourhood always united in the face of an external threat. The moment that Numerius' men set foot in the narrow alleys they would have been spotted and Milo would have been warned. It would have been impossible to find him if he'd chosen to hide. No, the only way to grab Milo had been to lure him out of his fortress and set a trap and it had worked.

Numerius beckoned Titus to his side as they swept down the street. The boy looked flush with excitement at what they had done.

"I shall have you educated Titus," Numerius said laying a hand on the youth's shoulder for support, "But it shall not be me who will be your teacher. Do you understand?"

Titus nodded. "You are ill Sir, I understand."

"Yes," Numerius nodded. "I am ill. What profession will you choose when your education is complete?"

Titus considered the question.

"An architect Sir, I shall raise buildings," he replied with a smile.

"Why not choose the law as your profession?"

Titus shook his head. "I am a Samnite. A man with my background will never win anything."

Numerius allowed himself a wry smile.

"Your mother and sister, are they in good health?"

"They are Sir, although my sister is rather wayward and my mother drinks too much."

"They will be safe in the place that I have arranged for them," Numerius replied. "Maybe when this is all over I shall meet them."

"Thank you Sir," Titus said, "We would be honoured."

Numerius grunted unintelligibly.

"A true Roman will lay down what he is doing and leave everything behind when Rome requires him to. A true Roman will never despair of our city. Are you such a man, Titus?"

The question caught Titus by surprise. Numerius had stopped to look at him and there was something hopeful in the old man's eyes.

"I am no deserter Sir. I saved a Tribune's life at Cannae and I will fight to protect my family. This I know."

The answer seemed to please Numerius and he started to walk again.

***

Milo was not a happy man. He swore and threatened the soldiers around him with the most terrible of fates but when he was dragged into the torture chamber of the Tullianum and saw the instruments of pain laid out on the table he became very quiet.

Numerius had Milo bound to a chair. Then he ordered everyone to leave except for Nicomedes the doctor, Titus and the three men who would do the torturing.

"Were going to talk," Numerius said as he stood behind Milo's chair. "We are going to talk about what you have been up to. If you cooperate there will be no need to inflict any pain but if you don't…"

Numerius left the sentence hanging in the air.

"I know half the Senate," Milo hissed, "You wouldn't dare touch me."

"Wrong answer," Numerius cried. He nodded to one of the gaolers who picked up a rod of white hot metal and pressed it against Milo's exposed shoulder. There was the hiss of burning flesh and a sickening smell and then a terrifying high pitched scream of agony that reverberated through the underground room.

"Fuck the Senate," Numerius said placing his mouth close to Milo's ear.

"Now do we understand each other?"

Milo was still screaming and his knees shook.

"You bastard, you burned me, you burned me," he shrieked.

"Tell me how you knew the man had tried to kill Quintus Fabius Maximus," Numerius said as he started to pace up and down behind Milo's chair with his hand's clasped behind his back.

"He told me, he told me that he had tried to kill Fabius," Milo screamed.

"Why would he tell you this?"

"I don't know," Milo howled, "But I believed him, he was that kind
of man who would do something like that."

"Why did you hide him," Numerius snapped, "the man had just tried to kill the leader of the Senate? Why did you not hand him over to the authorities?"

"No," Milo muttered beginning to master his pain. Sweat had accumulated on his cheeks and forehead.

Numerius raised his eyebrows and glanced at Nicomedes. The doctor's face looked like it was set in stone.

"What do you say doctor," Numerius said, "Do you think he will be strangled or thrown from the Tarpeian rock for aiding an enemy spy in war time?"

"The Tarpeian rock," Nicomedes replied weakly.

"For the final time, why did you hide him Milo, he was a Carthaginian, an enemy of Rome? Did you somehow forget about that?" Numerius raised his voice and smacked Milo over the head with his hand.

But Milo refused to answer. Numerius was about to order the torturers back to work when he was interrupted.

"Last night, how did the assassin manage to escape?" Titus raised his voice and stepped out of the shadows. "You yourself had made sure that all the doors were locked and guarded."

"Fuck off you little shit," Milo shook his head.

Numerius struck Milo over the head, "Answer the question."

Milo coughed. "He jumped from the first floor window. He was carrying someone. I think it was a woman."

"A woman," Numerius repeated. "Are you sure?"

Milo nodded.

A gleam of interest appeared on Numerius' face. "Now why

would a wanted man leave the nice safe place you had
    provided
for him, jump out of a window and run off into the middle of the
night carrying a woman? Can you explain that?"

"No", Milo muttered.

"Who was the woman?" Numerius said sharply. "What was she
doing at your house anyway? Women are forbidden from
leaving their homes by order of the Senate."

"I don't know who she was," Milo sneered, "they come and go.
I have a large household."

"There was an orgy," Titus interrupted, "the women came for
that," Titus pointed at Milo, "he organised it."

"You little dirty rat" Milo snarled spitting at Titus.

"Bacchanalian rites in the Subura," Numerius allowed himself a
smile, "not yet a crime but not something you would want to
boast about either. Tell me the name of this woman and where
she lives?"

Milo chuckled as if he'd heard something utterly absurd.

"Go fuck yourself," he cried in a loud voice.

"The woman's name, what is it?" Numerius persisted.

Milo chuckled again and there was incredibility in his voice as
he spoke.

"You want me to tell you who my clients are? Are you

completely mad? Have you lost it up here old man? I will tell you
nothing, nothing!"
Numerius grabbed the white-hot poker from the torturer's hand and pressed the hot metal into the prisoner's eye. There followed a sizzling sound like meat cooking in a pan. Milo screamed, a high-pitched scream of utter agony as the poker boiled away his eye. The scream made the hair on Titus' neck stand up. Numerius crouched at his prisoner's side, his face close to Milo's.

"I don't care whether you live or die," he said in a quiet voice, "I don't care about your powerful friends. You see Milo, I am afraid of nothing. I have sold my soul to the underworld. That's where I am going for eternity. Now tell me the name of that woman and where she lives."

Milo opened his mouth and screamed.

A few moments later the door to the chamber opened and a guard poked his head nervously around the corner.

"Sir, there is a man outside claiming to be a lawyer and acting for the Senate. He's been told his client is here. He's insisting that we release the prisoner right away."

Numerius glanced at his screaming prisoner and the gaping hole where his eye had used to be.

"Fine, I don't think he knows who she is anyway."

Numerius turned to Nicomedes whose face was a pale shadow of its usual colour. "Doctor, you will need to keep Milo in here for a few more hours. Don't release him until the last possible moment and under no circumstances are you to let that lawyer speak to him."

"But how do you want me to do that?" Nicomedes protested. "I am supposed to be your doctor Sir."

"You are an educated man," Numerius nodded confidently.

"Just find a way of stalling that lawyer."

Numerius beckoned to Titus, "Come we have work to do."

Chapter Twenty-two – The rotten system

The men of the Triumviri Nocturni rose to their feet as Numerius accompanied by Titus strode into the Tullianum's small courtyard. At the gates to the jail a small hawk nosed man with keen eyes stood watching them, his hands gripping the iron bars.

"The lawyer," Titus gestured.

"It didn't take Milo very long to call his friends for help did it," Numerius replied. Then he glanced thoughtfully at the troop of soldiers who had assisted his firemen in arresting Milo. "We had better take them along with us," he said.

"There is going to be trouble."

"Where are we going Sir?"

"I need to know the name of that woman," Numerius replied,

"She will know something about where our man is hiding."

"But Milo didn't know her name."

"Maybe he doesn't," Numerius nodded, "but Milo is a businessman, Titus. Remember what he said about knowing half the Senate? Information on these families will be very useful to him. If my hunch is correct he will have kept records on everyone attending his parties. If what he said about that woman is true, her name will be listed somewhere."

"Were going to raid his house?"

"Yes," Numerius replied, "but we don't have much time."

 The procession of firemen and soldiers led by Numerius and

Titus swept through the forum and into the Argiletum, the street of the book sellers. The crunch of the men's hobnailed sandals on the paving stones was loud and menacing and yet Titus had grown nervous. They were going back into the Subura. Milo's men would have raised the alarm by now. That was how Milo's lawyer had managed to appear so quickly and if they'd had time to organise that, then who knew what else was waiting for them in the alley's up ahead.

Numerius was right, there was going to be trouble.

"Show us the way to his house, Titus," Numerius said calmly.

As they entered the narrow alleys the people seemed to flee before them. Titus could see the doors being closed and bolted and heard the crash of shutters being drawn across windows. Mothers called urgently to their children and street vendors hastily packed up their goods and vanished.

Titus recognised people he knew but they all blanked him and he knew then that he had become an outsider, a traitor. The people of the Subura only had respect for their own. Whatever happened he would not be able to go back to the Subura after this was over. It was an intensely uncomfortable feeling but it was Milo who was the real traitor he reminded himself.

As they approached Milo's house a gang of armed men came out and formed into a group, blocking the doorway. Their leader, a huge, fat man wearing nothing but a belt and a loin cloth, folded his arms across his chest. In one hand, he held a club. "Stand aside citizen," Numerius snapped, "I have the authority to search this house."

But the big man shook his head and refused to move.

"You have no authority in this neighbourhood," he replied.

Numerius took the spear from the hands of a nearby soldier and with a speed and strength that surprised everyone he rammed the weapon into his opponent's stomach. The fat man blocking his way doubled up and the club fell from his fingers. There was a look of surprise on his face.

"But you are just a fucking lawyer..." he muttered in confusion. Then his eyes rolled in their sockets and without making another
sound he tipped over sideway's onto the ground like some falling elephant.

"Does anyone else want to die today?" Numerius bellowed. The rest of the gang blocking the doorway muttered angrily but the mass of spears, shields and swords behind Numerius was enough to deter them. "Get out of here." Numerius roared. They did as they were told, stumbling away down an alley.

"Break the door down," Numerius ordered, "Were looking for a book or any kind of written account. The first man to find what we are looking for will be rewarded with ten silver coins."

It took a few minutes to break down the door but once they were in the fire men and soldiers started to fan out through the building. Titus hung around the entrance to the apartment block.
He could hear the noise of the firemen upstairs as they smashed their way through the various rooms. What they were doing now would make them an enemy of Milo for life but if the men were aware of it they didn't show it. Once they would be done, everything of value in Milo's house would have been stripped and stolen but that couldn't be helped.

Titus glanced casually at Numerius. When he'd first gone to see Numerius he had expected to meet a scholarly and gentle teacher but the man he had come to know was utterly ruthless

and efficient. The man had not flinched from torture and breaking into people's homes and if it wasn't for the man's friendliness towards him Titus would have feared him.
The fire crew at any rate were scared of their boss. He had noticed it in the way they approached him. Some of the men had even talked about their boss having offered his soul to the gods of the underworld in return for the capture of the fugitive.

Titus moved further into the house and watched as several men broke into a strong box. Clothes were flung onto the ground and a bag of coins they found disappeared quickly into one of the men's pockets.

"What's up with the old man, is he always like this?" Titus said catching the arm of a passing fireman.

The fire-fighter glanced at Numerius down the hall.

"Don't you know? They say the assassin we are looking for killed his son.

That's why he wants to catch him so bad."

The man disappeared and Titus glanced again at Numerius. His new patron was not mad. He understood now why they were doing what they were doing.
His patron too, in his own way, was looking for a way out.

"Sir," the soldier's commander came up to Numerius looking worried. "I think we're going to have a hard time getting out of here. There is a mob gathering in the alleys. They are getting bolder and stronger by the minute. They don't give a damn about Milo Sir but they hate it when outsiders come into their neighbourhood like this. We'll have a riot on our hands soon enough and many of my lads are just half trained boys."

"If we have to fight our way out then that is what we will do," Numerius said, "but I am not leaving before I have what I came for."

"Sir, we should leave now," the commander insisted.

Numerius shook his head, "I will take full responsibility for what happens here. Go back to your post and wait for my orders."

There was an authority in Numerius' voice that the commander did not argue with. Instead he saluted, turned sharply on his heels and left.

A few minutes later the first roof tile smashed against the wall of the house close to the doorway. A moment later another tile clattered against the broken door. The two soldiers guarding the entrance ducked as a third projectile flew over their heads. Titus peered down the alley and saw it was thronging with armed men. Someone shouted in their direction.

"Riot Sir," the commander announced as he rushed past.

Numerius said nothing.

The tumult in the alleys outside had grown louder by the time one of the Fire crew came rushing down the stairs carrying a leather bound scroll. The man glanced anxiously into the alley as he handed the document to Numerius.

Numerius undid the leather seal and unrolled the parchment holding it up carefully between his two hands. For a moment all men's eyes turned to look at him as Numerius took his time to study the scroll.

"Well well, come and have a look at this Titus," Numerius said, "I
was right.

Milo has kept records, wonderfully detailed records."
As he continued to study the document another fireman came down the stairs carrying two more similar looking scrolls.

"That's all we could find Sir," the man stammered.

***

Numerius lost two men in the fight to get out of the Subura. Holding the precious records himself he led his men into the narrow alleys. They were met with a hail of missiles and a torrent of abuse but the large Legionary shields were an effective way of pushing the mob before them. When the troop finally emerged into the wider streets around the forum the news of the riot had already spread throughout the city. Soldiers were rushing to cover and bar all the exits into the neighbourhood. Citizens milled around in confusion and a few faint-hearted souls were crying that the Carthaginians were already in the city. As he led his men into the Sacred Way, Numerius was confronted by an angry looking Praetor.

"Are you responsible for this mess?" the government official growled.

"I am, but I have no time to discuss it with you," Numerius replied.

"You arrogant ass," the official hissed, "This disturbance is the last thing we need in the city right now."

"So sue me," Numerius retorted pushing his way past the man.

"There is a rumour that you had Milo arrested and tortured?" the official cried with incredibility in his voice as Numerius and his troop filed passed down the street, but Numerius did not reply.

At his HQ near the Capena gate the troop was met by Nicomedes. The doctor looked anxious as he half ran, half walked to Numerius' side.

"I had to release him," Nicomedes gasped, "The lawyer took him away. They are spreading the news of what you did around the city. Milo has threatened you with dire consequences Numerius. He has powerful friends. There is no doubt about it. The Senate won't like what you have done. I am sorry, but there it is."

Numerius placed a hand on the doctor's shoulder. "Thank you," he said, "You are a brave man and I will make sure that Fabius knows what you have done for me."

The doctor nodded apprehensively. "Did you get what you were looking for?" he asked.

"I did," Numerius replied with a triumphant smile.

The scrolls from Milo's house were a treasure trove of information. As Numerius and Nicomedes poured over them they marvelled at the magnificent detail of the records Milo had kept. The accounts went back for years and recorded names, places, payment and the particular's of the men and women involved. There were also payments to individuals with a coding system that they didn't understand.

"Bribes," Nicomedes whispered, his eyes widening.

Numerius nodded. It was clear that Milo ran a far more extensive racket than he had ever imagined. Some of the names in the accounts belonged to very senior members of the great Patrician families. Numerius was glad to see that Fabius' name however was not amongst them.

"This will make very useful evidence in court," he muttered.

Nicomedes glanced up at him with a look of astonishment.
"My friend," he gasped, "don't you realise that they will kill you to prevent this information from coming out. You have dirt on nearly every noble family in Rome not to mention their wive's affairs. This will cause the greatest scandal in the history of Rome."

"I didn't know the system was so rotten," Numerius sighed. "So this is what we have become, a nation where nobles take bribes from criminals and their wives fornicate with slaves. We are mocking our ancestors. It is no good Nicomedes. This is shameful, utterly shameful."

"What are you going to do with this?" the doctor said gesturing to the books.

Numerius looked down at the scrolls.

"I will give them to Fabius. He will have to handle their contents. But we are getting distracted my good doctor. Come let's have a look at the entries from yesterday. That woman's name will be amongst them."

"A man could become rich with this kind of information," Nicomedes said stroking his chin.

Numerius did not seem to have heard him as he studied the accounts and he did not see the little gentle smile the doctor allowed himself.

There were nineteen women on the list and they all lived in the wealthier neighbourhoods of the city. Nicomedes bent down over the scroll and in turn studied the names.

"How are we going to know which one he took with him?" he asked.

"That's easy," Numerius replied, "I will have Titus and my fire crew go to each house and speak to each lady in turn."

"And they are just going to confess to being at this ritual, this orgy?"

Numerius shrugged, "They may be reluctant but if they are we will tell them that we have proof that they were there and that they had better cooperate, if they don't want their names and reputations to be smeared in public."

"That's blackmail."

"Yes, it is blackmail," Numerius replied looking up at his doctor, "So what. The Punic spy is a direct threat to survival of the state. Nothing is more important than capturing him. We need that information and we need it quickly."

"You are going to upset a lot of powerful people. Is that wise?"

"Haven't I already done that, a few more won't matter," Numerius smiled. He straightened up as Titus entered the room. The young man halted before the desk and saluted smartly as if he was still with the army.

"I have got a job for you Titus. It will involve pissing off a lot of high borne women and their families. Can you handle that?"

"Sir," Titus replied and Numerius smiled. The boy was either a fool or just very brave. He didn't have a clue what he was letting himself in for and maybe that was just as well. He began to explain what he wanted done, indicating to the accounts, when suddenly he began to sweat. His body felt as if it was on fire. He staggered and grasped at the table to try and steady himself but there was no strength in his arms or legs. Then he was falling to the ground.

***

It was early in the evening when Numerius was strong enough to sit up on the couch.

"Did Titus carry out my orders?" was the first thing he said.

"He did a good job," Nicomedes replied mixing a potion in a cup before handing it to Numerius. "Twelve women confessed to returning home in the company of their own slaves. Four remained all night at Milo's. Two refused to acknowledge they had been out and one did not answer the door when our men came round."

"The two whom refused to confirm they'd been out. Do they have no reputation worth defending or do they think we are stupid," Numerius growled angrily.

"Titus told them they were lying," Nicomedes said with a tight smile. "That was after they threatened us."

Numerius could not help but smile as he pictured the young Samnite boy telling a rich Patrician woman that she was a liar in her own home. It would have gotten Titus into serious trouble if the circumstances had been any different. Well those bitches deserved it he thought. Their moral behaviour was outrageous.

He looked up as Nicomedes cleared his throat.

"One of the Praetors' has ordered that you be arrested Sir," the doctor said, "but they can't seem to find anyone willing to carry out the task."

"Bunch of cowards," Numerius grunted.

"You cannot rely on Fabius all the time Sir, eventually they will send someone to bring you in. It's just a matter of time."

"Good," Numerius said rising slowly to his feet, "No time to waste then. Let's start by going to pay the one who didn't answer a visit. What's her name?"

"Sir, you should rest," Nicomedes replied anxiously, "you are not fit to go anywhere. It's already nearly dark."

"Oh stop moaning like an old woman doc," Numerius grumbled slipping into in his sandals, "I can manage. Now what's her name?"

Nicomedes sighed with obvious disapproval.

"There really isn't much point in me being here if you won't follow my advice," he grumbled, "The woman is called Marcella something, married to a tax collector. Titus has the details."

"Of course you are needed," Numerius said laying a hand on the doctor's shoulder.

***

The small procession carrying burning torches made its way up the Caelian hill. The noise from the riot in the Subura had subsided but it was still all the talk amongst the people on the street. It was twilight and Titus striding along in the rear was beginning to feel tired. He'd been on his feet for most of the previous night. It had been an eventful day he thought. It seemed ages since he had joined the hunt for the Punic spy. He could never go back to the Subura now, not after what he had done. It saddened him for the neighbourhood had been his home but his family came first and he would build them a new home, a better home.

His fate and that of his family he realised, were now largely in the hands of the man who led the procession. His patron looked pale and fragile and Titus had gone from being a little afraid of the man to being worried about his health for if Numerius died he too would be finished. Milo, he knew would hunt him down even if he left Rome and ran all the way to the Alps.

The procession with their flaming torches came to a halt outside a modest town house in a smart street and Numerius stepped forwards and rapped loudly on the wooden door.

"Open up in there, we have official business," he shouted.

There was no reply from the house. Numerius nodded to the two firemen who had brought their axes. The men went to work on the door and for a minute Titus waited as splinters and pieces of wood flew into the street. Then with a final derisory kick one of the firemen broke down the remains of the door and they were in. Titus followed closely behind as the firemen carrying their torches clustered together in the atrium. The house was silent and shrouded in darkness. There were no signs of life. The flickering light from the torches created eerie shadows on the walls.

"Sir," a voice suddenly cried in alarm. "Here, Sir".

Numerius crossed the atrium and entered one of the rooms. A fireman was standing in the middle of the room holding a torch.

"Gods," Numerius muttered.

Lying on the bed was the naked body of a woman. The blanket around her was soaked in blood and her open eyes stared lifelessly at the ceiling. "I think we know why she didn't answer our calls Sir," one of the firemen blurted out.

283

"Gods, he killed her," Numerius muttered and Titus could see the sudden disappointment on his face.

"Should we search the house Sir?" Titus said.

"Yes, yes," Numerius nodded looking distracted. He turned and sat down on the edge of the bed moving the woman's legs to make space.

"If I examine her I can probably establish how she died," Nicomedes said trying to sound helpful.

"No, there is no point," Numerius replied. "Why did he kill her, he had a good place to hide here, why throw that all away?" Numerius said to himself running a hand through his hair.

"Maybe she discovered who he really was?" Titus offered.

"Yes maybe," Numerius nodded. He glanced at the woman's face and touched her cheeks gently with his finger.

"Show me the accounts again we took from Milo's house," he said suddenly turning to the doctor, "What is so special about her? Why did you choose her Caeso," he muttered to himself, "why her?"

Nicomedes undid the scrolls and in the flickering torchlight the two men bent over the accounts. Numerius ran his finger down the lists of names.

"What's so important about her?" he growled irritably. "Go back doc and see if her name crops up in any other parties or payments or the like. Go back years if you have to. Maybe she has a history, there has to be some connection somewhere."

"The house is empty, nothing has been touched," one of the firemen reported standing in the doorway.

"Alright," Numerius said. He turned and looked at the dead woman again and Titus could see that his thoughts were far away.

The minutes past in silence until suddenly Nicomedes yelped in triumph.

"Got it, she attended a party a few years ago, also hosted by Milo but at a different address," the doctor looked up and there was an odd excitement in his eyes. "You will never guess where?" he added.

"Where?" Numerius exclaimed turning to look at the doctor.

"Fabius' house," Nicomedes said, "it had a different owner then, a man called Pollio and the notes say that the guests used the secret entrance. What does that mean?"

Numerius was on his feet. "What Fabius' house on the Palatine?"

Nicomedes nodded. "That's what it says Sir. As Fabius' doctor I know the address well," and as he said the words the doctor's mouth opened in dismay. Numerius' eyes widened as he struggled to grasp the full extent of the picture that was now so tantalisingly close.

"Hurry, to Fabius' house on the Palatine," he cried suddenly lunging for the doorway, "the assassin has found a way into the house. He's going to try and kill Fabius in his own home."

"I know that secret entrance," the doctor gasped.

"So do I," Numerius cried.

Chapter Twentythree - Cloaca Maxima

Adonibaal had never been down into the sewers before. He'd heard about the Cloaca Maxima of course, the big drain, built by the kings hundreds of years before to drain the low-lying marsh land between the hills of Rome, but he had never imagined he would go down into it. Some people had said that the Cloaca was the entry point into the underworld. Others spoke of gangs of monsters and criminals who lived in its tunnels and who killed anyone who entered their world. Old wives tales Adonibaal thought dismissively; created to scare little children. Nevertheless he'd said a prayer to Cloacina, the goddess of the sewers and had left her a silver coin. Tonight, he would need the gods to favour him.

Marcella had told him about the inspection doorway that led down into the sewers. He'd found it close to the Senate house and the forum, a small non- descript bolted doorway in a wall. He'd returned to wait at her house until it was dark. Then when he judged the evening and the twilight to be far enough advanced to give him some cover he'd started out. They would be looking for him now he knew but even if Milo did eventually find her corpse it would be too late. He just hoped Fabius was at home as usual. As he'd sped towards the Palatine he'd heard from passers by that there had been a riot in the Subura. It was a good omen. Milo was angry. Hopefully with a riot on their hands the authorities would be too busy too look for him. His spirits had soared higher when he had walked past Fabius' house and seen a group of heavily armed soldiers standing guard outside the front door. The old man was at home.

Throughout that afternoon, as he'd hidden in her house he'd sat in a chair staring at Marcella' corpse lying on the bed. He'd had to kill her he knew, she had discovered who he was and he couldn't afford loose ends but killing a woman had been a distasteful act. She should have kept her mouth shut. He was a professional and he had a job to do. She had brought it on herself but her desperate pleading had still managed to unsettle him.

Now he stood upright in the main tunnel of the Cloaca. In his hand he held an oil lamp he'd taken from her house. Its flickering light cast a shallow circle around him beyond which there was only total darkness. The smell in the tunnel was not as bad as he had expected but what really surprised him was the size of the sewer, the tunnel was huge. He lifted his lamp above his head and grunted in disbelieve. Not only could he walk upright, a man could sail a boat down here he thought. He glanced at the huge blocks of stone and the vaulted ceiling that faded away into the darkness. When he'd last been in Rome, twenty four years before, the Cloaca had been an open ditch. Now, at least in this section, it had been covered over for the ceiling looked new. He reached out a hand to touch the walls and noticed that in places the stone work had been repaired. Whoever had constructed the Cloaca had done it with special care and pride and the sewers looked well maintained. It was a remarkable piece of engineering.

He stooped and fastened the end of the ball of string he'd taken from Marcella's house to a large stone at the base of the steps leading up to the doorway. It was a precaution. He had no idea how many tunnels there were or how complex the sewer system was. If his lamp died on him he would at least be able to find his way back. Idly he wondered about the old Athenian story of Theseus and the Minotaur. Better to die bravely than live forever in shame he thought.

He began to wade down the tunnel. The dirty water came up to his knees and he could feel a current pushing him along. The angle of the tunnel was fairly steep. Somewhere up ahead he knew that the Cloaca would find its way into the Tiber. He knew the rough outline. The sewer started somewhere along the Argiletum in the neighbourhood of the Subura and then made its way past the Senate house, cutting across the forum in the shadow of the temple of Jupiter on the Capitoline hill before following the street that led to the cattle market and the Tiber beyond. Marcella had told him that he would find a door in the wall where the Cloaca passed along side the Palatine. He was lucky that it was summer he thought as he waded along. During the months when the Tiber had normally flooded the valleys between the hills of Rome it was known that the river water often forced the sewage back up its ducts until the whole city was clogged in a tremendous stink.

The only noise was that of his legs wading through the water and the incessant, high pitched squeaking of the rats who unseen, scurried away before the approaching light. He moved slowly casting his lamp from side to side as he inspected the tunnel walls and as he moved he slowly unwound the ball of string. To his surprise the tunnel duct was not in a straight line but turned and twisted its way through the earth. Here and there he could see terracotta pipes lined with lead poking out of the walls and at one point he came across a side tunnel that seemed to have been blocked up on purpose with huge stone slabs.

Suddenly from out of the darkness a round metal door appeared in the wall.

He stared at it for a moment, struck by its very oddness. The round hole was not very wide, perhaps a yard across and it looked illegitimate. A pile of broken bricks had formed on the sewer floor just below the entrance and he guessed they had been left behind from when the door way had been constructed. He stepped forwards and wound the string around the broken bricks, wedging it so that it was secure and would not slip away. Then he straightened up and stared at the door. It had a handle. Gently he tugged at it and to his surprise the door swung open with only a slight creak from its hinges.

Adonibaal drew Centurion from its hiding place beneath his clothes and thrust the lamp into the doorway. He could feel his heart pounding away with excitement. A room, he was in a room. He stooped and pushed his way through the doorway and crouched on one knee, listening but he could hear nothing. Carefully he swung the lamp around him. The room was not very large and in one corner were a pile of old rugs. He swung the lamp back and saw what he had missed the first time. There in the corner was the narrow staircase disappearing upwards just as Marcella had described it.

Slowly and taking his time he began to ascend the stairs. They rose at a sharp angle and he had to bend his head to prevent himself from hitting the ceiling. Now and then he paused to listen but there was no sound apart from his own breathing and the gentle hiss of the oil lamp. It was getting late and people would be preparing for bed. He'd forced Marcella to tell him what she knew about the layout of Fabius' house. According to her it was a normal Roman house with an atrium at the centre, a garden at the back and the usual rooms radiating from the atrium. Adonibaal ran through his plan one final time. The tunnel emerged in one of the rooms off the atrium. That's what she had told him. His attack would rely on speed and sheer violence. He would emerge, locate Fabius and cut his throat and kill anyone who got in his way. Then he would escape back down the stairs and into the sewers. He was improvising he knew and would have liked to have had more time but he didn't have that luxury and this was the best plan he could think of. He pondered about the soldiers he'd seen at the front door but it couldn't be helped. He glanced at Centurion. He would rely on speed, surprise and if possible, silence.

He sensed the end of the staircase before he could see it and quickly extinguished his lamp and placed in on the stone steps. Then half crawling he slithered up the remaining steps until his hands came to rest on a wooden trap door. The square door was about a yard from the last step and as he crouched below it he paused to listen but all was quiet. Raising his hands his fingers traced the outline of the trap door and found the hinges. It opened upwards.

He took a deep breath and slowly began to exert pressure on the door. If it was locked his plan was doomed but to his relief the wood started to move. Ever so gently he pushed it upwards until a crack appeared and he could see into the room above.

The room was in darkness but lamps were burning in the atrium beyond flooding it with light. He could see no one. Again he paused to listen but there was not a sound. Too quiet he thought suddenly. It's too quiet. A warning screamed in his head but he didn't move. He was close now, close to finishing his job once and for all. This was not the time for cold feet. He peered through the darkened room into the atrium beyond familiarising himself with the house' layout. In a rich house like this the owners would normally sleep in the most secure rooms, the ones closest to the centre. Gently he raised the trap door another inch. There was something pushing down on it preventing it from lifting more easily. A carpet, it was a carpet. He bit his lower lip feeling his heart pounding away. This was the moment.

With a firm push he lifted the trap door above his head and using his elbows forced himself upwards and onto the floor of the room. He crouched on his haunches Centurion in his hand. The room he was in was a bedroom and it was empty. He slithered towards the doorway leading into the atrium and hid alongside the wall. When he dared risk a glance into the atrium he saw that although brightly lit it was empty. The house was silent. He rose to his feet and stepped boldly into the atrium, striding straight for the two rooms where he presumed Fabius would be sleeping. The first bedroom was empty and he felt the odd warning signal return but he had no time to think. He stepped through the doorway into the second room. A solitary oil lamp burned in a corner. There was a bed along the wall and in it lay a figure asleep covered by a blanket. A senator's toga lay draped across a chair. Adonibaal stared at the sleeping figure.

***

Numerius rushed into the atrium. His lungs were bursting and his breath came in ragged gasps. There was a man standing in the doorway to Fabius' room. He was holding a sword. Too late his mind screamed. After all this he was too late. There was nothing he could do to stop the assassin. The man just had to take a few more steps and Fabius would be dead. He had failed.

"Caeso," he panted.

The assassins head had turned at the sound of the intrusion. Alarm gave way to a look of shock as he recognised Numerius. His brother looked older than he had imagined, Numerius thought, but it was definitely him, the eyes were unmistakable.

"Caeso," he cried summoning up the last breath in his lungs, "You have a daughter."

His brother seemed to hesitate for a precious second. Then with a speed that took Numerius by surprise he sprang away across the atrium. Numerius was aware of the soldiers behind him, yelling and shouting as they poured into the atrium. He watched, unable to find the strength to move, as his brother vanished through the doorway into the darkened side room with the horde of guards close on his heels. He heard a thump and a groan of dismay and a voice shouted out.

"He's in the tunnel, the bastard got into the tunnel."

Numerius felt the strength return to his body.

"Fabius, where is Fabius," he cried struggling towards the old senator's bedroom.

"I am here," a stern voice growled.

Numerius turned to see the old man standing in the doorway to one of the room's normally used by the household slaves. He was clad in simple white night clothes. A couple slaves stood at his side holding knives in shaking hands.

"I don't understand," Numerius blurted.

"I decided to take some precautions," Fabius snapped. "One of them was not to sleep in my own bed. The body in there is a decoy. It's made of straw."

"So you weren't in your room after all..."

"No," Fabius shook his head, "And if you had let your brother enter my room he would have been trapped."

Numerius swayed and placed a hand on the wall to steady himself.

"But then you would be dead and I would have failed," he muttered quietly.

Fabius ignored him.

"So it's young Caeso who has been trying to kill me," Fabius said with a hint of bitterness. "How long have you known?"

"I was trying to save you," Numerius muttered without replying to the question.

Fabius grunted something unintelligible.

"We will discuss this later, now is not the time," Fabius said turning away, "Find Caeso and bring him to me when you do." Numerius became conscious of Titus at his side.

"Sir, he got into the tunnel before we could stop him," the young man said excitedly, "but the men don't dare to go after him. He can hold up a whole army down there in that confined space. What shall we do?"

Numerius took a moment to collect his thoughts.

"Have the men seal all the inspection shafts in the city. We will trap him down in the sewers."

"Sir," Titus frowned, "all the inspection shafts? How many are there?"

"Just do it," Numerius snapped.

***

Dawn found Numerius resting in Fabius' house. Titus and Nicomedes had done as he'd ordered. They'd posted guards and had found the door where Caeso had entered the Cloaca. Several parties of armed men had entered the tunnel but after hours of searching they had found nothing. Caeso had vanished once again. Exhausted and disappointed, he'd allowed his men a well deserved rest and they now lay fast asleep on the floor beside his chair.

The house was quiet now and only the hushed movement of the slaves preparing for the new day seemed to disturb the early morning.

Numerius sat in his chair, still in his clothes, staring into the room into which he'd watched his brother disappear. A heavy bench had been placed over the trap door and a soldier lay upon it asleep snoring gently. Numerius was exhausted. He stroked his chin with trembling fingers feeling the grey stubble of two days growth. His eyes looked feverish and dark bags had formed below them.

When he had first realised that his brother had returned to Rome and had returned to kill it had changed everything. Numerius knew he was partially to blame for what had happened to his father. It was a blame that had clung to him like a shadow ever since the murder. No one had known or noticed the fury he'd felt when Caeso had taken Flavia from him, and simmering with rage and jealousy, he'd sought revenge and had told his father about Caeso' marriage plans. Vainly he had hoped it would lead to Flavia coming back to me. It had been a foolish youthful notion.

But all of this had happened many years ago now. He could not have foreseen the tragic consequences. Painful as they were he was not responsible for Flavia's death in childbirth, he had not murdered his father and he had not forced his brother to flee. He was not responsible for the feud that had caused his father's death. If he had a share in the blame then Caeso had to burden a far greater share.

Numerius stirred and shifted in his chair. One needed more courage and strength than he had ever imagined in order to forgive he thought but it was the only way. It was the only way in which things could be put right. So he had prayed to the gods of the underworld that they should release him from his pledge of vengeance which he'd made after Publius' murder. His brother had not meant to kill Publius. It had been an accident. He understood that now. He would forgive Caeso for what he had done, however hard it may be but the Gods were greedy and fickle and he wasn't sure they would release him from his oath? Would Caeso want to be forgiven? But these were questions that he could never answer and therefore he would not dwell on them. What mattered, now he had made up his mind, was that he felt stronger and more purposeful, for without forgiveness there was no future, there would be no end to the suffering and death that was wrecking his family. Without forgiveness, his father's and Publius' deaths would be meaningless. He would do what he could and would continue doing what he could until his strength ran out.

"You are awake," a voice said behind him.

Numerius turned to look over his shoulder. It was Fabius. The old man however looked at him with cold, unfriendly eyes.

"I had all the entry points into the sewers guarded," Numerius replied rising slowly to his feet. "We had him trapped but my men have searched every inch of the Cloaca and they found nothing. My best guess is that he managed to get out into the Tiber before we got into the tunnels. He could be miles away by now."

"Maybe the fact that he is your brother has undermined your judgement," Fabius' voice cut through the air like a whip. "Since yesterday I have received nearly a dozen complaints about you. One of the Praetors wants to have you arrested for murder of a citizen in the Subura and the illegal torture of another. He also accuses you of starting a riot in the Subura. Tell me that these accusations are false?"

"I did what I had to do," Numerius replied.

"Damn you", Fabius' face exploded with rage, "I ordered you to find and capture a fugitive, not to send the city into turmoil. Do you know who these people are who are demanding your head? They are powerful men. They are not easily turned away."

"Then let them come for me," Numerius retorted.

"Don't tempt me," Fabius shouted, "don't you see what you have done? You know how fragile the mood in the city is right now. Did I not say that we should remain united during this desperate time? Your actions have caused mayhem and you have divided us. You have let me down Numerius. The survival of the Republic is at stake damn it."

"Fuck the Republic," Numerius snapped, "I have seen what she has become." And from the folds of his clothes he took a bundle of scrolls and placed them in Fabius' hand.

"What's this?" the old man muttered staring at the documents in surprise.

"Milo's records of his dealings with the Senate," Numerius replied as he turned and headed for the door.

***

Alone he made his way back to his house on the Janiculum. He needed some time to think about his next move and Fabius' house was not the right place to do that. The sun was rising behind him and the morning air felt crisp and fresh on his face. He crossed the Sublicus Bridge and started up the hill. A movement amongst the grave stones that lined the road caught his eye but he saw nothing. He was plodding up the hill when he heard running footsteps behind him. He cursed. He had forgotten to go out armed but when he turned he saw that it was Titus. The boy looked red in the face and his chest heaved as he came to a stop.

"Sir, you shouldn't be out on your own," the boy gasped.

Numerius felt a sudden surge of emotion.

"That is kind of you to think about me, but I will be alright."

"Nevertheless I shall stay with you," Titus replied.

299

Numerius raised his eyebrows. "If they want to take me, I don't think you will be able to do much to stop them Titus," he said.

"I shall walk with you," the boy replied.

Numerius studied the young man for a moment. Then he shrugged. "Very well if your mind is made up then follow me. I am going home."

"The assassin," Titus said as the two of them started out towards the gate, "they say that he is your brother and that he killed your son."

"Yes," Numerius nodded.

Titus was quiet for a while. Then he looked up.

"I would like to serve you Sir, when this is all over, as a free man."

"You will get what was promised to you," Numerius said.

But Titus shook his head.

"I shall educate myself," he said, "but I also wish to work for you Sir".

Numerius paused.

"And why would you wish to work for another man Titus," he replied.

"I shall learn from you Sir," Titus said confidently.

***

The first sign that all was not well came when Numerius saw his man servant sitting outside the front door with his hands clasped to his head. He stopped in his tracks and stared at his house.

"What is it?" Titus asked in alarm.

Numerius didn't answer. He stared at the slave on the porch. Then he started to run. As he drew nearer he could see that the front door was open.

"What's going on?" he yelled.

The slave looked up and jumped to his feet at the sight of his master. There were tears in the man's eyes. Then as Numerius approached he fell to his knees whimpering shamelessly.

"What's going on?" Numerius repeated in a steadier voice.

"Master, I am so sorry," the slave whimpered, "we did what we could and the gardener is dead. We tried to stop them but they were too many and they were armed. Forgive me, master, forgive us."

"Who did this?" Numerius stopped and stared through the doorway into his house with growing alarm.

"Armed men Sir, I don't know who they were."

"What were they after?" but as he asked the question Numerius already knew the answer. He staggered backwards as if someone had struck him.

"They took her away, they took Pompeia," the slave sobbed miserably.

"Oh gods," Numerius groaned.

Chapter Twenty-four

In the year of the consulship of Centho and Tuditanus

Adonibaal crouched in the darkness listening out for the tell tale sounds of pursuit but he could hear nothing apart from the high pitched squeals of the rats and the drip of water on water. The sewage had drenched the folds of his tunic. It was cold and disgusting. His torch had died and he was alone in total darkness. He could feel his beating heart as he recovered from his shock. He'd gotten so close to his target, so damned close. His brother's sudden appearance had utterly surprised him. It was as if Numerius knew his every move he thought despairingly, always showing up at the crucial moment. Twice now he had failed. Would he ever get close enough to Fabius for a third attempt? The man would take every precaution he could. His task was growing harder and harder. Numerius, Numerius, he thought fighting a sudden and growing sense of panic, was it his brother's role in life to always thwart him? Had some demon ensured that Numerius would always be against him?

He tried to calm himself. It was a simple of matter of survival. Fabius must die so that he could live. For how else could he Adonibaal return home and take back what belonged to him. How else could he give up this awful life which he had been forced to lead. There was no future for him in Rome as long as Fabius lived.

He spat into the darkness as he felt his resolve return. He would win. He always did. If his brother tried to stop him again he would kill him. Nothing and nobody was going to stop him now from taking back what was rightfully his.

He felt the reassuring presence of Centurion in his hand. The cold iron calmed him like only an old friend can do. Numerius had not dared to come after him into the narrow tunnel. His brother was scared and the knowledge seemed to give him some comfort. But Numerius was cunning. His brother had always been cunning. Instead of coming after him into the sewers and finishing it himself he would move quickly to seal off all the exit points and then starve him out. That was his brother's style. He would have to move fast Adonibaal thought, if he was to escape the net that was being drawn around him. He paused to think. His only real hope was to try and get out of the sewers where they flowed into the Tiber.

He spat again into the darkness and turned his head from side to side peering into the blackness. But which way should he go? There was no light and nothing in the darkness to give him a clue. If he blundered and went the wrong way it would all be over for him. With an effort he slowed his breathing and cocked his head but the noises in the Cloaca provided no clues either. Fuck. Then he felt it; the slight tug of a current at his clothes. He gasped in sudden elation. That was it! How stupid of him not to notice the current. All he had to do was to follow the current and it would lead him to the Tiber. Immediately he started forwards, feeling his way along the walls with his hands. The stone tunnel was slippery and seemed to turn frequently. It would not do to injure himself on sharp rock or other obstacle. He slowed his pace pausing now and then to listen but still there was no sound of a pursuit.

As he waded through the tunnel he was struck again by Numerius' odd shouted comment.

Caeso, you have a daughter.

If it had been meant to distract him it had worked. Now he pondered on the strange meaning. Whilst he'd been in Rome he had been faithful to Flavia. She had given birth to a daughter whom he'd never seen, but they had told him that the baby had died alongside Flavia during birth. Had the child survived then and grown into an adult? Had they lied to him about her death? Had those bastards hidden her existence from him? Was that what Numerius had been trying to tell him?

It was all tricks and lies he thought savagely. Tricks intended to distract and hurt him, lies to trap and finish him. It was just the sort of thing Numerius would do, the coward. He sighed as if in pain. But what if Numerius was telling the truth? What if his daughter had really survived? He steadied himself against the damp wall. Matters were becoming complicated. He had to hold onto the simple truths, Fabius had to die, so that he Adonibaal could live. That was the only truth that mattered.

Despite the darkness in the tunnel he forced himself to start moving faster. His clothes were soaked to the waist now as he splashed through the tunnel swearing as his feet banged into hidden obstacles. Minutes seemed to last for hours and still the tunnel continued. He passed a disused duct which had been blocked up. Then just as he was about to despair of ever finding the river he felt a gentle breeze touch his cheek. No his senses were not playing tricks. The air was becoming less foul. He splashed on holding his arms out in front of him like a blind man feeling his way along the walls. Then as he rounded a bend he noticed a tiny light. He waded towards it breathing hard and cried out in relief. As he drew closer he could make out the low vaulted tunnel exit and the passive waters of the Tiber beyond. The river level was low and reeds partially blocked the sewers path. He paused by the tunnel exit sucking fresh air into his lungs and allowing his breathing to calm. It was night and the sky was filled with bright stars.

The Tiber's current was strong and it took all his remaining energy to swim across to the far bank. He dragged himself ashore and lay panting on his back amongst the reeds. Upstream he could see the torch lights on the Sublicus and Aemilian bridges and he guessed the Cloaca's exit was somewhere between the two bridges for the current had swept him under one of them and deposited him a few hundred yards downstream. Behind him he could make out the dark shape of the Janiculum hill. He lay for a while watching the stars and recovering his strength and as he did so he realised something. He needed to know if Numerius had spoken the truth. The need to know was powerful. If indeed he had a daughter within the city then he needed to find her. He needed to see her, to know if she was indeed his.

"So you wish to bring us together do you, brother", he whispered. Oh Numerius was cunning alright, using the idea that he had a daughter as the bait with which he would trap and capture him. And yet as his eyes closed and he began to drift off to sleep, Adonibaal was aware that the dread of being captured had lost some of its potency.

It was light when he woke with a start. A small cargo ship was drifting by on the Tiber and he could see the helms man on her deck and the graceful row of oars dipping quietly into the water. His hand closed around Centurion and then he swore as he saw his surroundings. He was utterly exposed. He should have moved to a better hiding place during the night when he had the chance. He stared at the bridges upstream. There were armed men on them and as he watched them he saw a patrol of soldiers on the eastern shore inspecting the river bank. Directly across from him was the Emporium, the river docks where the traders loaded and unloaded their goods. Even at this hour it was a hive of activity.

He twisted onto his stomach and glanced up at the Janiculum. The road to Ostia led up the hill disappearing amongst the trees. The hill seemed to remind him of something, he frowned, something important. Something someone had told him. Then he remembered. Hadn't Janus said that his brother had a house up there? For a moment he stared towards the top of the hill. Then he smiled as he had a sudden idea. His brother was about to be out manoeuvred.

He began to crawl through the tall reeds towards the highway. As he drew closer he noticed the numerous grave stones with the names of the dead inscribed on them lining the road. He could see no traffic and as he reached the higher and rockier ground he got up and crouched behind one of the head stones.

A copse of trees higher up the hill caught his attention and he straightened up and half ran, half walked towards them. The trees were clumped together and just behind them was a shallow ditch. He dropped down into it and lay down on his stomach. From his hiding place, he had a clear view of the road leading up from the river. Satisfied he made himself as comfortable as possible and settled down to wait.

It was some time later when he noticed the solitary man coming towards him. There had not been much traffic on the road until then and Adonibaal had struggled to keep his eyes open. However there was something familiar about the distant figure that jolted him out of his slumber. The man had already crossed the bridge and was starting to ascend the hill. Adonibaals sharp eyes widened and he blushed with sudden uncharacteristic nervousness. The figure was that of his brother. Numerius was alone and he would be level with him very soon.

For a moment Adonibaal pondered what to do. His original plan had been to wait for Numerius to come up the road on his way home. He would then follow his brother to see where he lived and then wait until it was dark before breaking into the property and confronting Numerius in the privacy of his own home. His brother would know how to get to Fabius. The two men were friends after all. Now however, as Numerius approached rapidly, he realised that he hadn't expected him to be on his own. Maybe the time to take him was now on this road. Excitedly he peered at the approaching figure. Numerius seemed to be deep in thought, oblivious to his surroundings. He walked with a slight limp and he was unarmed. Not that Adonibaal was worried about that. His brother had never been a match for him when it came to a fight. He made up his mind and readied himself to burst out of the copse. Numerius drew level and Adonibaal was about to rise when he heard a shout and from the corner of his eye saw a man running up the road towards them. Instinctively he froze in his hiding place. Numerius was five yards away and turned to look at the newcomer who had called out his name.

The two men spoke briefly and then started up the hill. From his ditch Adonibaal watched them until they were nearly out of sight. Then silently he rose to his feet and followed. The two men continued up the hill until they came to a villa. As they approached the house Adonibaal could see a slave sitting beside the front door. The man had his hands clasped around his head as if he was in agony. That was odd. Adonibaal crouched beside a large boulder and watched his brother speak to the slave. They were too far away for him to hear their conversation accurately but he noticed how Numerius' shoulders seemed to slump. Then the two men rushed into the house and disappeared. They re-appeared again within a minute heading straight towards the place where Adonibaal was hiding. Adonibaal kept very still as they passed him, heading back towards the city. He caught a glimpse of his brother's face. Puzzled he watched Numerius disappear down the hill. He'd seen that same expression a thousand times before on the faces of his victims in Utica when they'd known they had been caught. It was a dangerous look. It was the look of a man with nothing left to lose.

When his brother had gone Adonibaal turned to look at the villa. He stood up, stretched and started towards the house. The slave had disappeared but the front door was still open. He paused at the entrance and wondered whether he should call out but it was not necessary. The slave had returned and stood looking at him blankly. The man had been crying. Over the man's shoulder he caught a glimpse of smashed and broken furniture and blood stains on the neatly tiled floor.

"Is this the house of Numerius Fabius Vibulani?" Adonibaal asked.

"He is my master," the slave sniffed, "What do you want?"

"What happened here?" Adonibaal gestured towards the broken furniture.

The slave folded his arms across his chest. "Who wishes to know?" he replied guardedly.

Adonibaal fixed his eyes on the man.

"Is your master at home?"

The slave hesitated. "He is not, he just left, if you have come from Rome you would have met him on the road," the man's face suddenly grew suspicious, "Who wishes to know?" he repeated.

"I have come from Ostia," Adonibaal said, "Tell your master that his brother called on him and that he sends his greetings."

The slave suddenly looked unsure of himself. He peered at Adonibaal curiously.

"His brother," he muttered to himself, "I did not know my master had a brother." Then he recovered his composure. "Will you care to wait till my master returns?"

"Yes I shall," Adonibaal said stepping past the slave into the hallway. He stopped and looked down at the blood-stained tiles.

"Maybe now you can tell me what has happened here?" he said glancing around the wrecked room.

The slaves face darkened and his lower lip trembled.

"The master of the house has gone to find his daughter," the man muttered, "We were attacked in the night and they took her away."

"Who attacked you?" Adonibaal turned sharply to look at the man.

"Men who have no respect for the sanctity of a vestal virgin," the slave replied bitterly. He turned away so that Adonibaal would not see his emotion and so he missed seeing the curious glint that had suddenly appeared in Adonibaals eye.

"Forgive my apparent ignorance for I have not seen my brother in many years as you will know," he said smoothly, "but remind me again the date on which our Vestal daughter was born?"

"The sixteenth day of March," the slave whimpered.

"And the year?"

"In the year of the consulship of Centho and Tuditanus."

"Thank you," Adonibaal said as the colour slowly drained from his cheeks.

Chapter Twenty-five – Captive

Pompeia rushed to the doorway of her room as she heard the strangled cry of alarm from the hallway. It was followed moments later by a loud crash and the splintering of glass. It was the middle of the night and she had been asleep. She was still clad in her night clothes, a long flowing white dress that was barely thick enough to hide her body. In the atrium with its small square fountain and fine mosaic floor her father's gardener was grappling with an intruder. Someone screamed. It was the cook's high pitched female voice. Then before she could open her mouth the intruder, a tall man clad entirely in a black tunic stabbed the gardener and pushed him to the ground. More men, also clad in black appeared from the hallway.

"Mistress, hurry, this way," her father's man servant shouted to her from the door leading to the garden. The man beckoned to her urgently but she didn't move. Instead she turned to face the intruders. There were six of them now, all clad in black and they were advancing towards her. She could see the knives in their hands. On the floor the slave lay still as a large pool of dark red blood spilled out onto the mosaic.

"How dare you enter my father's house like this," she cried angrily gathering the folds of her night clothes around her.

The intruders said nothing as they surrounded her. Then a huge man with a pockmarked face and thick protruding lips grasped both of her hands by the wrists forcing them together. Her hands were swiftly bound together with a length of rope.

"Who are you?" Pompeia said without struggling.

The man with the protruding lips sneered. "You are coming with us. The high priest has declared that you are to stand trial."

Pompeia knew it was pointless to resist. The men in black were hired men, probably working for the college of Pontiffs. It didn't matter. They had their orders. She was not surprised. She had been expecting them for some time now and now that they had she felt strangely relieved.

"It is alright," she turned to the man servant who was still standing in the doorway leading to the garden, "Tell my father what has happened and attend to the gardener. He was a brave man. My father should know what he tried to do."

The slave was crying and unable to answer.

"This way," the man with the lip snarled tugging at the rope that bound her hands.

"No," she said firmly, "I will not go to the temple like a common prisoner. Untie my hands and I shall promise not to try and escape."

The leader of the intruders paused as he thought about it.

"Alright, if you promise?" he growled.

She nodded. "And I wish to change my clothes," she said, "If I am to stand trial then I will do so in the robes of a Vestal Virgin."

***

The high priest and his secretary Metellus had been smart to have her arrested in the middle of the night she thought as she was marched into the city. At this hour the streets of Rome were deserted and there was no one about to see what was being done to her. Ever since Metellus had raped her she had known that the priests could not change their minds. She was being used like a sacrificial animal, supposedly to appease the angry gods and grant Rome fortune in battle, but in reality the priests were using her to further their own power. She wanted to laugh. The system was rotten to its core but Vesta would not allow her to die.

Her captors took her to the Regia, an irregular pentagonal complex in the forum just yards from the temple of Vesta. The Regia was the place where the old kings of Rome used to live. Now the spot was the official residence of the Pontifex Maximus, the supreme religious authority. It was here at the Regia that the college of Pontiffs would come to gather. It was here that the college's archives and administrative documents were kept alongside the complicated instructions on how to perform the sacred religious rites and the laws that governed marriage, death and wills. It was the place too where Mars, the god of war had his shrine and where his ceremonial spears were kept. The spears were only ever used when Rome declared war when they would be symbolically hurled onto enemy land. The Regia was a place where few liked to go for it was rumoured that people who entered through its gates had a habit of never being seen again.

The silent procession left the Sacred Way, passing through a covered antechamber whose iron gates swung open for them and into a paved courtyard. Pompeia stared at the grey stone walls that seemed to close in around her. The yard was open to the sky and some twenty yards long and eight deep. Torches burned from iron holders set into the stone walls. Two wells and a cistern had been sunk into the ground and at the far end she could make out the dark shape of the door through which one stepped when visiting the shrine of Mars. Only the high priest and the Vestal Virgins were allowed to enter the shrine and in her time as a Vestal, Pompeia had only once been to the shrine and that had been on the day when Rome had formally declared war on Carthage, some two years ago.

Metellus was waiting for her. He stood with his hands clasped behind his back, the hood of his purple tunic pulled over his head. As she approached him he averted his gaze.

"Why did you allow her to dress and walk freely?" he snapped at the man with the protruding lip.

The man shrugged. "She promised she would not escape."

"That's not the point," Metellus growled, "She has defiled the purity of Rome and she should not be allowed to show the dignity of her office. Lucky for you, that it was night time."

"Look at me Metellus," Pompeia said suddenly but the priest shook his head and kept his eyes averted. "You know that it is forbidden for us to look directly on a Vestal who is accused of breaking her vows," he replied. "Take her clothes and lock her up," he ordered.

***

Pompeia was led into a small room without windows and just a solitary stone bed for comfort. Her Vestal robes were taken from her and she was given a simple white Peplos, a sleeveless dress which was fastened at her shoulders with two large pins and had a belt around her stomach. Then she was left alone. She sat on the stone bed. She should be afraid she thought. It had been nearly a hundred years since the last Vestal had been buried alive beneath the cattle market but the rituals leading up to her death were well known. She would be condemned and then allowed to lower herself into the underground room which would become her tomb. A small quantity of food and water would be placed in the room and then the cavern would be quickly covered over and blocked up until no trace of her remained. The food and water were meant to keep her alive for a few days so that the priests could claim they had not actually executed her. Her death would be left for Vesta, as final judge, to decide. If Vesta decided the Vestal was innocent she would be resurrected and allowed to rise from her tomb. But no Vestal had ever risen from her tomb.

She slipped off the bed and knelt on the ground and quietly prayed to Vesta. The goddess was wise and merciful. She would not let her servant die and the more she prayed the calmer she began to feel.

She was half asleep when her first visitor arrived. She heard him shuffling outside her door and then the bolts were undone and a young nervous and distracted looking man was shown in. He bowed but did not move beyond the doorway.

"Yes," she said rising to her feet and straightening her dress. "I have been instructed to represent you at your trial," the young man declared avoiding her gaze.

"You are a lawyer?" she asked.

He nodded looking uncomfortable. Pompeia stared at him and then laughed but it was laughter devoid of any joy. It was clear that the man didn't want to be here. In all probability, he had been told he had no choice. The law still required her to have a defence even though the outcome of the trial had already effectively been decided.

"Do you wish to take my case?" she said with a sigh.

The lawyer hesitated and lowered his eyes to the ground.

"Do not worry," she said, "I do not require your services. I shall be defending myself. You may go."

The lawyer bowed his head and then with a look of relief he left the room.

Her second visitor came an hour later. It was Floronia. The young Vestal bowed politely as she came in and placed a tray of food and a small jug of water at Pompeia' feet. She looked nervous and tense but as she stepped back into the doorway she hissed a single word.

"Whore."

Before Pompeia could reply she had vanished.

Pompeia was not aware of time passing. The small room grew hotter and hotter until it was a stifling oven. She ate a little of the food that Floronia had brought and dipped her fingers into the jug of water before wiping her face in an effort to cool herself. The venom in Floronia' voice had caught her by surprise and saddened her. How quickly her friends seemed to have deserted her she thought. How quick people were to show their true colours when put under such pressure.

Her third visitor came a few hours later. Pompeia rose as she heard the bolts being undone wondering who was coming. It was her matron, the head Vestal. The old woman bowed graciously and opened her arms and touched Pompeia gently on the shoulders.

"My child, they have taken your robes," she said with a kind, compassionate voice.

Pompeia bowed respectfully and lowered her eyes. "Thank you for coming," she replied.

The matron nodded and glanced around the room.

"I have spoken with our father and they are going to put you on trial tomorrow at dawn. I have come to pray with you, kneel with me now child."

Pompeia did as she was asked and for a few moments the two of them knelt on the floor as the matron offered her prayer to Vesta.

"I did not do the things they accuse me of," Pompeia whispered when they were finished. "You do believe me, don't you?"

"I don't know what to believe child," the matron replied. Our father says that you have cavorted with this priest, this Cantilius."

"It's a lie," Pompeia whispered fiercely, "They are lying. You know what Metellus did to me in our home. You were there."

The matron swallowed nervously and nodded. "I shall keep praying for you child," she muttered.

The final visitor was Julia, the 12-year-old Vestal. Pompeia's face brightened up as she saw who it was. As the young girl came in tears appeared in her eyes and she rushed forwards flinging her arms around her older sister. Pompeia felt a tear begin to burn behind her eyes too but she forced herself to keep her composure. She did not want the young girl to grow more upset than she already was.

"It's so nice of you to come," she said as she held the young girl close.

She felt Julia shake as she cried.

"It's not fair, it's not fair," Julia sobbed.

Chapter Twenty-six – Revelations

Adonibaal wandered slowly through his brother's house as if he owned the place. Numerius' villa was modest and he'd learned that there were just three household slaves. In addition to his brother's personal servant who'd let him in there was a female cook and her assistant, a boy. The cook and her assistant were away buying food and would return at night fall. Adonibaal was pleased. None of them were a physical threat to him. All he had to do was wait for Numerius to return. There had been a fourth slave, the gardener but the man had been killed when the priests had come to take away Numerius's daughter. It was his blood that Adonibaal had seen on the tiled floor.

The servant had asked him to wait in the room specially designed for this purpose but he'd ignored the slave. It was curiosity of course. He wanted to know how his brother had lived all these years. He wanted to understand what sort of man Numerius had become. He entered the master bedroom. Numerius' bed was a simple couch covered with a couple of blankets and on the ground stood a bowl of half eaten broth. Adonibaal picked it up and sniffed. Fish soup, his brother's favourite. He smiled and placed the bowl back on the ground. The bedroom was a disappointment, there was nothing personal in this room and he stepped back into the Atrium. Through the hallway he could see the slave on his hands and knees scrubbing away with a cloth at the blood-stained tiles.

His attention was suddenly drawn to a closed door. All the rooms were open, all except this one. He crossed the Atrium and noticed that the key had been left in the lock. That was careless brother he thought. He opened the door and stepped into the room and gasped in shock.

Staring down at him from their alcoves were the faces of his ancestors.

For a moment Adonibaal was rooted to the floor. He felt the blood rush to his cheeks as he stared back at the long line of death masks. It had been such a long time since he had last seen them. Yes, they were all here, all fifteen…He stopped. There weren't fifteen, there were sixteen. Right at the end of the row, his father's face stared down at him. Adonibaal flinched instinctively, unable to look away as a torrent of memories came flooding back. He jutted out his chin and took a step towards his father's death mask as if challenging him to speak but the room remained silent.

"Ha," he said contemptuously.

Beyond his father's mask was one further alcove and this one was empty. Adonibaal looked away quickly as if suddenly ashamed. He was in a study. At the far end was a large desk and a chair and behind that a book shelf filled with books and papers.

Ignoring the mask's he strode over to the desk and looked at the book shelf. The books were mainly Legal texts but in between them were a couple of histories and a geography book. He took one of the papers from the shelf. It was a trial summary and strategy paper. He looked up.

"You are a lawyer," he muttered.

He placed the paper back on the shelf and sat down in the chair from where he could watch the doorway. The chair was comfortable. He stroked his chin as he tried to imagine Numerius sitting here whilst working on his cases. A modest comfortable house, a steady but hardly spectacular job, small staff and a quiet location outside the city he mused. Hardly the lifestyle that their father had prepared them for.

Idly he glanced at a pile of papers on the desk. They looked like letters from Senators, clients etc. As he disturbed the papers something fell of the desk and landed on the floor with a dull metallic ring. He bent forwards and picked it up and as he saw what it was he grunted in surprise. In his hand he held a small brooch but this was no ordinary brooch, it was a Phaleri, a military award. His military award! He stared at the brooch in amazement. It was the award he had won during the sea battle that had ended the first war with Carthage. He'd thought he'd lost it years ago but his brother seemed to have kept it. He shook his head and slipped the award into his pocket. Why would Numerius have kept his Phaleri?

"My master does not permit anyone to enter his study," a voice said from the doorway.

Adonibaal looked up to see the slave standing in the doorway. There was a disapproving look on the man's face.

"Is that so," Adonibaal said from behind the desk.

The slave nodded and waited for him to move but when Adonibaal made no effort to leave the servants face darkened but he said nothing as he turned abruptly on his heels and left the room.

Adonibaal sniggered and unsheathed Centurion and placed the blade on the desk beside the papers. Then he pushed his chair back and lifted his feet up onto the desk so that his sandals were facing the doorway. From the Atrium he caught a glimpse of the slave watching him.

"When do you expect my brother to return home?" he cried in a loud voice.

"I do not know," the slave answered from the Atrium.

Adonibaal sighed. He would sit here and wait for Numerius and when he came home he would know the reason why his brother had betrayed him all those years ago. And then what would he do? Would he kill him? He took the Phaleri from his pocket and examined it again. Why would Numerius have kept his award? It meant nothing to him.

"Why did the priests take our daughter?" he shouted.

There was no immediate reply from the Atrium and Adonibaal had to repeat himself before the slave answered.

"She is a vestal virgin," the slave's sour answer came back.

"There is only one reason for them to take a Vestal."

Adonibaal frowned. "Does she visit my brother often?"

"When she can," the slave's voice sounded reluctant.

Adonibaal looked thoughtful. Could it really be true? He'd acted on instinct when he'd asked about Numerius' daughter's birthday and year but the answer had thrown him. Pompeia had been born on the same day and in the same year as Flavia had died. The woman had to have been adopted for Numerius had never had a woman when he'd still been in Rome. He sighed. A coincidence perhaps but he didn't believe it. Nervously he tapped his fingers on the desk. Pompeia had to be his daughter. That was what Numerius had been trying to tell him.

He lifted his feet off the desk and turned his attention back to the bookshelf. On the top shelf were two small jars he hadn't noticed before. He took them down and sniffed the contents. They smelt like medicines.

"Is my brother ill?" he called out puzzled.

There was a long pause from the doorway. Then suddenly the slave was standing there looking confused.

"My master has Malaria. He is dying. I thought that was the reason why you had come to visit him?"

Adonibaal stared at the slave in utter surprise. Then he just shook his head and gestured for him to leave but the man didn't move and as he stood staring at Adonibaal the slaves face grew more and more suspicious.

325

"I asked you to leave." Adonibaal snarled.

The slave's expression turned hostile and he glanced at Centurion on the desk. Then without another word he vanished.

Adonibaal was vaguely aware that he would have to do something about the servant before he raised the alarm but he was still in too much shock to give it any thought. His brother was dying. Well that was news he had not expected. Had Numerius known for long? Then he had a strange thought. Was that why his brother had told him about Pompeia? He looked down at the Phaleri on the desk. His brother was trying to reach out to him. These things, he thought struggling in sudden confusion, were the actions of a man who still loved him. Unsteadily he leaned back against the book shelf and stared at the opposite wall. His brother wanted forgiveness.

He heard the noise of the front door opening. Then an urgent and emotional female voice cried out to her colleague. It was the cook returning from her errand.

"She's going to be put on public trial tomorrow in the Forum," the woman cried. "The master has gone to Fabius' house to plead with him. They say that Fabius is going to defend her."

Chapter Twenty-seven - Trial

They came for her at dawn. Pompeia had spent the night in prayer. She had asked the goddess to protect her father and her sisters. She had prayed for Cantilius and for justice and now as the footsteps of the guards approached she knew she was ready. They led her out into the courtyard of the Regia. It was a beautiful morning with a clear blue sky and a bright sun. She glanced up as a flock of birds rose noisily from the rooftops. Her guards said nothing. Their faces looked like they were made of stone. The college of Pontiffs were going to give her a public trial. Her crimes were not against a person but against the state. Metellus would be acting as the prosecutor the matron had told her and the judge would be the Pontifex Maximus.

They led her out through the iron gates and into the forum and they did so Pompeia gasped in astonishment. A vast crowd had gathered. There had to be thousands of people crammed into the forum. As she came into view a hush spread like a ripple through the crowds as eyes and heads turned and craned expectantly trying to get a glimpse of her. A narrow pathway had been kept open and priests armed with spears and shields stood along it at short intervals, facing the crowd. And amongst the crowd she noticed for the first time, were women. Had the restrictions on their movement been relaxed? A few men at the front of the crowd called out insulting her, but she refused to look at them. They would be hired men, hired by the priests to try and upset and rattle her. But here and there amongst the multitude she noticed a head bow in respect as she passed by.

A rectangular space had been cleared in the forum where normally the market traders would have had their stalls. Metellus flanked by his fellow priests sat upon a raised platform and to one side, by himself, sat the high priest, clad in a toga with a purple border that partially covered his head. Pompeia felt her heart sink. She had known him and every one of these men for years but today she knew she didn't have a single friend amongst them. Behind the priests Rome's wealthier citizens had gathered and to her right clustered around her matron were the five remaining Vestals. Her sisters stared at her, Aurinia with pity, Floronia and Opimia with tense hostility, Julia with sadness and Musa with curiosity. Her matron looked stern and disapproving. Pompeia glanced beyond her towards the crowds. The people were watching her intently, some were crying, others looked fearful, tight lipped and yet others scowled angrily. Her immorality and lack of virtue were to blame for the catastrophe of Cannae. It was her behaviour that had sent their sons and fathers to their deaths. She knew what they were thinking. A tense religious hysteria had spread throughout the city and as she began to understand the mood she felt her own spirits sink. They would never acquit her, not in a city which desperately needed reassuring that the gods had not abandoned them.

As she approached, the priests acting as one body averted their eyes and refused to look at her. She halted before the raised platform and the crowd seemed to hold its breath. It had been over a hundred and fifty years since the last Vestal had stood trial. At last Metellus rose to his feet, turned and waited for the high priest to signal the start of the trial.

Metellus began with a prayer to the gods. It was an ancient ritual and as he carefully pronounced the archaic words the crowds fell into an expectant hush. Pompeia stood before the raised platform, with bowed head. A cool breeze played with her long curly hair. When Metellus finished speaking the vast expectant crowds remained silent.

"What are the charges?" the high priest said gravely.

"Incest," Metellus cried in a loud voice, "We charge this woman with Incest."

There was a groan of dismay from the crowd. Their worst fears had been confirmed. As the Vestals were considered to be married to Rome any relations with its citizens was judged as incest. Metellus was about to continue when there was a disturbance. The crowd closest to Pompeia suddenly bulged outwards pressing up against the shields of the guards. In the midst of the disturbance a man appeared struggling towards the front and as he reached the line of guards an angry muttering rose up from the ranks of Patricians assembled behind the high priest. Some of the younger and bolder nobles jumped to their feet and shouted at the Praetor, the magistrate in charge of public order, gesturing towards the newcomer.

"Arrest that man." they cried.

Pompeia gasped as she saw the man who seemed to have caused the disturbance. It was her father. He looked agitated and there was wildness about him as he pushed his way through the crowd. He was searching for her she realised but it wasn't until he finally saw her that he seemed to calm down. As their eyes locked she felt the stir of some deep emotion. In that moment, she felt an overwhelming sadness for him, he looked so vulnerable and so alone amongst the hostile crowd, so exposed and in such danger and yet he had come to be with her. In that moment, it was as if they were united, two people sharing the same predicament, the same fate. He smiled sadly as he held her gaze and there was a knowing sparkle in his eye that nearly brought tears into her eyes. Across the divide and through the wall of shields she felt him reach out and suddenly she knew she was no longer afraid.

The Patricians were still shouting at the Praetor. The magistrate had begun to look distinctly uncomfortable but he didn't move and his predicament was only relieved by the booming voice of the high priest.

"Silence," the high priest roared rising to his feet.

Slowly the crowd settled back down and the Patricians reluctantly returned to their seats but the bad-tempered muttering would not entirely die down. Then Metellus' voice cut once more across the forum.

"The gods declare this vestal to be impure," he cried, "They have provided us with inescapable proof. This woman has allowed her impurity to infect our city and has brought down the wrath of the gods. This is what the Augurs tell us. This is what they have seen."

Metellus watched the crowds allowing his words to linger.

"These are terrible accusations," the high priest said gravely and then turning to Pompeia but without looking at her he spoke again. "What do you say to these charges? Well, are you still a virgin?"

Pompeia sensed the bitter delight in the priest's voice as if the man knew he had her cornered and knew that she knew it too.

"I have chosen to serve Rome," Pompeia' voice was strong as she turned to address the crowd and not the priests. "The welfare of our city is my only concern. I ask you to believe your eyes and your hearts and not the words of men who are wrong. You all know me. You have seen me on your streets. I am still the purest of the maidens of Rome. My love for this city is in my blood and whoever or whatever you think I am, I know this to be the inalienable truth. I shall not lie to you today. I shall love this city and always work for its people whatever verdict you decide upon. That is the only truth that will be spoken today."

"Answer the question," Metellus cried. "Are you still a Virgin?"

"I was until I was raped."

As she spoke a cry of disbelieve and anguish rose from the crowds but it was not in sympathy for her, it was the shock of hearing that the priests had been right. The people were fickle, she knew, they would care only for the health of the city.

The high priest raised his eyebrows and for a fleeting moment Pompeia gained the impression that the man had been surprised. Could it be that he didn't know what Metellus had done?

"Who raped you?" the high priest frowned.

Silently Pompeia raised her arm and pointed a solitary accusing finger at Metellus. Her action caused the court to erupt. Some of the priests jumped to their feet shouting angrily and waving their fists whilst from the crowds someone hurled a half-eaten apple at her. Slander one of the Patricians roared. Metellus just smiled and raised his hands for silence.

"Calm yourselves," he cried, "Can you not see that these are the words of a desperate woman. But what do you expect from such a creature, entrusted with the purity of Rome as she was, who has allowed her virtue to be taken so easily. This woman will say anything to escape her punishment. Look how easily she lies, how she wishes to accuse her accusers but the facts remain unaltered. Her guilt is confirmed. She admits that she has broken her vows."

But Pompeia stood her ground, her finger pointing resolutely towards Metellus and as the seconds passed and she didn't lower her arm the crowds began to mutter.

"No, I shall now tell you what really happened," Metellus shouted ignoring the accusing finger, "There was no rape and she did not perform a miracle."

One of the priests handed him a sieve similar to that which Pompeia had carried through the streets of Rome. Metellus held it high above his head so that all had a clear view.

"Filled with glue to prevent the water from running away," he shouted. "See how she mocks you all."

There was a surge of anguish from the crowds.

"But she did have a lover and he has confessed," Metellus continued. "Bring him here so that all can hear him."

A few moments later the badly beaten figure of Cantillius was dragged up to the front of the platform by two guards. The young man trembled, swaying on his feet and he looked terrified.

"Is this the man?" the high priest said.

Metellus nodded. On his platform, he seemed to tower above the trembling boy like some great shadow. Metellus looked down at Cantillius and as he spoke his voice was contemptuous.

"Tell this court how you defiled this Vestal," he ordered.
Cantillius stared up at the high priest and then suddenly he fell to his knees weeping and clawing at the paving stones.

"Forgive me father," he cried, "Forgive me for what I have done. It was madness."

"Get up boy and answer the question," the high priest retorted irritably.

Slowly Cantillius rose to his feet.

"I would meet her in the shrine to Terminus. She told me she wanted to have a baby. She seduced me in the shrine. The affair went on more than a year."

As he spoke a mutter of horror and disapproval spread through the crowd.

"How many times did she press herself upon you?" Metellus snapped as his dark eyes flashed triumphantly.

"Many times," Cantillius replied lowering his head.

A howl of outrage erupted from the crowd and the high priest shook his head in disgust. "Shame, you shame us," he growled. Then he rose to his feet and stepped off the platform. The high priest slowly circled the weeping young man who knelt before the court and as he did so a slave handed him a coiled whip.

"You have admitted your guilt," the Pontifex Maximus hissed,

"Your punishment is to be flogged to death," and with that he personally raised the whip and stepped back.

"No." Cantillius yelled as his head shot upwards in shock and he stared wild eyed at the high priest, "You promised..."

But his words ended in a high-pitched scream as the whip caught him across the face opening up an ugly red line across his cheeks.

"Cantillius," Pompeia cried suddenly, "I know what they have done to you. I know what they have told you to say, I know you are a brave man, show them you do not fear death. Tell us the truth. Do not go to the next world as a liar."

The whip cracked once more followed by another scream of pain.

Then as the high priest raised the whip for a third strike Cantillius staggered to his feet. His face and chest were bleeding heavily and one of his eyes was completely closed and yet he managed to half turn and look at her and in that split second she saw his deep haunting shame.

"Forgive me," he shouted raising his hand to try and protect his face, "Stop, the Vestal speaks the truth. I have lied."

The whip came in fast and furious and caught him across the chest spinning him around on his feet and yet Cantillius managed to stay upright. "I lied," he cried spitting blood from his mouth. He raised both his hands towards the sky as if imploring the gods and sank onto his knees as the whip struck faster and faster cutting and lashing his body to bloody pulp but despite the frenzy of the whipping his voice still managed to break free.

"She is still a virgin. I did not touch her. It was the other two, Floronia and Opimia, they came to me in the shrine. I defiled them both."

As Cantillius spoke those words the high priest, his face contorted with rage, hesitated in surprise, the crowds gasped, the matron rose to her feet, Floronia' face turned a deep red and Opimia fainted.

"What?" Metellus stuttered looking confused. The forum held its breath as all eyes turned slowly to look at the Vestals clustered around their matron. Then before anyone could speak the whip lashed out once more through the air and the force of its blow sent Cantillius tumbling to the ground.

"Lies," Metellus shouted staring at Cantillius' bloodied corpse,

"You all heard him. He confessed. He cannot change his mind now," but somehow Metellus' voice lacked its usual conviction.

"No, he speaks the truth," a woman's voice suddenly cried. "I have known it for some time."

Pompeia turned to see her matron. The old woman was still on her feet and staring defiantly at the priests on their raised platform.

"Silence," the high priest bellowed wiping the sweat from his face, "You do not have the right to speak."

But the matron did not back down. Stubbornly she thrust her chin outwards. "Pompeia is one of mine," she cried, "I will not idly stand by whilst she is falsely accused. Vesta has spoken to me. She has told me the truth. You are accusing the wrong woman."

"Nonsense," Metellus shouted but as he did he glanced at the crowds in surprise for suddenly voices could be heard; voices that were raised against him. The murmurs grew louder and Pompeia suddenly realised they were coming from the women in the crowd. Then the storm erupted and a single lower class woman's voice drifted across the forum.

"Listen to the goddess."

The shout was speedily picked up by the crowd. Metellus blushed and raised his hand for silence but the crowd ignored him. The Patricians gathered behind the platform began to cast nervous looks around them as they sensed the beginnings of a riot.

"Pompeia speaks the truth," the matron's voice seemed to rise above the tumult, "She was raped. I know because I was there."

"Shut up you stupid woman," Metellus hissed.

The high priest had begun to look alarmed. He glanced at Metellus who was trying to silence the crowd.

"Impossible. Do you have proof?" he asked lamely.

"Do I have proof?" the matron's voice came close to mocking him, "What proof can I offer but my own word as a witness that it is the truth."

"She lies Sir," Metellus shouted, "This is slander. I will not stand for this."

"Sit down Metellus," the high priest roared.

It was Pompeia who brought the court to order. For a moment she stared at Cantillius' broken and bloodied corpse. Then she half turned to look at her two sisters. Floronia' face was still a deep red and she looked in shock. The girl refused to look at her. Opimia was being helped up onto her feet. She should have suspected it Pompeia thought as she remembered Cantillius' comments about the two girls the last time they had met in the shrine to Terminus. It explained their hostility. It explained why they had been so competitive with her. They had all fallen for the same man. She felt a deep sadness. The girls were still so young and naive. They must have been unable to cope with their bodies natural desires. The discipline of being a vestal was tough for it prohibited so many earthly pleasures but over time a woman could get used to the regime. Perhaps Floronia and Opimia had not had enough time to learn the real value and happiness that could be found from serving the goddess.

"Vesta has spoken," she cried in a stern voice, "Hear her words and praise her wisdom," and as she spoke Pompeia knew that she had broken the bond with her sisters. A tear appeared in her eye.

The high priest had retreated to his chair. Metellus had ignored his master and was still on his feet. The crowds beyond the line of guards grew more and more restless as they waited for the verdict.

"Well?" a dozen or more voices cried from the crowd.

Metellus turned to the high priest with an almost pleading look that slowly grew in alarm. The Pontifex Maximus waved his hand in irritation.

"Acquitted," he muttered.

The crowd yelled that they had not heard him.

"Acquitted, the charges are dropped," the high priest shouted.

***

Pompeia bowed her head as she heard the verdict. Her relief was tempered by the sight of Cantillius' bloodied body and the knowledge of what now awaited her two sisters but she had little time to dwell upon their fate. The priests and the Patricians who had remained behind were in a state of uproar and confusion. Metellus stood on the platform looking lost as if he still couldn't understand how he had managed to lose the case. The high priest had sunk deep into his chair and was stroking his chin and staring moodily into space. His prestige had taken a serious blow she thought but it was his own fault for trusting his secretary. There would be repercussions for Metellus now and as the knowledge of that brought a faint smile to her lips it was as if Metellus had read her mind for suddenly he jumped down from the stage and advanced towards her with menacing strides.

"You bitch," he cried.

Then his path was blocked. The man seemed to come out of nowhere and suddenly the point of a Gladius was hovering over the priest's throat. Metellus lurched to a halt, looked down at the metal and then up at the man who threatened him.

"Are you the man who raped her?" Numerius said.

Metellus stumbled back in surprise as he recognised Numerius. Then he regained his composure.

"Careful old man," he snarled, "if you lay one finger on me you will die."

"I am not afraid of death but I think you are," Numerius said and with a speed that took everyone by surprise he slashed the priests cheeks with the point of the sword. Metellus cried out more in shock than pain and fell over backwards onto his arse. A line of dark red blood appeared across his cheek. He looked up at Numerius with growing horror.

"Did you rape her?" Numerius shouted raising his sword.

Pompeia was aware of a commotion. A party of patricians and priests were rushing to Metellus' aid. Some of them were armed and others were calling out to the Praetor to have his men arrest her father. It was spiteful. Just because they couldn't have her they were going to take her father instead. The crowd gaped in astonishment at the speed of the turn of events. No one had expected a fight to break out but now that it had their surprise quickly turned to feverish excitement.

"Father," Pompeia cried out in warning.

Numerius however had already seen the men rushing towards him for he stepped backwards to shield her with his body.

"Titus," he cried.

"Here Sir," a man's voice spoke from behind her. She jumped for she had not heard the stranger approach. The young man was holding a sword. "I've got your back," he said watching the approaching men.

Metellus had risen to his feet as his colleagues reached him. The priests were unarmed but the Patricians were holding knives and clubs. Hostile faces stared at Numerius and Pompeia could see the dark malice, hatred and spite in their eyes as the men spread out to surround her father. She didn't understand the reason for their hostility and she didn't care. Her father had been the only one who had been with her from the beginning, the only one who had never doubted her innocence.

"How is Milo?" Numerius called out to the men closing in around him, "Does your pimp master miss his eye?"

"Milo died this morning from his wounds," Metellus screeched regaining his confidence now that his colleagues had come to his aid. "You will stand trial for his murder. Praetor, for the final time, will you do your duty and have this man arrested or must we do it ourselves?"

The Praetor clad in the military uniform of a Tribune swallowed nervously. He glanced towards the high priest for support and guidance but the supreme religious authority chose to look away.

"Very well then," the magistrate shouted. "Lay down your arms Numerius. Spilling blood here today will do no one any good. You are under arrest for the murder of a fellow citizen. Seize him," he ordered.

As the Praetor's men stepped forwards to take their prisoner a solitary trumpet cut across the forum.

"Make way for the dictator Marcus Junius Pera," a deep voice commanded.

The crowd parted abruptly and twelve Lictors, clad in white togas and holding the symbols of their office marched into view. They were followed by the dictator on foot and then another twelve Lictors. Bringing up the rear was a full company of heavily armoured soldiers led by a Centurion. The crowd backed away as the heavy synchronised tramp of the soldier's boots reverberated through the forum.

No one moved as the dictator's men slowly filed into the open space and took up defensive positions around Numerius, Titus and Pompeia. The men sent to arrest Numerius glanced at their leader but the poor magistrate had gone red in the face and could not speak. The two camps faced each other across the forum. On one side the priests and the Patrician nobles gathered around Metellus whilst facing them were the governments stony faced and disciplined soldiers. The stand off lengthened without a word being spoken and as it did so the tension in the forum started to mount. At the fringes of the crowd people began to move away as they sensed the coming violence. It was a trickle at first but soon the crowds were in full flight, scattering in every direction as fast as they could. The fear of violence had proved too much even for those who had begun to relish the contest of power. The two parties however stayed put, confronting each other as all around them the crowd fled.

Pompeia was suddenly acutely aware that one false move could lead to a blood bath. She glanced at the Praetor, the man's whose responsibility it was to maintain public order and saw that he didn't know what to do. Behind the bands of priests and Patricians the high priests chair stood abandoned. There was no sign of the Pontifex Maximus. The coward had fled she thought with sudden disgust. As she stared at the empty chair she noticed that Metellus' party were being reinforced by a steady flow of armed men coming out of the side streets. It was as if the whole city was being sucked into the confrontation.

Before anyone could stop her she boldly stepped beyond the front line of soldiers.

"Men of Rome," she cried looking across at the opposing party, "Will you really strike against your elected magistrate? I do not think you will. Go home in peace and put away your weapons. Go home."

She stared at the closed ranks of her opponents and saw amongst them the faces of hard, tough and spiteful men but she didn't flinch. Instead she walked up to their front rank and as she approached the men parted to let her pass. She walked on into their midst and stopped, turning in a circle as all around men turned to look at her.

"Go home, the business for the day is finished," she said calmly.

The priests and patricians seemed unable to speak. Whether it was her courage or her status as a Vestal, whom no man was allowed to touch that persuaded them she didn't know but slowly the men started to disperse across the forum. Pompeia watched them go until she heard a noise behind her. Turning she saw the whole company of soldiers had begun to rhythmically bang their spears onto their shields.

"They are honouring you," the young man whom her father had called Titus said stepping up to her with a look of awe.

"Why would they do that?" she muttered.

"They are soldier's lady and they don't like killing their own people. Your words prevented bloodshed," the young man said.

Chapter Twenty-eight - Endgame

Some of the crowd had returned as Pompeia was escorted back to the house of the Vestals. They stood along the edge of the Sacred Way trying to get a glimpse of her. Some threw flowers onto the pavement ahead of where she was walking but most just watched with curiosity. She had reached the closed gates of the Regia when a hand from the crowd suddenly grabbed her arm. The action nearly jolted her off her feet. The hand's grip was tight and powerful and did not let go. She looked up into the dark eyes of a man. He was tall and well built with a white scar across his arm but as she made eye contact the strangest sensation seemed to come over her. It tingled all the way down her spine and made her shiver. There was something infinitely tragic about the way the man looked at her. As if he had known her all her life but that was impossible, she had never seen him before.

"Meet me by the Temple of Diane at midnight tomorrow," the man gasped.

She stared at him in confusion.

One of her escorts angrily advanced to her aid.

"I am your father," the man said. Then before she could reply he had vanished into the crowd.

***

Adonibaal stood on his brother's terrace looking down on the city of Rome. The city shimmered in the late afternoon heat. It

345

was a fine view he had to admit. His brother would have bought the house for this view. He could imagine Numerius relaxing and enjoying his retirement here. On this terrace, he would have entertained his guests, held parties and given advice to his clients. Yes, he could see how his brother would have enjoyed life up here.

He'd built himself a happy home, a modest, comfortable but useless and insignificant existence. The man who lived in this house had done nothing of any greatness. His brother had brought no glory to the family. He seemed to have hidden away behind obscurity and led a quiet, simple life. What a waste, Adonibaal thought. Who would remember his brother after he had gone? If he Adonibaal had remained in Rome, he would not have hidden away like this.

He would have made his ancestors proud. Glory, fame and greatness ran in the family. He would have made a far better heir to that tradition than his brother. But once Fabius was dead he mused everything would be as it should have been all those years ago. Hannibal would advance on the city and Adonibaal would collect his reward.

Adonibaal stirred from his thoughts as the man servant brought him the jug of wine he'd asked for. The slave said nothing and avoided his gaze with a sullen look. Adonibaal ignored him. He'd decided to let the man live. The slave may have his suspicions but he wanted his brother to know he'd been here. He wanted Numerius to know that he'd rifled through his most private of rooms.

Numerius however was not coming home today. He sensed it. Something had kept him in town. He would have to change his plans he thought. He raised the jug to his lips and took a swig. Some of the red wine ran down the sides of his mouth and onto his chin. If Numerius was seeking forgiveness it was a sign of weakness. Adonibaal was not ready to forgive his brother for betraying him all those years ago. If they thought he'd given up trying to kill Fabius then they were fools. He knew where Fabius was going to be thanks to the information that the cook had supplied. He sighed as he pondered the risk. Once, years ago in Utica, he had killed a fugitive and four of the man's guards in a direct surprise assault. It could be done if one chose the right moment and the right location.

***

The guards at the Trigemina gate were talking to the wagon driver. Adonibaal could hear them from his hiding place deep within the pile of hay which the wagon was carrying. It was night. He'd waited till it was dark before leaving Numerius' house. Wagon traffic was always heavy during the night for wagons were forbidden from entering Rome during daytime on account of the traffic congestion they caused. He'd spotted the lone driver on the road from Ostia and when the man had stopped to urinate in a field he'd slipped onto the wagon and hidden himself under the hay. Now he held his breath as the driver and guards conversed.

"Got to check your wagon I'm afraid," a voice said.

A moment later a spear point missed Adonibaal's head by inches. He could hear a man's laboured breathing close by and he tensed for the next thrust but none came.

"Be on your way then," a voice called out and the wagon started rolling forwards again. Adonibaal slowly relaxed his grip on Centurion and gently breathed out. The clatter of the wagon wheels on the paving stones told him that they had entered the city of Rome. He'd forgotten how noisy Rome could be at night. The clatter of wagon wheels on paving stones, the mewing of oxen and the cries of the drivers filled his ears. Then judging that he was approaching the cattle market, Adonibaal rose from his hiding place sending straw and hay tumbling onto the street. The driver cried out in sudden fright at the sight of the dark figure but before he could do anything else Adonibaal had leapt from the wagon and had vanished into the night.

***

It was starting to grow light when Adonibaal slipped up the steep staircase that led to the crest of the Palatine hill. He halted half way up the stairs as he reached the place which days earlier, when he'd done his initial reconnaissance, he had identified as a potential killing zone. He grunted in satisfaction as he noticed the short, narrow step to the door of the house and the bushes that shielded it. No one could see him from above or below if he waited on the doorstep. If Fabius decided to take this route from his house to the forum then the killing would take place here. He glanced down the stairs which he'd just climbed. The staircase was narrow and would force a party of men to climb it in single file. Fabius would come with bodyguards. He would have to let the first couple pass him, then kill them when they were moving up the stairs and their backs were turned before turning and killing Fabius. If he could do all that then at least he would have the advantage of the high ground against the guards who were bringing up the rear. The plan gave him a chance but it all depended on Fabius and the arrangements he'd made for his security and of those arrangements Adonibaal knew nothing.

He inspected the killing ground for a final time and then started down the stairs. It was time for him to make his way to the forum. Once Fabius showed up he would have a clearer idea of how many men were protecting him and their capabilities.

Dawn had turned into a beautiful morning with a clear blue sky. Adonibaal joined the multitude of people heading towards the forum. In the crowd he would be relatively safe from the watchers he knew would be out there looking for him. In the forum a vast mass of onlookers had gathered and he had to struggle to get a good vantage point of the judges. The crowd was tense and expectant and amongst them he noticed were women many of them dressed in black head scarves and dresses. As he waited for the trial to begin he suddenly felt nervous. What would she look like? What had Numerius told her about him? Did she even know that he was her father? He doubted she knew the truth. They would have lied to her like they had lied to him.

A hush rippled through the crowds as the she was finally brought out. Adonibaal craned his neck to get a glimpse of her. He was too far back to see her properly but noticed how she walked with a dignified step. Then he blushed with sudden emotion. His girl, they were putting his daughter on trial, he should have felt something, he should have wanted to stop the proceedings and rescue her but he felt nothing. With a shock he realised that the girl meant nothing to him. He didn't know her.

Adonibaal glanced at the judge and the prosecutor. Where was Fabius? The old man had not appeared. He frowned with sudden concern. Had he been misinformed? But he had clearly heard the cook in Numerius' house saying that he would be at the trial. He glanced at his daughter. Her back was turned to him and he could not see her face. Was she going to defend herself then? He hesitated in confusion.

The priests had begun to open the trial when there was a commotion in the crowd close to him. Adonibaal felt the press of bodies around him grow tighter and heard a few raised angry voices. Then the hairs on his neck stood up in sudden sheer horror. Just a few paces away from him, the man who had caused the commotion was forcing his way through the crowd. Adonibaal stared at him unable to look away. It was Numerius. There was fierceness and determination on his brother's face that he'd never seen before. Numerius however had not noticed him and after a moment Adonibaal started to breath again. His brother wasn't after him. He had come to be with her.

Recovering his poise, he glanced around. There was still no sign of Fabius. If the man was to act for the defence he should have been here by now. He's not coming Adonibaal thought with sudden insight. For some reason the old man was not coming. A wave of disappointment came crashing over him and his shoulders sagged in defeat. It was perplexing. Why had Fabius decided to stay away? He was the best hope the defence had.

Adonibaal stayed to watch the trial and as he did so he noticed the way in which Pompeia and Numerius acted and supported each other, one calm and composed the other fierce and emotional and slowly it dawned on him that even though they were not related by blood Numerius loved her more than he ever could. Numerius would always be her true father and the knowledge dispirited him even further until he felt utterly low and miserable. Would they leave him nothing which he could call his own?

***

Adonibaal fled from the forum after the judge had delivered his verdict. The only bright spot in the depressing black mood that was enveloping him was his happiness that Pompeia had been acquitted. He hadn't expected to feel like that about her but he had. Remorselessly however the black mood drove him away, despair mingled with a sense of hopelessness. His plan to kill Fabius was in tatters once again. Something strange was going on. Why had Fabius decided to stay away from the trial? But overshadowing all this and bearing down on him like the full weight of a horse was the knowledge that he'd discovered he had a daughter, only to learn that the girl would never love him like she did Numerius. But he was happy she was acquitted. Flavia would be happy too he thought. But his daughter's survival had nothing to do with anything he had done. If it had been up to him he would have allowed her to die. What sort of monster did such a thing?

His flight came to an end close to the Aventine. From the forum he could hear the tumult of the crowd. He glanced around him. His heart beat wildly in his chest as if he had been running. Suddenly he felt vulnerable. He had to get off the streets but he had nowhere to go. He was wanted by the authorities not to mention Milo's underworld thugs who would no doubt be searching for him. He had no friends, no places where he could hide. A sudden thought came to him and he groaned in desperation. Had it really come to this? But he had no choice. He looked up the street that led up the Aventine hill. It was a desperate decision.

He spent some time watching the front of the building. A fat woman was hanging out her washing and a few children were playing on a doorstep. He glanced upwards but saw nothing unusual. The street seemed to be going about its daily business. Mustering himself he stole around in a wide semi circle and found what he had hoped would be there, an alley that backed onto the house. He darted into it and felt his way along until he came to the backdoor. It was a flimsy construction. He pushed his ear to the door and listened. All seemed as it should be. He hesitated and glanced down the alley but he was alone.

With a splintering crash, he burst through the door into the back room. A woman squealed in terror and backed away from him. He barely gave her a glance as he stormed on into the front room nearly tripping over a horde of statues. A man had half risen from a workbench where he'd been working. There was a look of alarm on his face which changed to surprise as he saw Adonibaal.

"You." the man gasped.

"Are you alone, have they been here?" Adonibaal panted. Demetrius the Macedonian shook his head.

"You are safe friend," he said hurriedly. For a moment he stared at Centurion in Adonibaal's hand and then turned to look at his back door.

"I thought you had left the city days ago," he whispered turning his attention back to Adonibaal. Then he called out in a louder voice to the woman in the back room. "Its alright, he's a friend. See if you can fix the door."

There was an inaudible reply from the backroom. Slowly Adonibaal lowered Centurion.

"It doesn't matter," he said, "I need your help."

Demetrius raised his hands in acknowledgment and began stroking his chin.

"Sit, sit down, please," he muttered.

From the back room there was another inaudible noise.

Adonibaal remained standing.

"Of course, whatever you want," Demetrius looked away. The woman had appeared in the doorway and Demetrius moved to shoe her into the other room. She obeyed with ill concealed alarm.

"So what can I do for you?" Demetrius said.

"I need a place where I can stay for a couple of nights."

"You can stay here," there was something resolute and confident about Demetrius that surprised Adonibaal. That confidence had been lacking when he had first met the Macedonian. Had he misjudged the spy?

"And I need to know where Quintus Fabius Maximus is."

Silence descended on the room. Adonibaal watched Demetrius carefully. The Macedonian spy seemed to be thinking. Then he nodded slowly. "I do not want to know what Gisgo has instructed you to do," he said diplomatically, "I have no interest in your affairs." Demetrius took a deep breath and sighed. "When do you need to know by?"

"Now," Adonibaal replied.

Demetrius nodded. "I will speak with my contacts then. Give me a couple of hours and I should have some news for you."

It was Adonibaal's turn to nod. "Good," he said, "Go now then," he glanced towards the back room, "But know this Demetrius, if you betray me I shall kill your woman and then I will come for you."

"I will not betray you," Demetrius shook his head and turned for the front door. "Just give me a couple of hours."

Demetrius went out through the front door and Adonibaal was left nursing a deep sense of unease. He had been forced to reveal his hand to the spy. He didn't like the Macedonian but he'd had no choice and perhaps, just maybe the man would bring him back into the game.

***

Demetrius was back quicker than Adonibaal had expected. He came into the room with an excited look on his face. Sweat lathered his forehead.

"Fabius is at home on the Palatine," he gasped, "But they are going to move him out of the city tomorrow night. A man named Numerius oversees his security. They are going to take Fabius to his house. He lives somewhere on the Janiculum. They think he will be safer there."

Adonibaal's eyes glinted but he betrayed nothing of what he was thinking.

"And how did you find out this information?" he snapped.

Demetrius blinked in surprise and a little colour shot to his cheeks.

"One of Fabius's guards is fucking one of my girls. That's how I know," he muttered.

"How many guards will Fabius have?"

"I don't know," Demetrius muttered, "But I can find out."

"No," Adonibaal shook his head, "It would look suspicious if the girl asked him that sort of question."

Demetrius nodded quickly in agreement.

"Do you think Gisgo will keep his promises when this is all over," he said.

The question caught Adonibaal by surprise. He hadn't given the matter any thought but now that the Macedonian had raised it he grew annoyed.

"He will," he replied gruffly.

"Of course," Demetrius nodded and looked away.

Adonibaal paused for a long moment to think.

"I must go out now. There is something that I need to do but I will be back before nightfall."

As he left the house via the broken back door Adonibaal wondered again whether he could trust the Macedonian. There was something different about Demetrius that he just couldn't place but the man had proved useful. There was no denying that he was back in the game. The information that Demetrius had unearthed had given him another chance. And this time he would add an element of deception. He made his way towards the forum. Streams of people were coming the opposite way and there was an excited carnival like atmosphere in the air. The plan he had in mind was brilliant and if it worked it would completely wrong foot his brother. Up ahead he could see that his way was blocked by a crowd of people lining the street. The people were cheering. He stopped and craned his head to look down the road. Coming towards him was Pompeia. The crowd were throwing flowers onto the street ahead of her. Resolutely Adonibaal pushed his way through the crowd towards her.

Chapter Twenty-nine – Brothers

The Senate house was deserted except for a small group of men who clustered informally on the benches in the far corner. They looked serious and sombre as they listened to the man in their midst. Numerius sat a few rows back from the senators watching the historic meeting where Fabius was uniting the Senate and the people of Rome. The veteran leader was on his feet, pacing up and down.

"So we are all agreed then," Fabius said glancing at the faces around him.

Pera the dictator nodded solemnly. "Grachus and I will take the newly raised troops southwards and will keep an eye on Hannibal's movements but we won't risk battle unless the terms are highly favourable," he said.

"Don't let him trick you," Fabius replied, "Hannibal is the master of the ambush."

"There will be no more slaughter like Cannae," Pera said confidently.

"I will leave for Canusium tonight and take over command of the remnants of Varro's army," Marcellus, a dapper old general added.

Fabius walked up to the old general and laid a hand on his shoulder. "I know Rome can count on you, old friend. Treat Varro with respect, tell him that he is to return to Rome at once and that he is to lay down his consulship but tell him that the Senate thanks him for not despairing of the Republic."

Marcellus nodded. "I will," he replied.

"Once you have taken command move your men to Nola and fortify the town," Fabius said, "Hannibal will try and take it. It's of great strategic importance. I'm afraid though you won't be able to expect any reinforcements."

"I will hold Nola for the Republic," Marcellus said.

"An army will also need to be sent to Greece to check the Macedonians who are threatening to ally themselves with Hannibal. Another will need to keep an eye on the Gaul's in the north, two Legions should be sufficient, an army will also need to remain here to protect Rome and were also going to have to build a new fleet to support our allies in Syracuse," Fabius announced.

He paused as the vast scope and burden of Rome's commitments became obvious for all to see. This was the greatest war Rome had ever faced. Her armies would have to fight from Spain to Sicily and from Northern Italy to southern Greece against a host of enemies, Spaniards, Carthaginians, Celts, Macedonians and a growing list of former allies in southern Italy.

"We will do this, gentlemen, Rome will conquer," Fabius said gently as he sensed the mood.

The men solemnly nodded in agreement.

"Our strategy," Fabius went on, "will be to avoid battle with Hannibal himself. Instead we shall launch multiple attacks on the allies that he is now making in the south." A glint of cruel delight appeared in Fabius' eye.

"Hannibal is going to learn that he cannot be in two places at the same time and gentlemen, without the support of his allies he will not be able to remain in Italy. As for you young man," Fabius turned to the youngest of the distinguished men clustered around him, "Your father and uncle will remain in Spain with their armies. I know that some in the Senate would like our Spanish armies to come home to defend Rome but however popular that decision may be it will not win us the war. Your father and uncle have been ordered to prevent Hannibal's brothers from following him across the Alps into Italy." Fabius looked at the young man sternly. "I cannot let you go and join them. The Senate has a more important task for you. You will organise the new quotas of men and supplies which we are going to need from our Latin allies and our citizen colonies. It's vital that we begin to mobilize all our strength."

Scipio bowed gracefully but Numerius could see that he was disappointed. No doubt the young ambitious Patrician had been hoping to be given a role where he would be able to win glory on the battlefield. As if reading the youngster's mind Fabius allowed his eyes to linger on the Tribune who had only just returned from the south. "This is going to be a long war," he added.

"I shall win the war for the Republic," Scipio said boldly and the total self believe in his voice brought a few smiles onto the faces of the older men.

"Now with regards to internal matters," Fabius said turning to at a small wiry man whom Numerius didn't recognise, "The high priest has informed me, through his colleague here, that Metellus has been exiled for life for his despicable violation of one of our Vestals. He left the city this morning."

There was an audible sigh of relief from the Senators.

The wiry man rose to his feet and unrolled a scroll of parchment.

"I have been instructed to read this statement to you," he coughed. "The Pontifex Maximus," he began, "wishes you know that he fully supports the Senate's decisions and will ask the gods to grant Rome victory. He has instructed every priest and magistrate to carry out their duties with extra special care and attention." A bead of sweat ran down the priests face. "Regarding the two Vestals Floronia and Opimia, they will be put on trial but unfortunately one of them has committed suicide. The Vestal Pompeia, who was declared innocent, will be allowed to retire to private life. As she is no longer a virgin, she cannot continue to serve her goddess. The Vestals will therefore require three new girls to join their order and suitable invitations have already been dispatched."

The priest swallowed and turned to look at Numerius.

"The Pontifex Maximus wishes to compensate Numerius Fabius Vibulani. He offers a pound of Gold or ten acres of land near Telamon. Choose which you will accept and it will be so."

The priest lowered his parchment and looked up.

Numerius had risen to his feet. His face looked grey and old with large dark bags beneath his eyes.

"I want nothing from you," he replied, "If the high priest thinks he can buy my forgiveness with gold then he's more of an idiot than I thought."

The priest nodded curtly. "It is settled then," he said with the smooth indifference of a lawyer.

***

Fabius and Numerius were left alone in the Senate house as the senators and generals departed. The building was eerily quiet. They sat on the front bench staring at the speaker's chair. Through the open doors behind the speaker's chair, the first stars had appeared in the evening sky.

"I have seen two generations of your family take their seats in this hall," Fabius sighed. "Rome needs good men, and good men need Rome. If you truly understand what she is, Numerius, you will know that dedicating your life to her is easy. When we and all who come after us have long turned to dust and every word that we have ever spoken has been forgotten; men will still remember what Rome was."

"I am a dying man filled only with bitterness and regret," Numerius grunted.

Fabius sighed again and nodded. "Rome demands much from us it is true and still men come here to serve her and give all they have got."

"I have given Rome everything I had and she has left me with nothing."

Fabius rose to his feet and glanced at Numerius sternly. "You should not talk like this, old friend". He paused and laid a hand on Numerius' shoulder and glanced up at the roof of the great hall. "We are mere mortals and she is eternal, we should not expect anything from her."

Numerius lowered his head. "I must thank you for what you did to save my daughter," he said.

Fabius gripped Numerius' shoulder and smiled.

"What made you think I had anything to do with that?"

"You had the Senate relax the ban on women leaving their homes. You persuaded the dictator to have his men close by."

"Ah," Fabius nodded happily, "yes it all seemed to work out well." He paused. "There are still some in the Senate who would like to see you punished for causing Milo's death."

"He died from an infection. He was alive when I released him."

Fabius held up his hand, "There is no need to defend your self. You are not on trial. There are some in the Senate though who would still like to see you punished but their anger is shallow and will fade over time."

"What will you do with Milo' accounts?" Numerius asked.

"Nothing," Fabius replied curtly, "they have been locked away. We cannot afford to upset and divide the Senate at this time. It is vital that we remain a united force."

Numerius coughed.

"And what about my brother, what will be his fate?"

***

Adonibaal felt guilty. He could still feel the cool touch of her skin. It had been the first time he had seen her from close up. She had been quite beautiful but what he had not expected was how much like Flavia she looked. There had been something innocent about the way she had stared at him and for an insane moment he had believed that she actually was Flavia, so strong was the resemblance between daughter and mother. He had done what he had come to do and afterwards he had fled like a coward. Now as he made his way back towards Demetrius' house on the Aventine he could not contain the growing sense of guilt. He was using her. She had done nothing to wrong him. But now he was using his own daughter in his plan to kill Fabius. The plan was simple and effective. He had calculated that she would tell Numerius about the encounter and Numerius would then move to set a trap for him at the appointed hour and place. Except; he had no intention of going to meet her. The deception would instead be on his brother for whilst Numerius waited for him in vain at the temple of Diane he would enter the house on the Janiculum and kill Fabius. But now he felt guilty and the feeling confused him.

"Stick to the plan," he muttered to himself.

He stumbled on. People pushed past him but he was oblivious to his surroundings. It had been a very long since he had ever felt guilty about anything. It was a horrible feeling and in an alley he suddenly leaned against a wall and threw up. People stopped to stare at him and quickly he wiped his mouth on the back of his hand and stumbled on. A man's voice cried out in protest but Adonibaal didn't look back to see what it was about. He would make her understand he thought. When this was all over he would explain himself to her, he would tell her everything, about his life, what he had done and who he was. She would know it all, every last detail and as the thoughts gathered in his mind he felt the growing urge to explain himself building like some huge tidal wave. She would know him for the man he was supposed to have been and not the monster he'd become. She should know the truth. She should know the oath of loyalty he and Flavia had sworn to each other. She would know that he was loyal to that oath still.

He heard running feet behind him and in alarm whirled round. But it was just a group of children chasing one of their own. He wiped the sweat from his face and caught sight of an old woman sitting on her doorstep watching him. The lady was chewing on something and her eyes were just slits in a heavily wrinkled face. Adonibaal fled up the street alarmed by his own behaviour and his sudden inexplicable loss of confidence. He could not bring himself to admit it but his encounter with Pompeia had spooked him.

***

It was night and like a ghost Adonibaal stood hidden in the darkness of a vestibula. There was no moon. A perfect night he thought. Across the street a group of soldiers had gathered around the entrance to Fabius' house. Adonibaal had counted ten men. He could see them easily enough for most of them were carrying burning torches that lit up the entrance hall with eerie flickering devilish light. Ten armed men were too much to take on in one assault, even for him. Fabius was making sure he was well protected. The soldiers seemed to be waiting for something to happen but the door to the house remained firmly closed.

Adonibaal's thoughts wandered as he waited. Patience was something he had a lot of. He thought of Pompeia and Numerius. Would they be waiting for him outside the temple of Diane just like he was waiting now for Fabius? Would she be stood there alone beside the temple, like some goat staked to the ground whilst the hunters waited for the wolf to appear? The guilt he'd felt at getting her involved had never really gone away. It was wrong but the decision had been made and he would have to see it through to the end. The time to explain would come afterwards. If there would be an afterwards he thought grimly. But he had prepared for that too.

He'd remained all day at Demetrius's house and as he'd waited the tension had began to build. Demetrius' comments about Gisgo had unsettled him. The Macedonian's words had affected him like a slow acting poison and he'd hated the spy for it. He'd passed the time playing with Centurion, twirling the sword one way and then the other as he watched the Macedonian and his woman go about their business. They had not spoken much but he could see the tension on their faces too. It had been a relief therefore for all when he'd slipped out into the night to take up his observation post. He was going to kill Fabius tonight. Now he felt the calm familiar professionalism of a man who knew he was in control. He knew how to stalk his prey and he knew he was good. Fabius was going to die.

His attention was suddenly drawn to the soldiers across the street. The men had fallen silent. Then he saw why. The door to Fabius' house was open. A moment later Fabius appeared clad in his Senatorial toga. Adonibaal caught a quick glimpse of the man's white hair before his view was obstructed by the armed escort. Following him out of the door were four litter bearers carrying a closed litter and a gaggle of slaves with various boxes on their backs. Fabius was taking his personal belongings with him Adonibaal thought. That must mean he was planning to stay away for an extended period. He grunted in satisfaction as he saw no sign of his brother. Numerius must have taken the bait.

The door to the house closed and he saw Fabius slip quickly into the litter. The curtains were immediately drawn around him and with a synchronised effort the bearers raised the litter from the ground. Then the whole procession started off down the street. Adonibaal watched them go until he was certain in which direction they were heading. Then he emerged from his hiding place and began to run. The procession was heading for the Trigemina gate, the most direct route if one wanted to go to the Janiculum. It made sense. Adonibaal had scouted the route in advance and now his preparations paid off for he shot through the darkened streets and made it to the gateway well in advance of his slow-moving prey.

He could see them approaching long before he could hear them. The procession of torches bore down towards him. Adonibaal faded into the shadows as the litter halted before the closed gates. The guards whose duty it was to protect this gate conversed briefly with Fabius's men and then he heard a great creaking noise that told him the gate was being opened. He watched as the first of the torches passed on through and then coolly he stepped from the shadows and joined the tail end of the gaggle of slaves whom were carrying the boxes. No one challenged him. In the flickering torch light he must have appeared as just another slave following on behind his master's litter. He held his breath as he passed under the gateway. Still no one had spotted him. He kept up with the servants for a few paces beyond the wall and then suddenly faded back into the shadows. There was no sign of alarm. He felt a fierce sense of elation. The fools were half asleep. Amateurs! He resisted the thought of attacking the litter right away. He would stick to the original plan and break into the house and kill Fabius when his men thought he was secure and their guard would be down.

***

Adonibaal was glad for the moonless night. He crouched beside a tree some way off and studied the three guards who barred the front door to Numerius' house. The litter bearing Fabius had just been carried inside. In the torch light, he could see the shape of the men's helmets. He frowned at some cautionary instinct. The men were making no attempt to be discreet. He could hear their chatter and cocked his head, listening to the tone of their voices but the soldiers sounded relaxed. Maybe they were not expecting trouble. That left seven others within the house. Smoothly Adonibaal rose to his feet and flitted off through the trees until he came to the low wall that marked the boundary of his brother's land. Whilst he'd been in Numerius' house he'd taken the chance to thoroughly explore the house and garden and now his prudence was paying off for he knew the layout.

He crouched beside the wall and carefully raised his head above the parapet. More torches and men! With one quick glance he counted three guards beside the doorway that led from the garden into the house. But had they bothered to watch the servant's entrance? He crawled along the wall like a spider, smooth and silent until he thought he was in the right position. Slowly he raised his head. The side door leading from the garden into the slave's rooms was dark and looked deserted. He stared at the dark space where he knew the door was. Then he cocked his head but the only sound he could hear was the murmur of the guards and a gentle breeze that rustled through the trees and bushes. Six men outside, four within the house he thought. Plus the slaves but with luck they would be asleep. He lowered his head and turned to lean against the garden wall. Without a sound Centurion slid from its scabbard. Adonibaal felt his heart pounding away. Four men within the house but they would not be expecting him. He sighed and bent down and kissed the blade of his sword and muttered a prayer. The time to end it had come.

He was over the wall in one smooth leap. He landed on his feet and crouched like a wild cat, every sense straining to paint a picture of the darkness before him. Then half bent over he ran across the terrace and crouched beside one of the large flower beds. The night seemed peaceful. Nothing moved. He risked another glance at the door into the slave's quarters. There was no sign of anything unusual. He could hear the guards by the main terrace door; they were still talking amongst themselves.

It took him only a couple of seconds before he was beside the door. He leaned against the brick wall of the house and waited until his breathing had calmed down. Then he tried the door. It was locked. He had expected that and from a pocket he produced the key he'd stolen from the house when he had been waiting for Numerius. He knew it was the key to the slaves quarters for he had seen one of the slaves use it. The key crunched in the lock and then smoothly the door swung open. Adonibaal took a deep breath and then stepped into the house.

Cautiously he closed the door behind him and then glided down the hall. There was no sound from the darkened rooms that he passed. He felt his heart thumping away but he knew what he was doing. Up ahead a single oil lamp glowed in the atrium. Where were the four remaining soldiers? He paused beside the wall where the hall entered the Atrium. He could hear the steady drip of water onto water close by. His eyes by now accustomed to the dark picked out the pile of boxes he'd seen the slaves carrying. Beside them was the litter in which Fabius had travelled. He strained to hear every sound. Where were the four remaining guards? Then he heard them, the low murmur of voices coming from the waiting room beside the front door. Adonibaal tensed and cocked his head. Yes he had heard correctly, the unmistakable sound of a die being rattled around in a cup. The soldiers were playing dice.

Then he heard a sudden cough and his eyes were drawn towards Numerius' bedroom. In the room another oil lamp was burning. Was that where Fabius was resting? Adonibaal peeled away from the wall and crossed the atrium and as he did so he had the strangest sensation of déjà vue. He heard the man cough again as he closed in on the door. Centurion glinted. Fabius was sitting on a couch reading a book. He was still dressed in his senatorial toga which Adonibaal had seen him in earlier and his back was turned to the doorway. Adonibaal stepped into the room, raised Centurion and gently touched Fabius' neck with the cool steel blade.

Fabius froze at the touch. Then slowly he turned round and Adonibaal's eyes opened wide in shock. The man standing before him was not Fabius at all. He had been dressed up to look like Fabius.

"Please," the man stammered, "I am just an actor. They hired me. I am not the man you want. Please let me live Sir."

And as if to prove his point the man reached up to his head and pulled off a white wig.

Adonibaal's mouth opened in horror and he stumbled backwards wildly pointing Centurion at the imposter as if he were a demon. They had tricked him. He had been fooled all the way. They had lured him into a trap and he hadn't seen it coming. In despair he stood rooted to the floor waiting for the inevitable appearance of the guards. In a strange way he felt relieved. He would not run. He would fight to the end and die the death of a warrior that he was. That was the way he had always resolved to go.

"He is waiting for you in his study," the actor stammered edging back against the wall. "He said he wants to speak to you."

Adonibaal felt the sudden sweat on his forehead.

"Who?", he whispered hoarsely.

The actor swallowed nervously, "The master of this house," he replied.

***

Numerius sat alone in the library of his house on the Janiculum. It was night and outside the sky was black like tar. A few oil lamps bathed the library in a dim reddish glow. On the desk before him lay a bundle of scrolls held together by a wax mark and the imprint of the family's seal. The histories were done and the story he had started to write with Publius was finally finished. He smiled as he thought of Publius and with his desire to please and his dog like loyalty. He missed Publius but he was happy that he had found a new son. The young man called Titus would be his new son. The boy was sharp and ambitious but he had a good heart and Numerius had decided to write him into his will. Titus would inherit everything when he was gone. He smiled as he wondered what his ancestors would think of having a Samnite in the family.

He glanced at the long line of black masks which sat silently in their alcoves staring down at him. Pompeia had come to him and they had sat in his garden, like they used to do, and had talked. They were allowing her to quietly retire with a small state pension. The high priest was now apparently eager to forget the whole matter. He'd declared that no record of her trial would be kept. Numerius had asked her if she would now marry but she said she had decided not to. Cantilius had been her love and with his death something had changed in her. The rape had scarred her like no sword ever could and she would not trust a man to be with her again.

He'd listened to her words with sadness for he had grown concerned that she would not find happiness but she had surprised him. She was opening an orphanage she had told him and was going to dedicate her life to the well being of the city's children. She would find happiness in that she had told him and he knew she would.

Sitting together in his garden they had talked about Caeso. She had told him about the man who had grabbed her arm in the street and the words he had spoken. Pompeia had then asked him then to tell her the truth and finally he had. He had told her that Caeso was her father. He had told her how he Numerius had adopted her when she was a baby and he'd talked about her mother Flavia and what she had been like. Pompeia had been surprised but not disappointed. She had asked just the one question which was why had her mother chosen Caeso and not him. He had been unable to answer and she had said it didn't matter anyway for he would always be her true father and she had no interest in meeting Caeso.

Numerius leaned back in his chair and raised the cup of wine to his lips before pouring the contents down his throat. The wine was amongst his finest stock and for a moment he savoured the taste. The house was silent but he knew his visitor would be close by. He'd seen through Caeso' decoy plan right away and when the Macedonian double agent had come to him with news that his brother was hiding in his house he'd known what to do. It had been hard to resist having the house surrounded there and then but it was better if it happened this way he thought.

He touched the cloth of his toga. It was his best one, the one he would only wear on important occasions. Then he straightened up. He had heard a noise. Something moved in the darkened doorway. He sighed and slowly rose to his feet and from the folds of his toga he took a Spanish short sword and laid it on the desk.

"Hello Caeso," he said calmly.

The doorway was silent but then a figure stepped out of the darkness beyond, his black cloak materialising from the gloom like magic. Adonibaal was holding a sword. He looked uncertain and his eyes kept darting around the room.

"We are alone," Numerius said, "but Fabius has a hundred men surrounding this house. There is no way out, brother."

"There is always a way out," Caeso muttered raising Centurion.

"We have half an hour," Numerius said quietly, "then they will come for you. I arranged that much with Fabius."
Caeso smiled. "You hold all the cards brother," he retorted, "You led me into a fine trap. Tell me was it that Macedonian who told you about me?"

Numerius nodded.

Caeso' eyes smouldered. "And Fabius where is he?"

"Fabius left the city yesterday with the army that has gone south to watch Hannibal," Numerius said. "He has issued orders that you are to be taken alive and publicly executed in the forum as an example."

Caeso grunted in surprise. "An example?" he repeated in mock horror.

"But that is not going to happen," Numerius replied.

Caeso shrugged and then glanced at the line of masks in their alcoves.

"Still think Ambustus was the greatest do you?" he said with a faint smile.

"Yes I do," Numerius said glancing at the masks.

Caeso turned to look at his brother and his face suddenly hardened.

"So tell me how you sleep at night knowing what you did to me all those years ago," he snapped.
"I am not the one who killed our father," Numerius said, "I too loved Flavia, you took her from me, she made a bad choice when she chose you."

"A bad choice," Caeso grew angry, "I would have made her happy, I loved her, I am loyal to her still."

"You did nothing for her," Numerius interrupted, "You barged into her life like some Legionary assault. There was never ever going to be any chance of her marrying you. How could you make her happy when our father would never approve of it? You ignored the reality of our situation."

"Ha," Caeso spat onto the ground, "What do you know about it. You are just a jealous coward. She chose me because I was more of a man than you."

"Perhaps," Numerius stood his ground, "but if you had waited just one more year you would have been free to do what you wanted. Our father was a dying man. He hid it from us but he had the same illness that now infects me."

Caeso blinked in surprise. "I did not know that," he muttered.

Numerius nodded. "His doctor told me afterwards." He paused.

"Did you know that our father left everything to you in his will? He never changed it."

"No?" Caeso shook his head the colour draining from his cheeks.

"He loved us I think," Numerius continued, "I inherited everything in your absence and Janus was made a freeman."

"Janus told me he got the house," Caeso muttered.

Numerius shook his head. "No, he was lying. I sold the house. He must have purchased it from my buyer."

Caeso closed his eyes. "The bastard lied to me to make me jealous."

The room fell silent as the two brothers considered what had been said.

"And my daughter," Caeso said quietly, "Why was I not told the truth?"

Numerius looked down at the ground. "I was going to brother, I was going to but events moved too fast for me. I am sorry. Not a day has passed since then when I have not wished I had acted faster."

Numerius looked up at Caeso, studying him.

"I would like to see her," Caeso said but Numerius shook his head. "No, I'm afraid she will not see you."

Caeso's shoulders seemed to sag a little.

"What do you want?" he said lifting his head and looking at his brother.

Numerius swallowed. "Forgiveness," he said. "I want us to forgive each other for what has happened."

"Why, will that make you feel better?" there was a mocking tone in Caeso' voice but it lacked conviction.

"We should do it to honour our father and my son, both of whom you killed," Numerius said. "I do not want them to have died in vain. I would like to be your brother again like we once were. Can you do that? Can you find that in your heart?"

Numerius straightened up and looked at his brother. Caeso was watching him.

"Your son?" he inquired.

"Yes the boy you killed in your first attempt on Fabius."

Caeso nodded as he remembered then and he looked down at the floor.

"Forgiveness," he repeated the word rolling it around in his mouth. "I never thought about it," he looked up, "I wanted to come home and walk again in the forum and be someone people treated with respect," his eyes widened, "but now I think I never shall."

"You are a passenger on someone else's ship," Numerius said,

"You have no control over your destiny. Why not come home brother and be at peace," and with those words Numerius stretched out his arm.

Caeso stared at him.

"Home," he muttered sadly, "I have forgotten what home is."

Then slowly he took a step forwards and peered at the family masks that looked down on them in silence.

"Does my daughter know about me?" he asked.

Numerius nodded. "I have told the truth, she knows who you are and what you did."

Caeso ran his hand through his hair. "Good," he muttered, "I am glad."

He peered closer at the masks. "I see that both Hercules and Ambustus are present. Our father's library was different."

"Yes I added them. Somehow they reminded me of being a boy again and growing up."

Caeso was staring at the sword lying on the desk.

"So what now," he said with a faint sad smile.

Numerius swallowed. "Our time is nearly finished," he said. Fabius will have you executed tomorrow in the forum." Numerius paused, "But I will not let him do that." He paused again and glanced up at the death masks. "I think it is time that we stopped talking about them and go to meet them, brother," he said with a sad smile. "Let's go together, like brothers, and face our demons and show the spirits of the departed that we are not afraid."

A great burden seemed to lift from Caeso's shoulders. His eyes twinkled in the flickering light and then slowly he nodded.

"Hold my arm Numerius and do not let go," Caeso smiled wearily.

"I won't let go," Numerius replied.

***

Pompeia stood in the library looking down at the two dead men. It was morning and the soldiers and slaves of the house crowded behind her trying to get a glimpse of the bodies. Numerius lay on his side; his fine white toga stained dark red by blood and just beyond him was Caeso on his stomach, his face touching the floor. His left hand still gripped a bloodied sword and across the dividing space the arms of the two men were linked together in the Legionary way, held together with the firmness of death. Pompeia wiped at her eyes. In her hand she held the scroll that was Numerius' final will and within it the revelation that Caeso had been her father. Numerius had written that it had been his great hope that Pompeia would be the reason around which the two brothers could be reconciled. Now she crouched down and placed her hand over the spot where the men's hands still grasped each other so that all three of them were linked.

"Go and join them," she whispered. "And be at peace."

***

Later that day the two bodies were placed on a cart and taken across the Tiber to the family mausoleum where they were buried beside their mother and father in a stone vault facing south along the Appian Way in accordance with the instructions in Numerius' will.

The Shield of Rome

27360409R00223

Printed in Great Britain
by Amazon